Beatrix of Clare

John Reed Scott

Contents

BEATRIX OF CLARE

BY

John Reed Scott

BEATRIX OF CLARE

I
RUDDY TRESSES AND GREY EYES

Two archers stepped out into the path,--shafts notched and bows up.

"A word with your worship," said one.

The Knight whirled around.

"A word with your worship," greeted him from the rear.

He glanced quickly to each side.

"A word with your worship," met him there.

He shrugged his shoulders and sat down on the limb of a fallen tree. Resistance was quite useless, with no weapon save a dagger, and no armor but silk and velvet.

"The unanimity of your desires does me much honor," he said; "pray proceed."

The leader lowered his bow.

"It is a great pleasure to meet you, Sir Aymer de Lacy," said he, "and particularly to be received so graciously."

"You know me?"

"We saw you arrive yesterday--but there were so many with you we hesitated to ask a quiet word aside."

The Knight smiled. "It is unfortunate--I assure you my talk would have been much more interesting then."

"In that case it is we who are the losers."

De Lacy looked him over carefully.

"Pardieu, man," said he, "your language shames your business."

The outlaw bowed with sweeping grace.

"My thanks, my lord, my deepest thanks." He unstrung his bow and leaned upon the stave; a fine figure in forest green and velvet bonnet, a black mask over eyes and nose, a generous mouth and strong chin below it. "Will your worship favor me with your dagger?" he said.

The Knight tossed it to him.

"Thank you . . . a handsome bit of craftsmanship . . . these stones are true ones, *n'est ce pas*?"

"If they are not, I was cheated in the price," De Lacy laughed.

The other examined it critically.

"Methinks you were not cheated," he said, and drew it through his belt. "And would your lordship also permit me a closer view of the fine gold chain that hangs around your neck?"

De Lacy took it off and flung it over.

"It I will warrant true," he said.

The outlaw weighed the links in his hand, then bit one testingly.

"So will I," said he, and dropped the chain in his pouch.

"And the ring with the ruby--it is a ruby, is it not?--may I also examine it? . . . I am very fond of rubies. . . Thank you; you are most obliging. . . It seems to be an especially fine stone--and worth . . . how many rose nobles would you say, my lord?"

"I am truly sorry I cannot aid you there," De Lacy answered; "being neither a merchant nor a robber, I have never reckoned its value."

The other smiled. "Of course, by 'merchant,' your worship has no reference to my good comrades nor myself."

"None whatever, I assure you."

"Thank you; I did not think you would be so discourteous. . . But touching money reminds me that doubtless there is some such about you--perhaps you will permit me to count it for you."

The Knight drew out a handful of coins. "Will you have them one by one or all together?" he asked.

"All together; on the turf beside you, if you please. . . Thank you. . . And do you know, Sir Aymer, I am vastly taken with the short gown of velvet and sable--

you brought it from France, I assume; the fashion smacks of the Continent. I would like much to have your opinion as to how it looks on me--we are rather of a size, I take it--though I shall have to forego the pleasure of the opinion until another day. . . And now that I can see your doublet, I am enamoured also of it--will you lend it to me for a little while? Truly, my lord, I mind never to have seen a handsomer, or one that caught my fancy more."

De Lacy looked again at the archers and their ready bows.

"St. Denis, fellow," he said, "leave me enough clothes to return to the castle."

"God forbid," exclaimed the bandit, "that I should put a gallant gentleman to any such embarrassment--but you must admit it were a shame to have gown and doublet and yet no bonnet to match them. . ."

The Knight took it off and sent it spinning toward him.

"Note the feather," he said. "It is rarely long and heavy."

"I observed that yesterday," was the merry response.

"Is there anything else about me you care for?" De Lacy asked.

"Nothing--unless you could give me your rarely generous disposition. Methinks I never met a more obliging gentleman."

The Knight arose. "Then, as I am already overdue at Windsor, I shall give you good morning."

The archer raised his hand.

"I am sorry, my lord, but we must impose a trifle further on your good nature and ask you to remain here a while," and he nodded to the man beside him, who drew a thin rope from his pouch and came forward.

De Lacy started back--the leveled arrows met him on every side.

"You would not bind me!" he exclaimed.

The outlaw bowed again.

"It grieves me to the heart to do it, but we have pressing business elsewhere and must provide against pursuit. Some one will, I hope, chance upon you before night. . . Proceed, James--yonder beech will answer."

The Knight laughed.

"I thank you for the hope," he said--and, throwing his body into the blow, smashed the rogue with the rope straight on the chin-point, and leaping over him closed with the leader.

It was done so quickly and in such positions that the others dared not shoot lest they strike either James or their chief--but the struggle was only for a moment; for they sprang in and dragged the Knight away, and whipped the rope about his arms.

"Marry," exclaimed the leader, brushing the dirt from his clothes, "I am sorry they did not let us have the wrestle out--though you are a quick hitter, my lord, and powerful strong in the arms. I wager you showed James more stars than he ever knew existed."

James, still dazed, was struggling to get up, and one of the others gave him a hand.

"By St. Hubert," he growled, rubbing his head in pain and scowling at De Lacy, "if there be more I have no wish to see them."

In the fight De Lacy's forearm had struck the point of his own dagger, where it protruded below the brigand's belt, and the blood was scarleting the white sleeve of his tunic.

The leader came over and bared the wound.

"It is a clean gash, my lord," he said, "but will need a bandage." He drew a bow-cord around the arm above the elbow; then, "With your permission," carefully cut away the sleeve and deftly bound up the hurt.

De Lacy watched him curiously.

"You are a charming outlaw," he observed; "a skillful surgeon--and I fancy, if you so cared, you could claim a gentle birth."

The man stepped back and looked him in the eyes a moment.

"If I remove the bonds, will you give me your Knightly word to remain here, speaking to no one until . . . the sun has passed the topmost branch of yonder oak?"

The Knight bowed.

"That I will, and thank you for the courtesy."

At a nod the rope was loosed, and the next instant the outlaws had vanished in the forest--but De Lacy's cloak lay at his feet, flung there by the chief himself.

"St. Denis!" De Lacy marveled, "has Robin Hood returned to the flesh?"

Then he looked at the sun, and resumed his seat on the fallen tree.

"A pretty mess," he mused--"a stranger in England--my first day at Windsor and the jest of the castle. . . Stripped like a jowly tradesman . . . taken like a cooing babe . . . purseless . . . daggerless . . . bonnetless . . . doubletless--aye, naked, but for an outlaw's generosity . . . cut by my own weapon"--he held up his hand and looked at the abraded knuckles--"and that is all the credit I have to show--the mark of a caitiff's chin. . . Methinks I am fit only for the company of children."

He glanced again at the sun--it seemed not to have moved at all--then sat in moody silence; the wound was smarting now, and he frowned at it every time it gave an extra twinge. . . Would the sun never move? . . . He got up and paced back and forth, his eyes on the oak at every turn--truly that tree was growing higher every minute--or the sun was sinking. . . Not that he was in haste to return to Windsor. . . There would be a fine tale to tell there--no need to speed to it--it would speed to him quite soon enough. . . . But to get away from the accursed place--anywhere . . . back to Windsor even . . . what if some one found him here in this plight--and he not allowed to speak--unable to explain--dumb as that oak. . . Would the sun never move! The wound was stinging sharply, and the arm above the cord was turning black and swelling fast--the pressure must come off. He felt for his dagger; then flung out an imprecation, and tried to tear the cord asunder with his teeth. It was quite futile; it was sunk now so deep in the flesh he could not seize it--and the knots were drawn too tight to loose. . . Would the sun never move!

He fell to searching for a stone--a small one with an edge that could reach in and rasp the deer-hide cord apart--but vainly; though he tried many, only to leave his arm torn and bleeding. . . Yet at last the sun had moved--it was up among the thinner branches.

Of a sudden, back in the forest rose the deep bay of a mastiff . . . and presently again--and nearer . . . and a third time--and still nearer . . . and then down the path came the great tawny dog, tail arched forward, head up--and behind him a bay horse, a woman in the saddle.

"Down, Rollo, down!" she cried, as the mastiff sprang ahead. . . "Beside me, sir!" and the dog whirled instantly and obeyed.

De Lacy bethought himself of his cloak, and hurrying to where it lay he tried to fling it around his shoulders, but with only one hand and his haste he managed badly and it slipped off and fell to the ground. As he seized it again the horse halted behind him.

"You are wounded, sir," she said; "permit me to aid you."

He turned slowly, bowing as he did so--he dared not speak--then glanced up, and almost spoke in sheer amazement, as he beheld the slender figure in green velvet--the sweet, bow-shaped mouth, the high-bred, sensitive nose, the rounded chin, the tiny ear, the soft, deep grey eyes, and, crowning all, the great rolls of the auburn hair that sunbeams spin to gold.

"Come, sir," said she, "I stopped to aid you, not to be stared at."

De Lacy flushed and made to speak, then checked himself, and with another bow held up his arm and motioned for her to cut the cord.

"Merciful Mother!" she exclaimed, and severed it with a touch of her bodkin.

The blood flooded fiercely forward and the wound began to bleed afresh.

"The bandage needs adjusting--come," and slipping from saddle she tossed the rein to the dog and went over to the fallen tree. "Sit down," she ordered.

With a smile De Lacy obeyed; as yet she did not seem to note his silence. And it was very pleasant indeed--the touch of her slim fingers on his bare arm--the perfume of her hair as she bent over the work--the quick upward glance at times of her grey eyes questioning if she hurt him. He was sorry now there were not a dozen wounds for her to dress.

"There, that will suffice until you get proper attendance," she said, tying the last knot and tucking under the ends.

He took her hand and bowing would have kissed it; but she drew it away sharply and turned to her horse. Then she stopped and looked at him in sudden recollection.

"Parbleu, man, where is your tongue?" she demanded. "You had one last night."

Where she had seen him he did not know; he had not seen her--and it only tangled the matter the more, for now she would know he was not dumb. But how to explain?

He smiled and bowed.

"That is the sixth time I have got a bow when a word was due," she said. "There may be a language of genuflections, but I do not know it."

He bowed again.

"Seven," she counted; "the perfect number--stop with it."

He put his hand to his lips and shook his head in negation--then pointed to the sun and the tree, and shook his head again--then once more to the sun and slowly upward to the top of the tree, and nodded in affirmation.

She watched him with a puzzled frown.

"Are you trying to tell me why you do not speak?" she asked.

He nodded eagerly.

"Tell me again" . . . and she studied his motions carefully. . . "The sun and the tree--and the sun and the tree again . . . is that your meaning? . . . Ah! . . . the *top* of the tree . . . I think I am beginning to understand. . . . Where is your doublet?"

De Lacy pointed into the forest.

"And your bonnet? . . . with your doublet? . . . and your dagger? . . . gone with the others? . . . you mean your ring? and it went with them, too? . . . yes, yes--I see now--outlaws, and your wound got in the struggle." . . . She turned toward the tree. . . "Ah! I have it:--you are paroled to silence until the sun has risen above the highest branch . . . what? . . . and also must remain here until then? . . . I see--it was that or die . . . no? . . . Oh! that or be bound? . . . well, truly the knaves were wondrous courteous!" . . . She studied De Lacy's face a moment--then sat down. "Would you like company?" she asked.

Would he like company! Her company!

She laughed gayly--though a bit of color touched her cheek.

"Thank you," she said, "I can read your countenance better than your bows."

Then suddenly his face grew grave and he motioned no.

"Yes, and I can understand that, too," she smiled, "and thank you for it. It may be a trifle uncommon to sit here in the depths of Windsor forest with a man I never met . . . never even saw until last night . . . and who has never spoken a single word to me . . . yet" (glancing at the sun) "the time is not long and . . . the path is rarely traveled."

He smiled--but the concern lingered in his eyes and he shook his head questioningly.

"Nay, sir, do you not see your very urging me to go proves me safe in staying?"

He hesitated, still doubtful--then threw himself on the turf at her feet.

"I suppose it is for me to do the talking," she observed.

And as she talked he fell to watching the sun in her hair--the play of her lips--the light in her eyes. . . . Never before would he have believed that grey could be so deep and tender; or that a mouth could be so tantalizing; or the curve of a cheek so sweet; or ruddy tresses so alluring. . . . And her voice--was there ever such another!--soft, low, clear, like silver bells at twilight out at sea.

And in the watching he lost her words, nor nodded when he should--until, at length, she sprang up and went over to her horse. And when in sharp contrition he followed after to apologize, she met him with a laugh and gracious gesture--then pointed to the sun.

"The parole is lifted," she said. "Will you put me up?"

With his sound arm he swung her into saddle--and with Rollo in advance and him beside her they went slowly back to Windsor. And now he did the talking--telling first the story of the outlaws.

When the towers of the huge castle showed afar through the trees, De Lacy halted.

"Would you deem me rude if I went no further with you?" he asked.

She smiled kindly. "On the contrary, I would deem you very wise."

"I care not to proclaim my adventure with the outlaws. It would make me a merry jest in the hall."

"I understand--and yet, wounded and without bonnet or doublet, you will not pass unnoted; an explanation will be obligatory."

"The wound is easy," he said; "my own dagger made it, you remember--but the doublet and bonnet, particularly the doublet, are bothersome."

She looked at him with quick decision.

"I will manage that," she said; "your squire shall bring both to you here."

De Lacy's face lighted with sudden pleasure, and he put out his hand toward hers--then drew it sharply back and bowed.

"Still bowing?" she said naively.

"I have no words to speak my gratitude," he said.

"And I no ears that wish to hear them, if you had," she laughed. "This morning you have had much trouble--I much pleasure--the scales are balanced--the accounts canceled. We will forget it all. Never will I mention it to you--nor you to me--nor either to another. When we meet again it will be as though to-day had never been.

. . Nay, sir, it must be so. You have been unfortunate, I unconventional--it is best for both we start afresh."

"But am I not even to know your name?" he protested.

She shook her head. "Not even that, now, and I ask your word not to seek to know it--until we meet again."

"You have it," said he, "until we meet again--to-morrow."

She smiled vaguely. "It will be a far to-morrow . . . good-bye, my lord," and rode away--then turned. "Wait for your squire," she called.

"And for to-morrow," he cried.

But she made no answer, and with a wave of her hand was gone, the dog leaping in front of her and baying loud with joy.

II
RICHARD OF GLOUCESTER

But the morrow brought no maid, nor a fortnight of morrows--she had vanished; and seek as he might at Windsor or through the Tower he could not find her. Had he been privileged to inquire the quest would have been ended by a word--but she herself had closed his lips to questions.

Then the mighty Edward died, and all was confusion in the Court; and what with the funeral, the goings and the comings, the plottings and the intrigues, De Lacy was in a maze. The boy King was at Ludlow with Rivers, and it was Nobility against Queen and Woodville until he came for his crowning. And in the turmoil De Lacy was forced to cease, for the nonce, the pursuit of ruddy tresses and grey eyes, and choose where he would stand. And presently that choice sent him riding into the North--bearing a message to the man in distant Pontefract, upon whom, at that moment, all England was waiting and who, as yet, had made no move, Richard of Gloucester.

The day was far spent, and before a fireplace in his private apartments Richard sat alone, in heavy meditation. The pale, clean-shaven, youthful face, with its beautiful mouth and straight Norman nose, and the short, slender figure in its mantle and doublet of black velvet furred with ermine, rich under tunic of white satin, tight-fitting hose of silk, and dark brown hair hanging bushy to the shoulders, would have been almost effeminate but for the massively majestic forehead and the fierce black eyes--brilliant, compelling, stern, proud--that flashed forth the mighty soul within.

Although he had just passed his thirtieth year, yet his fame was as wide as the domain of chivalry, and his name a thing to conjure with in England. Born in an age when almost as children men of rank and station were called upon to take their sires' place, Richard had been famed for his wisdom and statecraft before the years when the period of youth is now presumed to begin. At the age of eighteen he had led the flower of the Yorkist army at the great battles of Barnet and Tewkesbury, and not the dauntless Edward himself, then in the heyday of his prowess, was more to be feared than the slight boy who swept with inconceivable fury through the Lancastrian line, carrying death on his lance-point and making the Boar of Gloucester forever famous in English heraldry. And since then his hauberk had scarce been off his back, and while his royal brother was dallying in a life of indulgence amid the dissipations of his Court, the brave and resolute Richard was leading his armies, administering his governments, and preserving order on the Marches of the Border.

Presently there was a sharp knock on the door and a page entered.

"Well?" demanded the Duke abruptly.

"May it please you, my lord," said the boy; "a messenger of importance who desires immediate audience."

Richard frowned slightly.

"Whose badge does he wear?" he asked.

"No one's, my lord, but the fashion of his armor savors of the Court. He bade me announce him as Sir Aymer de Lacy."

"The name, boy, is better recommendation than any fashion. Admit him."

De Lacy crossed to the center of the apartment with easy grace, and after a deep obeisance stood erect and silent facing the Duke, who eyed him critically. A trifle over the average height and rather slender, and clad in complete mail except for the bascinet which he carried in his hand, there was something in his appearance and bearing that impressed even the warlike Richard. His dark hair hung in curls to his gorget. His hauberk of polished steel was but partially concealed by the jupon of azure silk emblazoned with a silver stag trippant; his cuissarts and greaves glistened in the firelight, and his long sollerets bore on their heels the golden spurs of his rank. Around his waist was a broad belt wrought in gold, and from it, almost in front, hung a great two-handed sword whose point reached to within a few inches of the floor.

"You are welcome," said Gloucester. "A De Lacy should ever find a ready greeting at Pontefract. Of what branch of the family are you?"

"One far removed from that which built this fortress, most noble Duke," returned the Knight, with a peculiarly soft accent. "My own ancestor was but distantly connected with the last great Earl of Lincoln whom the First Edward loved so well."

"I do not recall your name among those who fought for either York or Lancaster. Did your family wear the White Rose or the Red?"

"Neither," said De Lacy. "Providence removed my sire ere the fray began aright and when I was but a child in arms. When Your Grace won fame at Tewkesbury I had but turned my thirteenth year."

"Where is your family seat?"

"At Gaillard Castle in the shire of Leicester, close by the River Weak--or at least it stood there when last I saw it. It is ten long years since I crossed its drawbridge and not twelve months of my life have been spent within its walls."

"Your accent smacks of a Southern sun," said the Duke.

"My mother was of a French house, and to her own land she took me when my father died;" and, observing the Duke glance at his spurs, he added: "It was from France's Constable that I received the accolade."

"Then right well did you deserve it; St. Pol gave no unearned honors."

"I was favored much beyond my deserts," De Lacy replied, although his face flushed at a compliment from the renowned Gloucester.

"Your modesty but proves your merit," returned the Duke. . . "And now your message. From whom come you?"

"From the Duke of Buckingham, my lord," said De Lacy; and the keen look that accompanied the words did not escape the Prince. But De Lacy did not know the man before whom he stood, else would he have wasted no energy in any such attempt. As well try to read the visage of a granite cliff as to discover the thoughts of

Richard Plantagenet from the expression of his face. And if the royal Duke were in aught concerned as to the communication of the powerful Buckingham, there was no evidence of it in his voice or in the eminently courteous and appropriate question as he instantly responded:

"How did you leave His Grace and where?"

"He was most hearty when we parted at Gloucester; he for his castle of Brecknock and I for Pontefract."

"He had been in London?"

"Yes, my lord, since before King Edward's demise."

"Then are his letters very welcome."

"Your pardon, sir," said De Lacy, "but I bear no letters;" and as Richard regarded him in sharp interrogation he added: "My message is by word of mouth."

"And why," said the Duke in the same calm tone he had employed throughout the conversation, "should I credit your story, seeing that I neither know you nor recall your silver trippant stag among the present devices of our land."

"My bearing," returned De Lacy tranquilly, "comes to me from my mother's family, of which she was the heiress, and on English battlefield it has never shone. And unless this ring attest the authority of my message it must be unsaid," and drawing from his finger a broad gold band, in which was set a great flat emerald with a swan exquisitely cut on its face, he handed it to the Duke.

Richard examined it for a moment, then returned it with a smile.

"You are sufficiently accredited," he said. "I will hear your message. What said Stafford?"

"The Duke of Buckingham," replied Aymer, "sends to the Duke of Gloucester his most humble greeting and his very sincere condolence upon the death of Your Grace's great brother and sire."

"Pass over the formalities, Sir Aymer," interrupted the Duke curtly. "It was scarce for them you rode from London to Pontefract."

Aymer bowed. "Buckingham's message was in these words: 'Tell the Duke of Gloucester to hasten to London without delay. I have conferred with the Lords Howard, Hastings, and Stanley, and we are of the one mind that he must be Lord Protector. Tell him we pledge to him our whole support if he will give us his countenance in this crucial struggle against the Woodvilles.'"

"Did he say nothing as to the present status of the situation?" inquired Gloucester quietly. "I am far from Court and know little of its happenings."

"With them, my lord, I am fully acquainted," said De Lacy, "both from my own observation and by the Duke himself."

"How stands the matter, then?"

"Rather favorable to the Queen's faction than otherwise. The King's coronation has been fixed for the first Lord's Day of the coming month and His Majesty is to be escorted from Ludlow by two thousand men. The Marquis of Dorset has seized the treasure in the Tower and Sir Edward Woodville has been tampering with the navy, and methinks not without result. The Queen and the whole family are catering to the populace and spare no effort to win their favor. Only action sharp and sudden will enable the Barons to prevail."

For a moment Gloucester made no response, but sat with his head bent upon his bosom, as was his habit when in thought. Presently he said:

"How do you know that the King's escort will number two thousand?"

"The Council so fixed it, and very much against the wishes of the Queen."

"She wanted more, I doubt not," said the Duke meditatively.

"She long held that less than five thousand would not be fitting the dignity of a King."

Gloucester looked up with a trace of a smile around his eyes.

"Will the Earl of Rivers accompany his nephew?" he asked.

"It was so reported to His Grace of Buckingham; and further, also, that they would not start from Ludlow until the feast of St. George had passed."

"Did Stafford advise no plan in case I fell in with his desires?"

"None. The lords will follow whatever course you fix. All that they urge is haste."

"How long does Buckingham remain at Brecknock?"

"Until he receive word from you--or failing in that, until there be but time sufficient to reach London for the coronation."

"Was it his purpose that you should carry my answer?"

"Nay, my lord Duke," said De Lacy. "Here ends my mission for Buckingham. It was but as friend for friend that I bore this message. I am not of his household nor was it his business that brought me here."

"What brought you to Pontefract then, Sir Knight?" said Richard sternly. "As Buckingham's messenger you have received due honor; that aside, your name alone commends you."

"I sought Pontefract," De Lacy replied, "for the single purpose of tendering my sword to the Duke of Gloucester, hoping in his service to brighten the dimmed lustre of my House."

Not for an instant did the searching eyes of Richard leave the young Knight's face.

"Why do you prefer the Boar of Gloucester to the Stafford Knot? Buckingham is most puissant."

"A De Lacy, my lord," answered Aymer proudly, "follows none but Plantagenet."

"Bravely spoken," said Gloucester, suddenly dropping his stern air, "and worthy of the great name you bear. I accept your sword. Nay, kneel not, sir; Richard Plantagenet deems himself most fortunate to have you at his side."

At that moment the arras was drawn aside and a young and slender woman entered. Her gown was black, unrelieved by any color, save the girdle of gold; her face was almost flawless in its symmetry; her complexion was of a wondrous whiteness; and her eyes, of the deepest blue, soft and melting, and shaded by lashes long and heavy, were of the sort that bespeak the utmost confidence and know no guile. She hesitated as she saw De Lacy and was about to withdraw when the Duke glanced around.

"Nay, sweetheart," said he, rising and going toward her; "do not retire. . . . Sir Aymer de Lacy, I present you to the Duchess of Gloucester."

De Lacy advanced and sinking upon one knee touched his lips to the hand she extended to him.

"Surely, Sir Knight," she said, in a voice whose sweetness struck even his Southern-bred ear, "a De Lacy should ever be welcome in the halls of Pontefract."

"Your words, most gracious lady," answered Aymer, "are almost those used by my lord, the Duke, and to a wanderer's heart they are very grateful."

"You are an errant, then; a Sir Guy or Sir Lancelot," said the Duchess.

"Nay. Only a poor and simple Knight whose highest honor is that he may henceforth follow the banner of your great husband."

"Then must hauberk sit easy as velvet doublet or I know not my lord," and she smiled at Richard.

"Do not," said he, "give to Sir Aymer the notion that he has nothing but hard blows before him--although, indeed, he rode hither on scarce a peaceful mission, since he bears from Stafford and the Nobility the tender of the Protectorship and the insistence that I proceed to London without delay."

As he spoke the face of the Duchess suddenly became grave, and stepping swiftly to his side she put her hand upon his arm.

"You will not go, Richard?" she begged.

"Why, sweetheart, what ails you? Why should a journey to London and a possible exchange of blows alarm you?"

"It is not the journey, dear," she answered. "Many a time have you taken it; and, for the blows, did I not speed you to the Scottish war? Yet I have a foreboding--nay, smile not, my lord!--that upon your course in this matter hangs not only your own fate, but the fate of Plantagenet as well. Accept it not," taking his hand and speaking with deep entreaty; "the Protectorship can add nothing to Richard of Gloucester, and it may work not only your doom but that of the great House of Anjou."

"Nay, Anne, you are ill, surely," said Richard, putting his arm around her. "What has put such uncanny notions into your mind?"

"I do not know; yet I implore you to humor me in this. . . . You have not already despatched an answer to Buckingham?" she suddenly demanded.

"No--not yet," then turned sharply to De Lacy. "It seems, Sir Aymer, that you are to be admitted to my confidence as well as to Stafford's. So be it, for I trust you. Yet, believe me, it is well sometimes to forget."

De Lacy bowed low, saying simply, "I have forgotten."

"Forgive me, Richard," said the Duchess. "My heart so ruled my head that I quite lost myself."

The Duke took her hand and pressed it affectionately. "Think no more now of the matter; we will consider it to-morrow."

"And you will make no decision until then?"

"None, by St. Paul!" and striking the bell he ordered the page to summon the Duchess' lady-in-waiting.

In a moment she appeared: a slender figure in dark blue velvet, with ruddy tresses and deep grey eyes--the maid of Windsor Forest.

De Lacy caught his breath and stood staring, like one bereft of sense, until the dropping of the arras hid her from his sight. Then he saw Gloucester regarding him with a smile.

"You are not the first," he observed, "nor, I warrant, will you be the last."

"Her name?" said the Knight so eagerly the Duke smiled again.

"She is Beatrix de Beaumont, in her own right Countess of Clare, and save our own dear spouse no sweeter woman lives."

"In truth do I believe it; else has God sent a plague upon the Nobles of England.'"

"If disappointed love and blasted hopes can be so reckoned," said Richard with a shrug, "then does many a fair lord suffer from the disease. See that you do not become affected also."

"Nay, my lord Duke," replied De Lacy; "I know better than to allow a poor Knight's mind to dwell upon the charms of a great heiress--and she the Countess of Clare."

"Pardieu!" said Gloucester; "be not so humble. Your birth is equal to her own; it was only for your peace of mind I cautioned you."

III
THE VOICE ON THE RAMPARTS

On quitting the Duke, De Lacy dispatched a page for his squire and was then conducted to his quarters on the floor above.

Tossing his gauntlets and bascinet upon the high bed that stood in the corner near the door, he crossed to the small deep window and swung back the sash. Below him lay the broad bailey, that at this hour was alive with the servitors and retainers of the Duke. Before the dwellings against the inner wall children were playing, and through the fading light of the April afternoon rose a medley of sounds. From the direction of the distant gateway sounded the ring of steel-shod hoofs, and presently a body of horsemen cantered across the stone pavement and drew rein before the keep. A gruff command followed, and just as the rank was broken and the soldiery dispersed the sweet tones of the bell of All Saints' Chapel came floating over the walls.

The Knight crossed himself instinctively, and then, leaning on the ledge, his thoughts turned to his family's past and to why he, though of the blood of one of the Conqueror's favorite Barons, was a stranger in England.

The main branch of the House of Lacy, once so powerful in Britain, had become extinct almost two centuries before; and although Sir Aymer's ancestor had borne an honorable part in the wars of the Third Edward yet, like Chandos, he was content to remain a simple banneret. When the Second Richard went down before his usurping cousin, the then head of the family had stood, to the last, true to his rightful King; and hence it was small wonder that to Sir Richard de Lacy the atmosphere of the Court of the new Monarch was not agreeable. When Henry of Monmouth brought France again under English rule, Sir Richard rode no more to the wars; and the heir being but an infant, his retainers were mustered under a stranger's banner. During the later struggles of Bedford and of Warwick to retain the fast relaxing hold of England upon the domains beyond the Channel, the then Baron had done his devoir full knightly, but it is not in a losing struggle that families win advancement, and, to the last Lancastrian King, Sir Edward de Lacy was not known. Then came the Wars of the Roses and, ere Aymer's sire could bind the White Rose to his helmet, a sudden illness stilled his hand in death; and thus, again, had the House lost an opportunity to rise in fame and power. Much honor had Sir Aymer won in the recent small wars and constant fightings of the Continent, and in the right of his mother's family he might have aspired to high rank at the French Court; but Louis, "the Fell," was not a warrior's King, nor had long residence in a foreign clime bred in Sir Aymer forgetfulness of the land of his birth.

And so, at length, he had furled his pennon, and followed by his faithful squire and a few of his retainers he sought the English Court. And with him went the solemn purpose either to restore the once great name he bore to its place among the chivalry of England or to let it perish utterly with him. Within a few weeks of his arrival, Edward's sudden death occurred, and he had been quick to appreciate that his opportunity lay with Gloucester in the North. A friendship formed with the Duke of Buckingham some years previous in Paris, and which had been renewed in

London, had stood him in good stead; for being acquainted with De Lacy's purpose of seeking Pontefract, Stafford had to his great satisfaction made him his confidential messenger in the very matter which was then so near to Richard's heart.

The entry of the squire broke in on the Knight's thoughts, and he turned from the window.

"Make haste, Giles," said he, "and get me out of this steel."

With the skill of long practice it was quickly done; and removing the suit of thin yellow leather worn under the harness, De Lacy donned a doublet and short gown of black velvet, and then, throwing himself upon the bed, he awaited the summons to the evening meal.

Meanwhile, the squire had laid aside his own armor and stood forth in his leather suit that was creased and soiled by the iron weight.

Giles Dauvrey was no fledgling whose apprenticeship had begun among the dainty pages of my lady's bower. A Gascon, and lowly born, he was a simple man-at-arms when, in a small affray on the Italian border, he had chanced to ward from Sir Aymer de Lacy's head the battle-axe that, falling on him from behind, must else have cleft him to the gorget. The young Knight had thereupon obtained the man's transfer to his own following and--becoming assured of his bravery and martial fitness--he had made him his squire when, a few months later, an Italian cross-bolt had wrought a vacancy in the post. Stocky in build, wonderfully quick and thoroughly trained in arms, he also had the rare faculty of executing an order without the slightest evasion, and could be trusted in any emergency either of discretion or valor. Right often had the two stood side by side in the press of skirmish and the rush of battle,--for they had ever sought the locality of strife--and there had come to be little choice for the foeman between the accomplished axe-play of the master and the sweeping blows of the sturdy squire. And as among the veteran soldiery of the French-Italian borders no name stood higher than De Lacy, so also was no wearer of the silver spurs more respected than he who bore the banner of the Trippant Stag.

"It is a great fortress, Giles," said the Knight. "Never have I seen a stronger."

"Marry, no; nor one, I ween, wherein the discipline was sterner. Are all castles in this land of yours, my lord, so conducted?"

"All wherein the Duke of Gloucester holds command."

"Of a truth, then," said Dauvrey, "the tales I have heard of this Prince are not so wide of the clout."

"What were the tales?"

"They were many and various, yet I gathered that he was a great warrior and fit to be a ruler of men."

"And you gathered truly," returned De Lacy. "He is the best soldier and shrewdest man in all this island Kingdom."

"How looks he to the eye, my lord?"

"You may judge that for yourself; observe him at the evening meal. Here comes the summons."

A step came rapidly up the stairs and a page halted at the half-opened doorway.

"His Grace requests that Sir Aymer de Lacy join him in the great hall," he said.

The Knight arose and flung his short cloak about him.

"Lead on," he ordered; "we follow."

When they entered the hall the Duke was already seated on the dais, surrounded by the officers of his household. On the right, De Lacy recognized Sir Robert Wallingford, to whom, as Constable of Pontefract, he had been conducted upon his arrival; but the others he was not able to identify, although, of course, he knew by reputation several who should be among them. The chair on Richard's left was unoccupied, and he motioned for De Lacy to take it.

"Sit you here," he said. . . . "Gentlemen, I present Sir Aymer de Lacy. He is fresh from London and, I doubt not, can give you much news of the Court and Capital."

All arose and bowed to De Lacy, who bowed back at them.

"My knowledge, such as it is," said he, "is freely yours. Yet as I was only a few weeks in London my budget may be very meagre. But if you will ask, I will gladly tell you what I know."

And they did not hesitate to ask, and he was kept busy answering questions upon every conceivable subject, from the details of the funeral of the dead King to the fashion of the latest gown. Indeed it was not until the meal was almost over that he had an opportunity for a word aside to the Duke.

"May I ask Your Grace the name of the fair-haired man yonder?" he said.

"I cry pardon," Richard exclaimed. "I forgot you were a stranger in England. He is my Chamberlain, Sir William Catesby. . . The black-moustached Knight with the scar on his forehead, who has just put down his wine glass, is Sir Richard Ratcliffe. . . The elderly man beside him with the gray hair and ruddy countenance is Sir Robert Brackenbury. . . The one with the thin, dark face and broad shoulders is Lord Darby of Roxford.--The rest are younger men and of less prominence. . . The one beside Darby is Sir Ralph de Wilton, next to him is Sir James Dacre, and on Dacre's left is Sir Henry de Vivonne."

He pushed back his chair and arose.

"Gentlemen," said he, "you are excused from further attendance." Then he called to De Wilton.

"Sir Ralph," he said, "Sir Aymer de Lacy is of the Household. Give him some idea of his duties, and then sponsor him in Her Grace's presence chamber."

And Aymer liked De Wilton on the instant, with his courteous manner and frank, gracious smile, and for an hour or more they sat in pleasant conversation. Then Sir Ralph was summoned to the Duke, and De Lacy, postponing, perforce, his presentation to the Duchess' household until the morrow, went for a stroll on the ramparts.

Night had settled down; the sky was clear and through the cool, crisp air the stars were shining brightly. The turmoil in the bailey had subsided, but from the quarters of the soldiery rose the hum of voices that now and then swelled out into the chorus of some drinking or fighting song. There were lights in many of the dwellings where lived the married members of the permanent garrison, and from them ever and anon came the shrill tones of some shrewish, woman scolding her children or berating her lord and master. For a while Sir Aymer paced the great wide wall, reflecting upon what had occurred since he came to Pontefract and the matters he had learned from De Wilton. But through it all a woman's face kept with him and led his thoughts awry, and presently he turned aside and leaned upon the parapet.

He had found her--and by accident; and had lost her the same instant. Beatrix of Clare, the greatest heiress in England, was not for him--a wanderer and a stranger. She had warned him plainly that day in Windsor Forest--though he, not knowing her, had missed the point till now. He might not presume to speak to her until properly presented--nor even then to refer to what had passed or so much as intimate that they had met before. . . And yet had not Gloucester himself bade him be not so humble--that his birth was equal to her own? Why should he not aspire . . . why not seek her favor . . . what more favorable conditions would he ever know than now? How extraordinary it was that she should be in Pontefract--the length of England from where he saw her last. Surely the Fates were kind to him! And had she recognized him? No, for she had not even given him a glance. He had thought to meet her in the presence chamber this very night; and now--he must wait until the morrow. Yet the morrow was sure . . . and then he would see again that sweet face, those ruddy tresses and grey eyes . . . would hear that silvery voice. . .

Hark! he heard it now.

"Why so abstracted, sir?" it seemed to say.

He stood quite still--would it come again?

St. Denis! there it was!

"Is she so far away, Sir Ralph?" it asked.

Sir Ralph! What had Sir Ralph to do with this music?

There came a soft laugh and a touch of a hand on his shoulder.

He whirled around--and stared in wonder at the woman of his dream.

"Oh!" she said. "Oh! I thought you were Sir Ralph de Wilton . . . the night is dark--pray, forgive me."

De Lacy bowed low.

"I am Sir Ralph de Wilton," he said.

The Countess smiled.

"You are very good," she said, and moved away.

"May not Sir Ralph walk with you?" De Lacy asked.

She stopped and with head half turned looked at him thoughtfully.

"Yes, if he wish," she answered.

For a space they walked in silence; she with head averted. . . Presently she laughed.

"Silence is new in Sir Ralph," she said.

"He was waiting leave to speak."

"And that is newer still."

"You like the new?" he asked audaciously.

"Oh! it is variety for the moment"--with the faintest lift of the chin--"though doubtless it would get tiresome in time."

"Let us enjoy the moment then," said he. "I was thinking of you when you came."

"I regret, Sir Ralph, I may not be equally flattering."

"So does Sir Ralph."

"Though I will admit my thoughts were of a man."

"He shall have my gage at sunrise."

She shook her head. "They were not worth it--only idle curiosity concerning a new member of the Household I noticed in the Duke's chamber this afternoon." . . . She became interested in her cloak. "I do not now even recall his name," she added negligently.

De Lacy smiled and looked at the stars.

Presently she shot a quick glance up at him.

"Did you not meet him at the evening meal, Sir Ralph?"

"He was there--on the Duke's left," De Lacy answered carelessly.

"And his name?"

"De Lacy---Aymer de Lacy."

"A good North of England name," she commented.

"Aye, it once ran with Clare in Yorkshire," he answered.

"The Clares are done," said she, and sighed a bit.

"And the flower of them all bloomed last," he added gravely.

But she put the words aside.

"Do not be foolish, Sir Ralph. You know I dislike compliments. Tell me about this Sir Aymer de Lacy--I never heard of him at Court."

"He has lived all his life in France."

"Patriotic, truly!" with a shrug.

"As to that," said the Knight, "it is fit that he should answer for himself, and not through Sir Ralph de Wilton; though either Richard of Gloucester entirely ignored the point or else he was quite satisfied."

She laughed. "Then it is not for me to raise it; so tell me why he came to Pontefract."

"To take service with the Duke, I fancy--and methinks he has already found one more reason for staying than for coming."

"The Duke is reason enough for a soldier who wants a man for a master," she said. Then suddenly faced about. "Let us hasten--I fear I have overstayed my time."

As they rounded a bastion near the keep they encountered Lord Darby.

"Ah, Beatrix, well met," he said, offering his arm and nodding carelessly to De Lacy. "Her Grace desires you."

"Did she send you for me?" the Countess asked, ignoring his arm and hurrying on--and De Lacy noting it, kept beside her.

Lord Darby forced a smile. "Not exactly; I volunteered to go for you."

"You are very kind," she said rather tartly; "a moment longer and you would have been saved the trouble."

Darby's smile failed completely and he made no answer.

In the doorway the Countess halted--and gave De Lacy her hand.

"I thank you for the walk," she said, as he bowed over it; then a merry gleam came in her eyes--"Good night, Sir . . . Aymer."

IV
TRAILING CHAINS

"Women are queer creatures," De Wilton remarked, as he turned away from the window and sat down beside De Lacy, who having just completed his first tour of duty in the Household as Knight-in-waiting was still lounging in the antechamber.

"It seems to me," said Aymer, "I have heard that idea advanced once before in France--or maybe it was in Italy."

"Doubtless--but the present proof of it is yonder," De Wilton answered, nodding toward the window. "The Countess has just gone for a ride with Darby."

De Lacy looked up from the dagger he was idly polishing on his doublet sleeve.

"And the proof in particular is what?" he asked. "Her costume, her horse, or her escort?"

"I gave her the horse," said De Wilton.

"That absolves the horse, and as it could not be the costume, it must be . . ."

De Wilton brought his fist down on the bancal with a smash.

"Darby--and may the Devil fly away with him! . . . Oh! it is not jealousy," catching Aymer's quick glance. "We were children together at her father's castle, and she is like a sister to me."

"And so, as usual, ignores a brother's advice touching her suitors?" De Lacy observed.

"Touching only this one."

"Then you should feel flattered."

"I offered no advice as to any other."

Aymer sheathed the dagger and adjusted his cloak.

"I suppose," said he, "one may assume you are not over-fond of Darby."

De Wilton nodded. "That you may--and yet if you were to ask my reasons I could give none, save a thorough detestation."

"And the Countess has asked for the reason?"

"Many times."

De Lacy laughed. "I see," he said. "Now tell me about this Darby--I think you mentioned he was not of the Household."

"Thank Heaven, no--or I would not be of it. He has some power in the West Riding, and came by special summons of the Duke. But that business ended two days ago--it is the Countess that holds him now."

"Well," said De Lacy, "I, too, would linger if it meant a ride with the Countess of Clare and the favor that implies."

"Oh, as to that, he is favored no more than a dozen others. What irks me is that she favors him at all."

"What would you say if I, too, tried for a smile?" De Lacy asked.

De Wilton ran his eyes very deliberately over the handsome figure beside him.

"That you will win it," he said, "and may be more than one--and the chains that trail behind. . . Beware, the chains are very heavy."

De Lacy shook his head. "Strong they may be--strong as life--but heavy, never."

Sir Ralph looked at him in wondering surprise--then clapped him on the shoulder.

"French skies and French blood! Pardieu, man, go in and show this Darby and the others how the game is played."

"But the chains------"

"Wrap them about her also. And by Heaven, why not?--the last of the Lacys and the last of the Clares. St. George, it would be like old times in Merry England."

"Nay, Sir Ralph," said Aymer, laying his hand upon the other's arm, "your words are quite too flattering. I must be content with the smile."

De Wilton raised his eyebrows. "You brought the chains across the Channel with you?"

De Lacy arose. "No, but maybe I have found them since."

Suddenly De Wilton laughed. "My mind surely is getting weak," he said. "I clean forgot you had never seen the Countess."

"Oh, yes, I have--on the wall last night."

"Was it possible you were near when Darby found her?"

"I was with her."

"With her!" said De Wilton incredulously. "Surely you do not mean it."

De Lacy's face straightened. "Be a little more explicit, please," he said.

"Tut, man, I meant no offence," was the good-natured answer. "You do not understand the matter. The Countess never walks alone on the ramparts after dark with any man save the Duke and me."

"St. Denis, I forgot. It was *you* she walked with," said Aymer.

De Wilton stared at him. "Are you quite sane?" he asked.

De Lacy linked his arm within the other's. "Come over to the window and I will tell you how, last night, Sir Ralph de Wilton chanced to walk with the Countess of Clare on the ramparts of Pontefract."

"And I suppose then it was you, and not I, who talked with the Duchess in her presence chamber all the time the Countess of Clare was gone."

"No, I was on the ramparts, too," De Lacy answered. "Listen--here is the tale."

"Good!" exclaimed De Wilton at the end. "She punished Darby well--I wish I could have seen it; and it cut him to the raw, for all his suave indifference." Suddenly he struck the wall sharply. "And yet--she rides with him to-day. St. George! We are back where we started. Women are queer creatures!"

Just then Sir James Dacre stopped at the corridor door.

"Who is for a ride?" he asked.

"I am," said De Lacy, "if Sir Ralph will excuse me."

De Wilton nodded. "Go, by all means; it was good of you to keep me company even for a moment."

"I might venture to guess," said Dacre, as they cantered across the bailey toward the gate, "that that black of yours was never foaled in England."

"I got Selim in Spain," De Lacy answered, "and with him the story that he came from the stables of the Soldan of Granada--but of that I cannot vouch--nor do I care," patting the shining shoulder; "he is my good friend and companion, and he has never failed me."

Dacre looked at the small head, with its bright, full, kind eye, broad forehead, tapered muzzle, thin, sensitive nostrils and ears; at the arched neck, the deep chest, the rather short barrel, the narrow waist, powerful flanks, and sinewy, springy, slender legs.

"He is beautiful," he said. "Methinks I never saw so perfect a horse."

"And his intelligence is in kind," said Aymer. "He has many accomplishments, but the one most satisfactory to me is the way he understands my voice. . . Observe------"

He dropped the reins over the pommel, and at the word, Selim, without touch of knee or shift of bit, went through all the gaits and facings, ending with the most difficult of all--the seven artificial movements of the horse.

Sir James Dacre's rather cold face warmed with admiration and he reined over and stroked the black's soft muzzle.

"You are a wonder, Selim," he said. "Your equal is not in the Kingdom; though, in a short dash, the Countess' bay mare might put you to your speed."

"Very likely," said Aymer, "but I will wager there is none in England can beat him from the Solway to Land's End."

Dacre smiled--"I would rather share the bet than take it."

Then the talk led to the horses of France and Spain, and thence to the life there in general, for Sir James had never crossed the Channel, and he plied his companion with questions. And so they jogged along in pleasant converse, and De Lacy saw that the reserved and quiet Dacre was in fact as sincere and good-hearted as the generously impulsive De Wilton. And he warmed to them both; for he had antici- pated cold looks, hatred, and jealousy, such as under like conditions he would have met with on the Continent.

And as they rode there came a faint hail from the front--and thrice repeated. The track at that point led through a wood and was straight away for half a mile, then it swung to the left. Just near the turn were two horsemen; and the rearmost, when he saw his cry had been heard, waved his hat and gesticulated violently to- ward the other, who was several lengths in front. Both were coming at top speed.

Sir James Dacre puckered his eyes and peered ahead.

"My sight is rather poor," he said, "but from yonder fellow's motions, I take it he wants us to stop the other--an escape doubtless."

Just then the one in the lead shot through a patch of sunlight and both Knights cried out.

"A woman!" said De Lacy.

"The Countess!" exclaimed Dacre. "What may it mean?"

"She went riding with Lord Darby shortly after mid-day," said Aymer.

"And that is Darby," added Dacre, as the sun hit the second horseman. "Par- dieu! I do not understand--it cannot be she is fleeing from him."

They drew rein, and watched the approaching pair.

"Well, if she is, she is succeeding," Aymer observed. "She is gaining on him at every jump. St. Denis! how that horse of hers can run!"

"It is Wilda, the bay mare I spoke of. But see, Darby still waves. What in Heaven's name ails the man? Can it be the mare has bolted?"

De Lacy shook his head. "The Countess is making no effort to control her; the reins are hanging loose."

Then they heard the first faint beat of the hoofs, growing louder and louder, and presently with it Darby's cry:

"Stop her! Stop her!"

"Maybe, my lord," said De Lacy, leaning forward, his eyes intent upon the

Countess; "if the lady wish it she will signal."

Two hundred yards away now came Wilda running at terrific speed, but straight and true. Suddenly De Lacy swung Selim around.

"It is a runaway," he called to Dacre, "the reins are useless." And even as he said it the Countess told him the same by a motion of her hand.

A moment more and she swept between them; but beside her went the black, leap for leap with the bay. Then Aymer saw the trouble--the bit had broken in the bar, tearing the mouth badly, and from each cheek-strap dangled a useless half, which striking the frightened mare on the muzzle kept driving her to top speed.

The Countess gave De Lacy a quick smile.

"I am trying to enjoy it," she said, "but I think I am dreadfully frightened."

Aymer glanced at the road--it was straight and level for another four hundred yards, then it disappeared, and he remembered it pitched sharply forward in a rough and twisting descent. Whatever he did must be done quickly--no horse ever foaled could carry its rider down that declivity at such a speed.

"Death waits yonder," he said, pointing to the brow of the hill. "I must lift you to my saddle. Will you risk it?"

She hesitated; then suddenly loosed her foot from the stirrup.

"I am ready," she said--and smiled again.

De Lacy dropped his reins.

"Closer, Selim, closer," he commanded.

The black; drew over until his master's boot was pressing the Countess's saddle girth.

"When I give the word," said De Lacy, "free yourself from the pommel and catch me around the neck."

The Countess nodded. "I understand," she said, and gave a quick look forward. The hill was getting very near.

He reached over and wound his right arm about her slender waist. "Now!" he said sharply.

For a second the Countess hung in the air between the plunging horses; then the bay shot ahead alone--and she rested safely across De Lacy's saddle, his arms about her and hers about his neck.

Of his own accord the black had instantly slackened speed, and now at the word he stopped, and the Countess dropped lightly to the ground.

"How can I ever thank you?" she said, giving Sir Aymer her hand.

"By not trying to," he answered, dismounting and kissing her fingers almost reverently. "Fortune has already blessed me over much."

She turned to Selim, who was standing quietly beside his master.

"I may at least thank you, you beauty," she said, and kissed his soft black muzzle.

De Lacy smiled. "Never before have I wished I were a horse," he said.

A bit of color flashed into her cheeks and she busied herself in twisting into place a roll of ruddy hair that had been shaken from its fastenings. It took an unusual time, it seemed, and just as she finished Sir James Dacre rode up.

"I claim a share in the rescue," he said gayly, and gave the Countess her hat, that had been lost when she changed horses. Then silently he held out his hand to De Lacy; and afterward he petted the black and whispered in his ear. And Selim answered by a playful nip, then rubbed his nose against his master's palm.

At that moment Lord Darby dashed up, his horse blown, its sides bloody with rowelling and flecked with foam.

"Thank God, Countess," he exclaimed, "you are not injured."

"Not so much as scratched, thanks to Sir Aymer de Lacy."

"Aye, Sir Aymer, it was cleverly done," said Darby; "a neater rescue methinks I never saw."

De Lacy bowed. "Whatever credit there may be, belongs solely to Selim," he said. "But for his speed and intelligence I had never reached the Countess." Then he led the black forward. "And he asks the honor of carrying her back to Pontefract."

"Not so," Darby interrupted; "that is my privilege," and he swung his own horse around.

The Countess was struggling with her hat.

"But Wilda," she protested.

"Is at the castle now, if she made the hill in safety," said Dacre, watching the scene with the glint of a smile.

The Countess still hesitated--and Darby stepped confidently forward and dropped his hand to put her up.

"Come, my lady," he said.

De Lacy made no move, nor spoke, but his eyes never left the Countess's face. And she, if she felt any irritation at the awkward situation so foolishly forced by Darby, concealed it completely and punished him with a smiling face.

"You may put me on Selim, Lord Darby," she said. "He has carried me part way home, and since he wishes it he shall carry me all the way."

Darby's dark face flushed and for a moment he drew back his hand in refusal--then quickly offered it again. But the delay lost him the favor; for De Lacy, seeing the opportunity, instantly presented his own palm, and the Countess accepted it, and he swung her to his saddle.

Then she looked at Darby. "If you are very good," she said, with a little laugh, "you may put me down at the castle."

And Darby laughed, too. "But you must give me time," he replied. "I am not so nimble as Selim's master."

And so they made their way back to Pontefract, De Lacy walking beside the Countess, and Lord Darby and Sir James Dacre following on horseback just behind. Wilda had evidently got down the hill unhurt; in the soft earth at its foot the deep marks of her running hoofs were very evident; and a little way from the castle they came upon her, calmly browsing beside the track. She had lost her bridle and her fright was quite gone--for she answered to the Countess's call, and permitted De Lacy to put a strap around her neck and make her captive.

As they crossed the drawbridge the Duke of Gloucester was standing near the gate tower and he called Lord Darby to him--and Dacre offering to take Wilda to the stables, Sir Aymer and the Countess were left to go on alone to the keep. As they drew up at the entrance, and the Countess shifted position in the saddle, she dropped her kerchief; De Lacy secured it and put it in his doublet, then reached up to lift her down.

She shook her head.

"The kerchief first," she said, with calm finality.

There was no mistaking the tone, and without a word he gave it to her. She slowly tucked it in her bodice, looking the while toward the gate.

"I thought Lord Darby was to put me down," she said, and giving De Lacy a dazzling smile--"but if you care to act as his substitute, I suppose you may. . . Good-bye, Selim." She gathered up her skirt and moved toward the steps. On the bottom one she turned. "Do you not think, Sir Aymer, it is about time for you to be presented?" she asked--then ran quickly up the stairs and through the doorway.

V
THE CAPTURED FAVOR

St. George's day was dropping into night. Since early morning the castle had been busy in the various ceremonies with which mediaeval England observed the feast of her patron Saint; the garrison had been paraded and inspected; the archers had shot for a gold bugle, and the men-at-arms had striven for a great two-handed sword; there had been races on foot and on horseback, and feats of strength and wrestling bouts; and the Duke himself had presided at the sports and distributed the prizes.

It was almost sundown when the last contest was over and the great crowd of spectators that had congregated within the outer bailey began to disperse. Richard had dismissed his attendants, with the exception of Ratcliffe, and leaning on the latter's arm he sauntered slowly across the stone-paved courtyard toward the keep.

"Methinks," said De Wilton, as he and De Lacy followed at some distance, "that the order we have so long expected must come to-morrow. And I, for one, shall be well content; it is many a long day since I saw London."

"Why so certain of to-morrow?" De Lacy asked.

"Because if His Grace intend to be present at the coronation, he may dally here no longer. . . Say you not so, Dacre?" as the latter joined them.

"Verily, yes," said Dacre, "and I have already directed my squire to prepare for the journey. Marry! it will be a joyous time in London."

"It is long since there was a peaceful crowning in fair England," observed De Lacy, "and I shall be glad indeed to see the pomp."

"It may not equal the splendors you have seen in France," remarked Dacre, "but there will be a goodly show nevertheless; something rather brighter than Yorkshire hills or Scottish heather."

"I have no quarrel with the heather," replied De Wilton, "but the hills are . . .

well, not--so soft as the cheeks and eyes of the dames of the Court."

"In sooth," said De Lacy, "I am with you in that. To me a pretty face was ever more attractive than a granite crag."

"Both are handy in their places," said Dacre with a shrug. "Yet, Pasque Dieu! of the two it were not hard to choose the trustier."

"Go to!" exclaimed De Wilton; "it was not a gallant speech. You will have to mend your mind in London."

"Nay, Sir Ralph, my words, perhaps, but scarce my mind."

"It is the same thing there," De Wilton laughed.

At that moment the Master of Horse suddenly left the Duke and turned toward the stables.

"Busk yourselves for the road, fair sirs," he called, as he passed. "We march after matins to-morrow."

The news spread like the wind through the castle, but it occasioned neither confusion nor even bustle. The personal following of Richard of Gloucester were selected from veteran soldiers who were ever ready. They had but to don harness and mount horse when the route was sounded; and they could have ridden across the drawbridge at sundown, just as readily as the next morning.

In the antechamber that evening there was much discussion by the younger Knights as to the Duke's probable course; would he head the Nobility; would he aim for the Protectorship; would he remain quiescent and let the Woodvilles control? Those older in his service, however, were content to bide patiently the future, for long since had they learned the folly of trying to forecast the purposes of their silent leader.

And Sir Ralph de Wilton and Sir Henry de Vivonne were hot in the argument when Sir James Dacre arose and clapped De Lacy on the shoulder.

"Come along," he said. "These two gentlemen are vastly entertaining, doubtless, but I am for the presence chamber to make my adieux."

The Lady Mary Percy was reading aloud Chaucer's "Knight's Tale" when they were announced, but she quickly laid aside the heavy tome, and the Duchess paused in her embroidery and greeted them with a smile.

"I have seen nothing of you since you saved the Countess," she said, giving each a hand to kiss, "and I owe you both a heavy payment."

"And which, then, does Your Grace rate the higher: the Countess or her hat?" Dacre asked.

"I do not quite understand," said she.

"Sir Aymer de Lacy saved the Countess, and I saved the hat," he explained.

"And what did Lord Darby save?" the Lady Mary asked pertly.

Dacre smiled placidly.

"Nothing--not even his temper; the Countess saved that for him," he answered; and every one laughed--even the Duchess; though she shook her head at him, the while, in mock reproof.

"That forfeits your share of the reward," she said; then turned to De Lacy. "Some time, Sir Aymer, I must have a gallop beside the wonderful Selim."

De Lacy bowed low. "Why not on him?" he asked.

"Well, perhaps--when we all are together again."

"In London--or at Windsor?"

A faint shade of concern came into her eyes, and De Lacy's thoughts instantly recurred to the scene in the Duke's chamber the day he arrived.

"At Windsor, let us hope; the roads are charming there," she said, and then she resumed her embroidery.

"Be seated, sirs," she commanded.

"Come hither, Sir Aymer de Lacy," called the Lady Mary, who was sitting beside the Countess of Clare. . . "It just occurred to me to-day that I heard of you a year or so ago from a friend in France."

"It seems to me," said De Lacy, taking the low stool at her feet, "that I have a sure quarrel with your memory, either because it is laggard or because it is not."

"And which do you think it is?" she asked.

"I might guess the better if I knew your friend's name."

"Marie."

"Half the women of France are Maries."

"You were then at Blois."

"At the Court, you mean?"

She nodded. "And but lately returned from an expedition into Navarre."

De Lacy shook his head. "I cannot guess."

She gave him a knowing smile. "Who of the Princess Margaret's maids, think you, it might have been?"

"It might have been any one of three," he said, "but I will guess Mademoiselle d'Artois."

"At last! At last! . . . How rapidly your mind works under pressure. I wonder, sir, if you will remember us so promptly a year hence."

"Suppose we wait and see," De Lacy answered, and tried to catch the Countess' eye, but failed. Indeed, save for a quick smile of greeting when he joined them, she had given him not a single glance, but had kept her head bent over her needle.

Lady Mary drew down her pretty mouth. "If you can forget Marie d'Artois so soon, what chance have we?" she asked.

"But I have not forgotten her; we were quite too good friends for that."

"And she was quite too fascinating," the Lady Mary laughed.

"Aye, and quite too beautiful."

"Goodness, Beatrix, listen to the man," she exclaimed. "He has the bad taste to praise one woman, to another."

The Countess looked up. "Sir Aymer was lauding Mademoiselle d'Artois to me, last night," she said.

"Can it be, Lady Mary," De Lacy asked, "you do not know that two months since, Marie d'Artois was wedded to the Duc de Boiselle?"

For a moment Lady Mary was taken aback; then she laughed gayly and arose.

"I will leave you to discuss the other two Maries," she said, and moved away. . . "Perhaps they, too, are married," she added, over her shoulder.

De Lacy looked after her contemplatively.

"I wonder," said he, "why the Lady Mary Percy resents my preferring you to her."

"Do you?" the Countess asked--then held up her hand. "Stop, sir, you may not answer--I did but jest."

"And may I not answer . . . in jest?" leaning toward her.

She shook her head. "No, sir, you may not; and if you attempt it, I shall leave you instantly."

"Pardieu!" said he; "you are the most alluringly tantalizing woman I have ever known. The evening of the ride you would scarce look at me, but talked with Lord Darby all the time."

"He was making his farewells; he left the following morning."

De Lacy laughed. "Two hours of farewells! Doubtless, you were delegated to receive them for the Household."

The Countess was busy with her needle. "He seemed to wish it so," she said.

"And the next evening, when I asked you to walk on the wall, you well nigh froze me with the chill of your refusal."

"And will do so again to--Sir Aymer de Lacy."

"And the following morning, at the first asking, you rode with me for leagues."

She flashed a smile at him. "And may do the same again."

"And yet that very evening, when by accident I touched your hand, you turned your back upon me and ignored me for a day."

"And will do the same again," she answered calmly.

"And the next evening you talked with me for hours."

"And am ready to do the same to-night. You, too, may take your farewell of the entire suite through me--unless, of course, you have tired of my foolish vagaries."

"Methinks I am quite satisfied to be classed with Lord Darby in the matter of farewells; and as for the vagaries, they may be tantalizing but, believe me, they are far more winning."

She held up a cautioning finger.

"I prefer your arraignment to your compliments," she said. "Methinks I told you once before of my dislike for flattery."

"That was to Sir Ralph de Wilton . . . the night you walked with him on the wall."

"True, so it was," she laughed; "but you were there and heard it."

He casually picked up a skein of silk that had slipped to the floor, but finding her eyes upon him gave it to her straightway.

"Why not walk now on the ramparts with Sir Ralph?" he asked very low and earnestly.

For an instant she seemed to hesitate; then she looked at him and shook her head.

"I may not," she said. "I have promised the evening to Sir Aymer de Lacy . . . for two hours of farewells."

But the two hours were very brief, indeed; for almost immediately De Vivonne and De Wilton arrived, and shortly thereafter came Sir Richard Ratcliffe and Sir Robert Brackenbury, and the talk became general. And presently Richard himself entered; and when he withdrew the Duchess went with him and the gathering broke up; and De Lacy got no more than a casual word of farewell from the Countess.

In the morning all was activity. The bailey resounded with the stamp of hoofs, the neighing of horses, and the rattle of armor, as the three hundred and more men-at-arms assembled before the keep, awaiting the order to fall in. The under officers stood apart conversing, but glancing, ever and anon, toward the main stairway in anticipation of the coming of the Duke or one of his suite. Presently the dark face of Ratcliffe appeared at the door; and after a quick glance about he waved his hand. Instantly the blare of the trumpet lifted every man into saddle; and in another moment, that which seemed but a confused mass had disentangled itself and swung into a square of glittering steel, over which the morning sunbeams rippled in waves of silver as the horses moved in restlessness.

De Lacy was standing before the entrance, watching the soldiery, when a page hurriedly summoned him to the Duke.

He found Gloucester in the lower hall, booted and spurred for the road, and pacing slowly back and forth, his head upon his breast. He was dressed entirely in black, and his heavy cloak, lined with fur, lay on a near-by bancal. He carried his gauntlets in his right hand, and every step or two would strike them sharply against the top of his high boot. Catesby, Brackenbury and Ratcliffe were gathered a bit apart, talking in low tones. They glanced up when De Lacy appeared, and as he halted just within the doorway, waiting for the Duke to address him, Brackenbury spoke:

"My lord, Sir Aymer de Lacy is here."

Richard wheeled abruptly. "Come hither," he said, and led the way toward the window. "Do you know the country or people in the region of Kirkstall Abbey?"

"No, my lord," said De Lacy. "I have never been north of Pontefract."

"Then you are the one for the purpose. A dozen men-at-arms have been detailed for you; take them and proceed direct to Craigston Castle and deliver to Sir John de Bury this letter. I ride to York to-day and South to-morrow. If you hasten, you can rejoin me at Nottingham. Do you understand?"

"Perfectly, my lord."

"Then away. Come, gentlemen!" and the Duke walked briskly to the stair-way.

As he came within view of those in the courtyard, there arose a mighty shout that echoed from the walls and keep. Gloucester's calm face relaxed in a slight smile and he waved his hand in response. Then scarce touching his foot to the stirrup which Catesby held he leaped into saddle. The trumpet rang out, and the horsemen, breaking from square into column, filed out of the courtyard and across the outer bailey.

Gloucester had tarried, meanwhile, to speak a final word to Sir Robert Wall-ingford; and when he had finished, the last clatter of hoofs on the drawbridge had ceased. As the Constable stepped back with a farewell salute, Richard's quick eye discerned the face of the Duchess at an upper window. Swinging his charger in a demi-volte, he doffed bonnet and flung her a kiss with his finger tips.

"*Au revoir, amante*," he called.

She smiled sweetly upon him and answered his kiss; then stood watching him as he rode rapidly away, followed by his attendant Knights, until the dark arch of the distant gateway hid him from her sight.

A few moments later Sir Aymer de Lacy came riding across the courtyard with his escort. He had changed his suit of velvet for one of steel; for being ignorant both of the country into which he was about to travel and of what manner of adventure might lie before him, he had deemed it well to have something more than silken doublet between his heart and a cloth-yard shaft. His visor was raised, and as he passed the keep, he looked up at every window. All were deserted, however, and he was about to turn away when, suddenly, a casement swung open and the Count-ess of Clare appeared in the stone-framed opening.

"*Au revoir*," she cried, and waved her kerchief.

Then by some mischance the bit of lace slipped from her fingers and floated slowly downward. She made a quick grasp for it, but it had sunk beyond her reach. A puff of wind spread it wide and carried it out toward De Lacy. He watched it as it dropped, bringing Selim almost to a stand to keep beneath it, and at length it rested upon his extended hand.

"I claim my favor, fair Countess," he called, and wound it round the crest of his helmet--then loosened rein and dashed away.

VI
A WAYSIDE SKIRMISH

For a space Sir Aymer rode alone at the head of the column without even casting a glance behind or addressing a word to his squire. Presently the road forked and turning half around in his saddle, he inquired: "Which leads to Kirkstall Abbey?"

"The straightaway one, my lord; the other would carry you back to Wakefield," said the elderly under-officer, whose hair, where it had strayed from under his casquetel, was silvered, and across whose weather-beaten face, from chin to temple, ran a bright red scar.

"The battlefield?"

"The same, sir."

"Ride beside me," said De Lacy. "Did you fight at Wakefield?"

"I did, fair sir--it was a bloody field."

"The Duke of York died that day."

"Aye, sir--I stood not ten feet from him when he fell. He was a brave knight, and our own Gloucester much resembles him in countenance."

"You have seen many battles, my man?"

"Since the first St. Albans I have missed scarce one. It is a trade that came into the family with my grandsire's sire."

"And do your children follow it, as well?"

"Not so, my lord. Raynor Royk has none to succeed him. And by your leave it is small matter. In a few years there will be but scant work for my calling in this land. England has seen her last warrior King--unless------"

"Unless what?" said De Lacy.

The old retainer glanced shrewdly at his young leader; then answered with apparent carelessness.

"Unless Richard of Gloucester should wear the crown."

De Lacy looked at him sharply.

"Small likelihood of that, my man," said he. "Edward left a goodly family."

"In truth yes, my lord," was the answer. "Yet there would be more joy among the soldiers in the North if Gloucester were our King."

Doubtless the speech merited rebuke,--it was over near to treason,--but the man was honest in his devotion to the Duke, and likely meant no particular disrespect to the young Edward. So De Lacy let it pass, but straightway changed the subject.

"Do you know Craigston Castle?" he asked.

"Most thoroughly."

"Where is it?"

"On the North bank of the Wharfe, a short three leagues beyond Kirkstall Abbey."

"And the Abbey?"

"Five leagues or more from Pontefract."

"A proper distance--we can taste the good monks' hospitality and still make Craigston before night. Is this the Aire I see shining ahead?"

"The same; the ford is easy."

De Lacy nodded; and the veteran taking that as his dismissal drew back and resumed his place in the column.

The nones bell had already sounded some little time when they drew rein before the lodge of the great Cistercian Abbey. The gates were closed, but the wicket was open and at it was the rotund face of the brother who served as porter.

"Be so kind, worthy monk, as to say to your superior that a Knight and his attendants crave refreshment ere they travel further," said De Lacy.

"Enter, fair lord," returned the porter, swinging back the gates. "Bid your men repair to the buttery yonder, while I conduct your worship to the holy father."

They found the Abbot pacing the gravel path between the cloister and the church, with his chancellor at his side. His cowl was thrown back and the white gown of his Order, which hung full to his feet, was fastened close to the throat. His face was pale, and the well-cut features and the small hands betokened his gentle birth. He was, possibly, about fifty years of age, but his step and bearing were as easy as De Lacy's own.

"*Benedicite*, my son," said he, as the Knight bent head to the uplifted hand, "you are welcome, and just in time to join us at the noonday meal."

"It was to ask refreshment for myself and my men that I halted, and your reverence has in kindness anticipated me," said De Lacy.

The Abbot turned to the porter: "Brother James," he said, "see that all are provided for and that the horses have a full allowance of grain.--And now, there sounds the horn for us. Sir------"

"Aymer de Lacy," filled in the Knight.

"A goodly name, my son; and one dear to Yorkshire hereabouts, although, now, near forgotten. Have you seen Pontefract?"

"I quit it but this morning."

"In sooth!" said the Abbot, with sudden interest. "And is His Grace of Gloucester still in presence there?"

"He left shortly before I did."

"For London?"

"Nay, methinks I heard he rode to York," replied De Lacy, who had learned enough on the Continent of the ways of churchmen not to tell them all he knew.

"To York!" said the Abbot in some surprise. "How many men did he take with him?"

"I was not present when the Duke departed and I did not see his following," returned Aymer.

The Abbot's keen eyes tried to read behind the answer, but evidently without success, for his next remark was: "I do not recall your face, Sir Aymer, among the many Knights who have traversed these parts."

"Your memory is entirely trustworthy," said De Lacy. "I came from France but lately, and have never seen this section until to-day."

"Fare you not to the coronation?"

"In truth, yes, your reverence; Deo volente."

"Then must you soon turn bridle; London lies to the South, my son," said the Abbot, with a smile.

De Lacy laughed. "Never fear--I shall be there--Deo volente."

"You have learned the Christian virtue of humility, at all events," said the priest, as they entered the hall, where the monks were already seated around the long tables, awaiting the coming of the Abbot. Upon his appearance they all arose and remained standing while the Chancellor droned a Latin blessing. Then he took his carved chair at the smaller table on the dais, with the Knight beside him, and the repast began. During the meal, the Abbot made no effort to obtain his guest's destination or mission, but discussed matters of general import. He, himself, contrary to the usual habits of the monks of his day, ate but little, and when De Lacy had finished he withdrew with him.

"You are anxious to be on your way," he said, "and I will not detain you. These roads are scarce pleasant after night-fall."

In the courtyard the men-at-arms were drawn up awaiting the order to mount.

"Verily, you ride well attended, my son. The roads need not bother you," said the Abbot, as he ran his eyes over the array. . . "Methinks I have seen your face before," looking hard at Raynor Royk.

"Like as not, your reverence," said the old retainer calmly; "I am no stranger in Yorkshire."

At that moment Dauvrey led the Knight's horse forward, and Aymer turned to the monk before he could address another question to Raynor.

"I am much beholden, my lord Abbot, for your kindly entertainment and I hope some day I may requite it. Farewell."

"Farewell, my son," returned the monk. "May the peace of the Holy Benedict rest upon you."

He watched them until the last horseman had clattered through the gateway, then turned away.

"My mitre on it, they are Gloucester's men," he muttered.

When they had quit the Abbey, De Lacy again summoned Raynor Royk and questioned him regarding the Abbot of Kirkstall. The old soldier, like the majority of his fellows who made fighting a business, had a contemptuous indifference to the clerical class. A blessing or a curse was alike of little consequence to men who feared neither God, man, nor Devil, and who would as readily strip a sleek priest as a good, fat merchant. Raynor's words were blunt and to the point. He knew nothing of the Abbot except through the gossip of the camp and guard-room, and that made him a cadet of a noble family of the South of England, who for some unknown reason had, in early manhood, suddenly laid aside his sword and shield and assumed Holy Orders. He had been the Abbot of Kirkstall for many years, and it was understood had great power and influence in the Church; though he, himself, rarely went beyond the limits of his own domain. He was, however, regarded as an intriguing, political priest, of Lancastrian inclination, but shrewd enough to trim successfully to whatever faction might be in power.

Two of the remaining leagues had been covered, and they were within a mile or so of the Wharfe when, rounding a sharp turn, they came upon a scene that brought every man's sword from its sheath. The narrow road, at this point, was through a dense forest of oaks and beeches that crowded to the very edge of the track and formed an arch over it. The trees grew close together, and the branches were so interlocked that the sunlight penetrated with difficulty; and though the day was still far from spent, yet, here, the shadows had already begun to lengthen into an early twilight. Some two hundred yards down this road was a group of figures that swayed, now this way, now that, in the broil of conflict, while from it came the clash of steel. In the road was the dead body of a horse, and, upon either side of it, lay two men who would never draw weapon again. The one had been split almost to the nose by a single downright blow, and the other had been pierced through the throat by a thrust of the point.

At a little distance, with his back against a tree and defending himself vigorously from the assault of half a dozen men, stood a tall and elderly Knight. He was not in armor, except for a light corselet of steel, and already he had been more than once slightly wounded. His bonnet had been lost in the melee, and his grey hair was smudged with blood along the temple. Two more men were dead at his feet, and for the moment the others hesitated to press in and end the fight. That huge sword could make short work of at least another pair of them before the hands that held it would relax, and the uncertainty as to which would be the victims stayed their rush. Suddenly the Knight leaped forward, cut down the one nearest him, and was back to the tree before the others had recovered from their surprise. Then with a roar of anger they flung themselves upon him, and the struggle began anew. In their rage and impetuosity, however, they fought without method, and the Knight was able for a short interval, by skilful play, to sweep aside their points and to parry their blows. But it forced him to fight wholly on the defensive, and his age and wounds left no doubt as to the ultimate result. His arm grew tired, and the grip on his sword hilt weakened. . . His enemies pressed him closer and closer. . . A blow got past his guard and pierced his thigh. He had strength for only one more stroke; and he gathered it for a final rush and balanced himself for the opportunity. So fierce was the conflict that no one noticed the approach of De Lacy until, with a shout of "*Au secours*!" he rode down upon them. He had out-stripped all his escort, except his squire, and even he was several lengths behind. Taken by surprise, the assailants hesitated a moment, and so lost their only opportunity for escape. With a sweep of his long sword he shore a head clean from its shoulders, another man went down before his horse's rush; and then, swinging in a demi-volte, he split a third through collar-bone and deep into the breast. Meanwhile, the old Knight had slain one and Giles Dauvrey had stopped the flight of another. But one escaped, and he, in the confusion, had darted into the forest and was quickly lost amid its shadows.

"By St. Luke, sir!" said the old Knight, as he leaned heavily on his sword, "your coming was most opportune. My strength was almost spent."

"It was a gallant fight," said Aymer. "I feared every instant they would close ere I could reach you. . . But you are wounded!"

"Nay, they are only scratches and will heal shortly--yet the leg grows heavy and I would best rest it," and he seated himself on the turf at the foot of the tree. "This comes of riding in silk instead of steel--certes, I am old enough to know better."

De Lacy dismounted and aided him to examine his wounds. The only one of any consequence was in the leg; it had been made by a sword thrust; and the point having penetrated only the fleshy part of the thigh, no material damage was inflicted.

"Were you alone when assaulted?" asked De Lacy, the while he was binding a scarf around the injury.

"Yes--and another piece of childishness. I had despatched my squire on a sudden errand, a short ways back, and had no notion of danger, when these rogues suddenly set upon me. I made short work of two of them and would have got through, without difficulty, but for the death of my horse. They stabbed him, as you see. Then I got my back against the tree and managed to keep them off for a period. The rest you know. And to whom am I so heavily indebted?"

"My name is Aymer de Lacy."

"By St. Luke! John de Bury is glad that it is to a De Lacy he owes his life."

"Are you Sir John de Bury of Craigston Castle?"

"The same--although, but for you I would be of the Kingdom of Spirits instead."

"It would appear that my coming was very timely for us both," said De Lacy, "for my mission in these parts is with you."

"With me?" Sir John de Bury exclaimed, struggling to his feet. "Then, if you will let me have a horse, I will ride beside you to the castle--it is less than half a league distant."

"One moment, Sir John," said Aymer. "Did you recognize any of your assailants?"

"Not one, by St. Luke," said De Bury. "Some rascally robbers, I fancy; there are enough of them in these parts."

De Lacy motioned to Raynor.

"Do you know this carrion?" he asked.

The veteran dismounted and examined the bodies; turning with his foot those that had fallen face downward.

"They are strangers to me, my lord," he said. "I never saw hair of them before. But, perchance, this fellow can give you some information," and suddenly stooping, he seized one of the seeming dead men by the neck and jerked him to his feet. "Answer the Knight, rogue," he said. "Raynor Royk has seen too many dead bodies to be fooled by one that has not a scratch upon it."

"By St, Denis!" said Do Lacy, "he is the one my good horse knocked over. I clean forgot him. How now, fellow," he continued sternly, "what mean you by assaulting a Knight upon the King's highway; and who set you up to such work?"

The man, who had been simulating death, hoping so to escape, regarded De Lacy with a frown and in sullen silence.

"Speak," said Raynor, giving him a shake that made his teeth rattle.

For answer he suddenly plucked a small dagger from a concealed sheath and, twisting around, struck full and hard at the old soldier's face, which was unprotected by the steel cap. Raynor sprang back and avoided the blow, but in so doing he released his hold, and the rogue dashed instantly for cover. No one was in his way and his escape seemed certain, for the heavily armed men of De Lacy would have no chance in a foot race with one lightly clad. With two bounds he had reached the line of trees and was almost secure when, like a flash, Giles Dauvrey drew his heavy dagger and hurled it after him. The point struck full in the centre of the neck and sank deep into flesh and bone. With a gurgling cry he plunged forward and lay still--dead before his body touched the turf.

"By St. Peter! a neat throw, Sir Squire," said Raynor, as he jerked out the weapon and handed it to Dauvrey. "I mind never to have seen a better."

"Toss the other carrion by the roadside," said De Lacy; "we tarry here no longer."

VII
A FAVOR LOST

When De Lacy, armed for the road, sought his host the following morning to say farewell, he found him in an easy chair near the fireplace in the hall, with his wounded leg resting on a stool, and the answer to Gloucester's letter in his hand. The old Knight made as though to arise, but the younger quickly placed his hand upon his shoulder and held him firm in his seat.

"Not so, Sir John," he insisted. "Do you remain quiet; I know the way to the courtyard."

"It grieves me sore that you cannot stay with me longer," said De Bury, allowing himself to be persuaded. "Yet I hope that we shall soon meet again. Craigston Castle is ever ready to receive you."

"And it shall have the chance, I assure you, when I am again in these parts--though our next meeting is likely to be in London; His Grace will scarce soon return to the North."

"Mayhap," replied Sir John; "but for the present, my wound and my duties keep me here. And, to speak truly, I am not unwilling; when you have reached my age, Sir Aymer, you will care little for the empty splendor of the Court--and that reminds me: you may meet there my niece, the Countess of Clare, and if you do--verily, you have met her," as De Lacy smiled, "and have been stricken like the rest. Beware, my son, your corselet is no protection against the shafts of a woman's eyes."

"In truth, I know it," De Lacy laughed. "I have met the Countess and . . . it is needless to say more. Yet it was at Pontefract and not at Windsor that I saw her. She is with the Duchess of Gloucester."

"In sooth! . . . And you are with the Duke of Gloucester," said De Bury, with a shrewd smile. "It is either fortune most rare or fate most drear. By St. Luke! I believe the debt has shifted and that you should thank me for having had the opportunity to save her uncle's life. Nay, I did but jest," he added hastily. "You have seen many a face, doubtless, in sunny France fairer far than hers; yet is she very dear to me and winning to my old eyes. Should you see her as you pass Pontefract--if you return that way--say to her that I am here, and that a short visit from her would be very welcome."

"It may be that the Duchess has left the castle," replied Aymer, "but your message shall reach the Countess."

"Best deliver it in person," said Sir John, kindly.

"Trust me for that," De Lacy answered--"and now farewell."

"A most gallant youth," said De Bury, when Sir Aymer was gone, "and of the right fighting stock; yet, if I mistake not, that sweet niece of mine is likely to make trouble for him."

The shorter route to London was by Sheffield, but De Lacy chose to go by way of Pontefract. It would, of course, bring him upon the main highway between York and London further North than by the Sheffield road; yet he took the chance of the Duke being delayed an extra day at York, in which event he would be able to await him at Doncaster, and join him at that place instead of at Nottingham.

It was still wanting something of noon when the low white walls of Kirkstall glinted before them. De Lacy rode steadily on, however, nodding pleasantly to the porter, who was standing in the gateway, but declining his invitation to enter. It was better, he thought, that Abbot Aldam should have no opportunity to question his men as to their destination of yesterday. When they reached the banks of Aire, he ordered a short halt; then swinging again into saddle, they splashed through the clear waters and breasting the opposite bank resumed the march at a rapid walk. Presently a body of horsemen hove in sight and, as they approached, De Lacy eyed them carefully. They were less than a dozen in number, and though they displayed no banner, yet the sun gleamed from steel head-pieces and chamfrons. The man in front, however, was plainly not in armor and his horse was strangely small. Then, as the distance was reduced, the horse became an ass and the rider the Abbot of Kirkstall.

"You travel early, Lord Abbot," said Aymer, as they met and halted.

"It is of our calling, my son. Religion knows no night. But you also must have risen early--on your way to the Coronation--Deo volente?" with a quizzical smile.

"As fast as horse will carry me."

"Perchance you may overtake the Duke of Gloucester; he left York to-day, I believe."

"He has rather a long start, methinks, for a stern chase," replied Aymer.

"Six hundred men move not so quickly as twelve, my son," said the monk. "Indeed, you might come up with him at Nottingham," he added carelessly.

"Peradventure, yes--Deo volente," wondering how much the Abbot knew of the matter and how much was shrewd conjecture. "But will not your reverence attend the Coronation? There is sure to be a brave array of churchmen there."

"No doubt," returned the Abbot; "but I care little for such gay scenes or for the intrigues of the Court. A country priest has no training for such traps. However, I trust we shall soon meet again; and, meanwhile, Kirkstall's gates are always open to you. *Pax vobiscum*."

"Hypocritical liar," muttered De Lacy, when the two troops had passed. "I would think twice ere I trusted myself in your power if I chanced to be an obstacle to your schemes. Giles, what think you of yon Abbot?"

"He is much of his kind and I like not the breed," replied Dauvrey. "Methinks he resembles rather his brethren of Italy than those I have seen in this land of mist and fog. He has been meddling with us, I warrant."

The Knight laughed.

"He has shown a most Christian solicitude for us, at all events," he said.

When De Lacy drew rein before the barbican of Pontefract, there was no need to wind horn to gain entrance, for the drawbridge was down and Lord Darby, with a score of attendants, was just departing.

"Now what in Satan's name brought him back?" Aymer muttered--though he knew the answer well enough. Then he raised his hand in salute. "I give you greeting, my lord," he said.

And Darby was even less pleased, for he was going and De Lacy was coming; but he, too, masked his face, and gave the welcome back in kind.

"Methought you would be with the Duke," he observed, drawing aside to let his men pass.

"And methought you were by now in London," De Lacy returned.

Darby smiled at the evasion. "Are you not for the Coronation?" he asked bluntly.

De Lacy nodded. "Indeed, yes--unless I am untowardly prevented."

"If you fare further to-day," said Darby, "I will wait and we can ride together to Doncaster--a short delay will be well repaid by your company."

It was but a play to know if De Lacy intended to stay the night at Pontefract, and it got its answer instantly.

"Your Lordship tempts me sorely," said Sir Aymer, "but I am obliged to remain here until the morrow." Then he smiled blandly at him; "it is unfortunate you have already started," he added.

Darby's black eyes brightened.

"Yes," said he, "it is."

He glanced quickly toward his escort, which was now at the foot of the hill, and laid his hand upon his bugle, as though to sound the recall--then he gave a mocking laugh.

"The luck is yours, this toss," he said; and with a wave of his hand, that might have been as much a menace as a farewell, he spurred away.

There were no faces at the windows as De Lacy crossed the courtyard, and he despatched a page to acquaint the Countess of Clare of his arrival and of his desire for a short interview. Presently the boy returned with the information that the Countess was with the Duchess, and that she could not see him before evening.

He sought the presence chamber at the usual hour, but it was deserted; and after waiting a short while he was on the point of leaving when the arras suddenly parted and the Countess entered.

"I am glad to see you," she said, giving him her hand, "even though you are a laggard and a thief."

"Why laggard?" De Lacy asked.

"Because you should be with the Duke and not here."

"Granted," said he. "Did you call Lord Darby laggard, too?"

"You will have to ask him; I do not now remember."

"I passed him at the gate, and from his temper I might guess you called him even worse."

"At least I know I did not dub him thief." Then she held out her hand. "The kerchief," she said peremptorily.

De Lacy slowly drew forth the bit of lace.

"Rather would I lose a quartering," he said very gently, "yet, in honor, I may not keep it against your will."

"And honor," said she seriously, as she took the kerchief, "is dearer far than all our quarterings. . . What brings you back to Pontefract?"

"You," said De Lacy, smilingly.

"Of course! but what else?--be serious."

"I am serious. But for you I would be riding fast and hard after the Duke. I stopped at Pontefract for two purposes; of which, one was to deliver to you a message from that gallant Knight, Sir John de Bury."

"My uncle!" she exclaimed. "He is in Scotland."

De Lacy shook his head. "He is now at Craigston Castle, whence I have just come, and bring you his loving greetings."

"The dear old man! How is he?"

"As strong as an oak, save for a slight wound."

"Wounded! How--where?" she demanded, with sharp concern.

"Only a sword thrust in the thigh, got in a skirmish with some brigands about this hour yesterday," said De Lacy; and told her the story of the fray in detail.

At the end the Countess arose.

"I must go now," she said. "The Duchess will need me; but first, tell me the other purpose that halted you here."

"The other," replied De Lacy slowly, "has been accomplished."

She looked at him questioningly.

"How so, if it were on my account you tarried?"

Aymer smiled.

"That I shall leave for you to guess," he said.

To his amazement the Countess did not reprove him, but blushed and looked away.

He bent eagerly toward her.

"My lady," he said, "in all the years I have worn spurs, I have yet to ask gage of woman. To-morrow I fare where there may be fightings enough, as you well know. Grant me, I pray, some token, and let my first sword stroke in England be as your Knight."

"Did you strike no blow yesterday?" she asked.

"None of which a soldier may be proud--it was but a lot of *canaille*."

For a moment the Countess looked him steadily in the eyes--then answered in those tones of finality from which he knew there lay no appeal.

"Sir Aymer, you ask for that which no man has ever had from me. Many times--and I say it without pride--has it been sought by Knights most worthy; yet to them all have I ever given nay. Beatrix de Beaumont bestows nor gage nor favor until she plight her troth."

With a smile, whose sweetness De Lacy long remembered in after days, she gave him her hand, and he bent low over it and touched it to his lips. Then suddenly she whisked it from him and was gone behind the arras.

VIII
THE INN OF NORTHAMPTON

When De Lacy--now in ordinary riding dress, his armor having been relegated to the baggage beasts--reached the main highway the following morning, he looked in vain for the dust of Gloucester's column or the glimmer of sun on steel. The road was deserted. Not a traveler was in sight, and there being no means of ascertaining if the Duke had passed, he adopted the only safe course and took up the march for London. Presently, upon cresting a hill, they met a pair of Black Friars trudging slowly along towards York; but little information was obtained from them, for they had not been on the road yesterday, having spent the last week at a neighboring monastery, which they had quit only that morning. It was rumored there, however, that the Duke of Gloucester had passed southward the prior day with a great train of attendants. This, at least, was some slight indication, and thanking them courteously De Lacy jogged on; but it was not until they reached Doncaster, about noon, that accurate knowledge of the Duke was obtained.

Halting before the inn of the "Silver Sun," a ramshackle old house, from over whose door, as proclaiming the character of the place, projected a long pole with a bunch of furze on the end, De Lacy called, "Ho, within!"

The landlord, a big, blear-eyed rogue, much the worse for wear and ale, came shambling out at the summons. His listlessness vanished quickly enough, however, at sight of the Knight and his following; and bowing to the ground he asked how he might serve them.

"With food and drink, good fellow," said De Lacy; "and that right quickly."

"Your worship shall be accommodated immediately with what I have," said the man with another bow that almost overbalanced him, "but if it is meagre, blame the Duke of Gloucester and his men."

"His Grace has passed?" asked Aymer.

"God's truth! he has," said the fellow. "He precedes you by a day. And, saving your lordship, if you travel to the Coronation, methinks you will have but scant fare along the road. They eat things clean as they go--but pay good silver for it."

"How many has the Duke in his train?"

"At least six hundred, I should say."

"He has doubled his force since he left Pontefract," observed Aymer to his squire, as the inn-keeper retired. "And there may be truth in what the rogue says--we may find slender provision in the wake of such a column."

"If there be enough for the horses, we can soon overtake them," said the squire; "for the men, it matters little: we all are soldiers."

De Lacy nodded. "We will push on steadily, and though I know little of this country, I fancy we will come up with the Duke by to-morrow night."

"By your lordship's permission," said old Raynor Royk respectfully, who had overheard the conversation, "we shall not see the White Boar banner this side Leicester town, and we shall scarce reach there before the evening of the second day from now."

And the old veteran, as events proved, was correct in his calculation.

When De Lacy entered Leicester, he hailed the first soldier he chanced upon and was informed that Gloucester lodged at the "White Boar," near the center of the town. It was a large and handsome stone house, with the second floor of timber overhanging the street; and before it swung the painted sign: a white boar and a thorn bush, indicating that the place was named in honor of the Duke. And De Lacy smiled as he thought how, to his own knowledge, at least half a dozen inns on the Continent had been hastily compelled to rechristen themselves when, from some cause or other, the particular individual whose name or arms they bore fell suddenly into disgrace. That such might happen in this case, however, never crossed his mind.

Passing the guards, who knew him and saluted, he entered the house, but was stopped at once by two strange squires, who informed him that the Duke was at present engaged. But even as they spoke, the inner door opened and Sir Richard Ratcliffe came out.

"Welcome back, Sir Aymer," he exclaimed. "The Duke has inquired for you. Why were you not announced?"

"I was told he was engaged," said Aymer.

"That was because they did not know you were of the Household. Come--" and himself admitted him.

The Duke was alone, seated before a rough table with his head upon his hand, and he did not stir until De Lacy stood directly before him. Then raising his eyes he fastened them intently upon the young Knight's face, though without sternness.

"You stopped at Pontefract," he said.

"I did, so please you," replied Aymer promptly. "I could gain but little by going farther that evening."

"And might gain much by staying," said Gloucester, sententiously. "However, I am glad, since you can give me word of the Duchess. How fares she?"

"As when you left, my lord. She sent her loving wishes to you."

Then drawing out De Bury's letter, he presented it without remark.

Richard read it carefully, and inquired regarding the journey to Craigston Castle. De Lacy narrated briefly the incident of the attack upon Sir John, but detailed at length the conduct of the Abbot of Kirkstall. The Duke, however, seemed more interested in the assault than in the priest, and asked particularly concerning the assailants. But on learning that neither De Bury nor the veteran Royk had recognized any of them, he dropped the matter with the remark:

"You have profited by your experience on the Continent. Not many would have thought to investigate these seeming outlaws."

De Lacy thanked the Duke for his words, and after being informed that he was to lodge at the inn with the rest of the suite, and that the march would be resumed an hour after daybreak, he withdrew, and having dismissed the squire with the horses went in search of Dacre or De Wilton.

It was a brave array that passed out of Leicester that Tuesday morning behind the royal Duke, and in soldiery fitness, man for man, its like was not in England. But it was a peculiar march, withal. No flourish of trumpets heralded the advance; no gaudy costumes clothed the attending Knights. The bugles were hushed, save where necessary to convey an order; the banners were bound in sable; upon every man was the badge of mourning; Richard himself was clad in black, and the trappings of his horse were raven-hued. Not since the great Henry died at Vincennes, sixty and more years before, had England mourned for a King; and as they passed along the highway and through the straggling villages, the people wondered at the soberly garbed and quiet column, forgetting, for the moment, that Edward the Fourth was sleeping in the chapel of St. George at Windsor and that his successor was not yet crowned.

All morning Gloucester rode steadily onward, halting near noon at a wayside hostelry for refreshment. The keeper, unnerved at the sudden advent of such a guest, could only stand and stare at the Duke, forgetting in his amazement even the accustomed bow with which he would have greeted an ordinary wayfarer, until a sharp word from Catesby brought him to his wits.

When the meal was almost finished, a sudden commotion arose outside, and the door was opened to admit one whose appearance showed every evidence of a rapid ride.

"Speak," said Richard.

The messenger saluted. "So please you, my lord, His Majesty will reach Northampton by four o'clock this afternoon."

Gloucester nodded; then arose and drew on his gauntlets.

"Gentlemen," said he, "we may not dally longer. Order up the horses, Ratcliffe, and let the route be sounded; we must be at Northampton ere the vespers chime."

"There will be some shrewd tongue play, methinks, and perchance sharp action this night," remarked De Wilton to De Lacy as, late in the afternoon, the towers of Northampton lifted before them. "Rivers and Grey are with young Edward--it will be Woodville against Plantagenet, and England for the stakes."

"A royal game, indeed," said De Lacy; "yet, surely, Edward's kingdom is secure."

"Pasque Dieu!" exclaimed De Wilton, "I can answer that better after he is crowned. All that I think now is that the situation is very grave. This meeting in yonder town is big with fate."

"I fear I am too new to my native land to appreciate the present situation," replied De Lacy; "yet I hope that war may be averted. There has been bloodshed enough in this fair land since the Roses were plucked."

"By St. George! my heart is with yours," returned De Wilton instantly; "yet, mark me, this night will make history for England. If not, then I mistake the Duke of Gloucester. It is obvious now that, to him, this meeting is no accident--it was timed for most adroitly. Why did he tarry so long at Pontefract, unless because it were easier to prick the Woodville bubble at Northampton than in London?"

"You know the Prince far better than I," said De Lacy, "but perchance you do not know that with Rivers ride two thousand men. If Gloucester intended such a course, why did he not bring a larger following? He was fully advised of the number of the King's escort."

"Because it would have aroused instant suspicion and left him no recourse but to force. He has some other plan, I warrant. Yet, should it come to blows, Richard himself is equal to a thousand men."

"Scarce so much as that, I fancy," said De Lacy, with a laugh. "Nathless, sooner will I ride behind the Boar of Gloucester with six hundred swords than under the Woodville banner with thrice the number."

"Well said, by St. George!" De Wilton exclaimed. "No Lancastrian upstart for me."

"Be not so energetic, Sir Ralph," said De Lacy, as Ratcliffe, hearing the words, looked back. "But tell me, I pray, who are these that approach?"

"Your eyes are keener than mine," returned De Wilton, "for I can scarce discern them at all. Is there any banner displayed?"

"Aye, but I cannot yet distinguish the device. . . . There are at least fifty of them, and they are riding most marvellously fast. By St. Denis! they cannot travel far at such a pace. When the sun next falls athwart the banner, I will try to make it out. . . There . . . Pardieu! it is a queer bearing: *argent, a la fasce-canton a desire de gueules*. Do you know it, or have I not read it aright?"

"Nay, your heraldry is not amiss," said De Wilton. "It is the red fess and canton of the Woodvilles. Yonder comes Lord Anthony of Scales and Rivers."

"Then the struggle is on, I ween," remarked De Lacy. "Let us move closer to the Duke. I would not miss this meeting."

When the horsemen were a short distance away, they broke from a hand gallop into a walk, and then all halted except the two who were in front. Of these, one was a man nearing middle age, of most courtly bearing and noble countenance; while his companion, who resembled him somewhat, was considerably younger. Meanwhile, Gloucester had kept steadily on; but when the others dismounted and advanced on foot, he instantly drew rein, and as Ratcliffe threw himself from the saddle and held the stirrup he stepped to the ground.

"Welcome, noble Rivers and Grey!" he exclaimed. "How fares His Majesty?"

The two men bent over the Duke's hands, and the elder replied: "Fit as a King, and most anxious to greet his great and noble uncle."

"Not more than is his uncle to greet him," said Gloucester; and Rivers read two meanings in the words. "Therefore, let us proceed; and do you and Sir Richard ride beside me; I have questions by the score to ask."

Presently, as they neared the gate of the town, Gloucester turned to the Earl.

"Where does the King lodge--at the castle?" he asked.

"His Majesty," replied Rivers, with a quick glance at the Duke, "has a boy's eagerness to reach London, and insisted upon pushing on as far as Stoney Stratford--this afternoon. He had already left Northampton when we learned of your approach. A moment more and we also would have been gone, for it found us with foot in stirrup."

There was a smile on the Duke's lips as he listened to this unexpected news.

"I do not wonder at Edward's haste," he answered lightly. "Who would not be impatient when a crown is waiting for him?--though I regret that it postpones our meeting till the morrow."

"You will not follow the King to-night?" asked Rivers quickly.

"No, I shall lie here if you and Sir Richard will bear me company. But if you rejoin him, I must perforce go, too--for me now to remain here alone would be discourteous."

"Your Grace honors us overmuch; we shall stay and gladly," replied Rivers readily. "Edward has the others of his Household, and can spare us for one night."

"Marry, yes!" said Richard. "Vaughan and Croft and Worcester's Bishop can hold him tight enough, else has the Welsh air changed them greatly."

At the large inn near the market-place the party halted, and Gloucester, after a few words aside with Ratcliffe, summoned Catesby and retired to his room. An hour later he descended and requested Rivers and Grey to join him at the evening meal.

Scarcely had it begun when down the street came the rattle of bridle-rings and the click of many hoofs. Rivers glanced apprehensively at the Duke, and then at Grey, and then back again at the Duke, who was sipping his wine apparently quite oblivious of the approaching noise. In another moment, at the outer door an imperious voice demanded:

"Is His Grace of Gloucester within?"

At the tones, Rivers started and dropped his knife upon his plate; his brows contracted slightly and a troubled look dawned in his eyes.

"Ha, De Lacy, well met!" came the voice again.

"By St. Denis! my lord, I am glad to see you," was the response. "It is a pleasure I had not counted on this side of London. Have you seen the Duke?"

"I arrived but this moment. Will you take me to him?"

"Assuredly--he is now at supper, but I shall venture to admit you."

They crossed the outer room, the door opened, and De Lacy stepped within and announced:

"The Duke of Buckingham!"

The man who entered was full six feet in height and slender, and bore himself with the easy assurance of one accustomed to respect and deference. His face was handsome in general outline and effect, though the features were not accordant with one another. Beneath a mass of ruddy hair, a broad, high forehead arched a pair of shifty grey eyes and a large, full nose overhung a mouth of indifferent strength, while the whole was gripped by a chin that was a fit complement to the forehead. He paused for an instant, as his glance fell on Gloucester's companions, and his surprise was very evident--then he doffed bonnet and came forward.

"By St. Paul!" exclaimed Richard, rising and extending his hand, "it is so long since I have seen the Duke of Buckingham that it was well to announce him formally."

"It is only those with the fame of a Gloucester that require no introduction," replied Stafford, with a graceful bow that included also Rivers and Grey.

"Come, come, Sir Duke!" said Richard, "this is too much of a family gathering for the turning of compliments."

"In truth, yes," returned Buckingham--"a half-brother and three uncles of our King--but, pardieu! where is His Majesty? Methought you traveled with him, fair brother-in-law."

"Edward lies to-night at Stoney Stratford," replied Rivers.

"Aye, it is unexpected all around, this meeting, it seems," said Richard suavely. "And, by St. Paul! a happy chance indeed. Come, Buckingham, the gross chare grow cold; take place and fall to. . . Catesby, tell the cook to sauce another capon and unbrace a mallard."

In all history there scarce had been a supper party such as this. There, about that table in this humble hostelry, were gathered four noblemen--three of them the most powerful in all England--who were arrayed against each other as leaders of the two factions that were playing for the highest stakes a mortal knows. Every one knew the relative positions of the others (for Rivers naturally judged Gloucester to be against the Woodvilles); that, within a few short days, the final move must be made; and that all their gayety and jocosity were hollow, and assumed but as a mask. At that very moment, while they smiled and played at friendship, Rivers and Grey were consumed with anxiety at this sudden appearance of Buckingham, their arch-enemy, and were hating him and Richard with fierce intensity; Buckingham was regarding them with all the fervid resentment the old Nobility had for this upstart family; while Gloucester, with neither hatred nor resentment in his mind, but with the cool, calm judgment that ever rose above the pettiness of personal feeling, was viewing them only as pawns that hampered his game of statecraft and therefore must be swept from the board.

It was near midnight when they quit the table and retired to their rooms above. Richard dismissed Catesby, who as Chamberlain was waiting for him, and drawing the rude chair to the many-paned window he opened it, and sat looking out upon the street below. Comparative quiet had settled over the town, broken now and then by a noise from the camp, or the shouts of some roistering soldiers far down the road. Around the inn there was only the tramp of the guards, the rattle of their arms, or the low word of greeting as they met. Presently there came an easy knock upon the door and Buckingham entered and shot the bolt behind him. Gloucester had turned his head at the first sound, but said nothing until the Duke was beside him. Then, pointing toward the heavens, he remarked, as he closed the casement:

"It will be a fair day to-morrow."

"All days are fair for some purposes," said Buckingham quickly; "and the sooner the day the fairer to my mind."

Richard smiled. "Patience, my dear Stafford, patience. It will come soon enough even for your eagerness, I fancy. Did I not say to-morrow would be fair?"

"You are pleased to speak in riddles."

"Not so; you used the riddle and I but spoke in kind. However, trifles aside. Your arrival was well timed; you should have seen Rivers' face when he heard your voice; it was worth a Knight's good fee. For the first time he began to see how he had blundered. By St. Paul! a child could have done better. The game is easy now."

Buckingham looked puzzled.

"What do you mean, my lord?" he said. "I have been following blindly your direction in this affair, and I must admit that the point is very hazy to me."

"Do you not see," said the Duke, "that by remaining here and sending young Edward ahead at my approach, Rivers and Grey have overreached themselves completely? In their desire to keep me from the King--for plainly they did not know of your coming--they have separated themselves from Edward and his two thousand men; and in so doing have lost both Edward and themselves."

"Yet the two thousand men are still with Edward, are they not?" Buckingham insisted. "I have three hundred, but methinks even though you ride with twice that number we would be utterly outmatched."

"Nay, you do not perceive my plan," said Richard. "It will not be necessary to fight. I could win now with but a hundred men. We will------"

At that moment a clear voice came up from the street. Richard listened an instant and then opened the casement.

"De Lacy," he called, "come hither. . . I want you," he said when the young Knight entered, wrapped in his long cloak, "with all possible secrecy, to secure all the doors of the inn and bring the keys to me. At any that cannot be locked, post two of my personal retainers with orders to permit no one to depart the place. That done, take fifty men and station them along the road to where it joins the Roman highway this side the Ouse. Bid them allow no one to travel southward ere sunrise without express authority from me. Act instantly."

IX
THE ARREST

De Lacy found the landlord dozing beside the chimney in the kitchen. The fire was still smouldering on the hearth, and the big black kettle gave forth an odor of garlic and vegetables that made the air most foul. On the floor, in promiscuous confusion, lay various members of the establishment, of both sexes, who never even stirred at the Knight's entrance, either because they were too deep in sleep to hear him or too tired to care if they were trodden upon. Arousing the host, Aymer demanded all the keys of the inn, in the name of the Duke of Gloucester, and before the half-dazed fellow could respond he seized the big bunch that hung at his girdle and snapped it free. Bidding him mind his own business and go to sleep, he proceeded to execute his orders; and then hastened to the house where, by accident, that evening he had noticed Raynor Royk was quartered.

Twenty minutes later he rode out of Northampton and crossed the Nene with the fifty retainers behind him. To Dauvrey and Raynor Royk, he repeated the Duke's order just as it had been given, deeming it well, if he were incapacitated, that those next in command should know what to do. Leaving five men on the south bank of the Nene, he dropped bands of four at regular intervals along the road, with instructions to patrol constantly the intervening distances on both sides of them. The remaining five men he posted at the Roman highway, with orders not to separate under any circumstances.

Leaving Raynor in charge of this detail, De Lacy and his squire jogged slowly back toward Northampton. Hanging in an almost cloudless sky, the full moon was lighting up with its brilliant uncertainty the country around. The intense calm of the early morning was upon the earth, and there was no sound but the tramp of their horses, varied, at intervals, by the approach of one of the patrols or the passing of a sentry post.

About midway to the Nene the squire's horse picked a stone. It stuck persistently, and he swore at it under his breath as he tried to free it. Presently it yielded, and he had raised his arm to hurl it far away when a sharp word from De Lacy arrested him. They had chanced to halt in the shadow of a bit of woodland which, at that point, fringed the east side of the road. To the left, for some distance, the ground was comparatively clear of timber, and crossing this open space, about a hundred yards away, were two horsemen. They were riding at a rapid trot, but over the soft turf they made no sound.

"There," said De Lacy, waving his hand.

The squire swung noiselessly into saddle.

"Shall we stop them?" he asked.

"Of course--be ready if they show fight."

Suddenly Dauvrey's horse threw up his head and whinnied. At the first quaver, De Lacy touched Selim and rode out into the moonlight toward the strangers, who had stopped sharply.

"Good evening, fair sirs," said he; "you ride late."

"Not so; we are simply up betimes," replied one, "and therefore, with your permission, since we are in some haste, we will wish you a very good morning and proceed."

"Nay, be not so precipitate. Whither away, I pray, at such strange hours and over such strange courses?"

"What business is it of yours," exclaimed he who had first spoken, "whether we come from the clouds? Out of the way, or take the consequences," and he flashed forth his sword.

"You are hardly courteous," replied Aymer, "and therefore scarce angels in disguise, even though you prate of the clouds. So if you wish to measure blades I shall not balk you. Nathless," as he slowly freed his own weapon, "it is a quarrel not of my making."

"Will you let us pass then?" said the stranger.

"I never said I would not; I but asked your destination."

"And I refused to answer--stand aside."

"Nay, nay! do not get excited," said De Lacy calmly. "Consider a moment; you ask all and grant nothing. I wish to know whither you ride--you wish to ride. It is only a fair exchange."

"It is very evident that you are seeking a quarrel," the other exclaimed; "and by the Holy Saints! you have found it. I shall ride on, and if it be over your carcass, on your head be it."

"I have seen a few dead bodies in my time, fair sir," replied Sir Aymer with a laugh, "but never one that stood upon its head. It is a pity then I may not see my own."

The stranger made no reply, but settling himself well in saddle charged in. De Lacy, without changing position further than to drop the reins over the saddle bow, so as to leave both hands free to wield his sword, awaited the rush. Saving a thin corselet of steel beneath his doublet, he wore no armor; and as his antagonist was, outwardly at least, entirely unprotected, a single stroke of the heavy weapons would likely decide the matter.

For a space, De Lacy contented himself with parrying the blows aimed at him and with blocking the other's advance. Repeatedly he could have ended the fight, but always he forebore. The man was no possible match for him, and with soldierly generosity he hesitated either to kill or to wound grievously one who showed so much pluck and grit even when the struggle was plainly lost. He was waiting the opportunity to disarm him.

"Will you not yield?" he asked at last, as again he brushed aside the other's weapon.

The only answer was a swinging blow that just missed his forehead.

De Lacy frowned, and his patience began to ebb. For the first time he assumed the offensive. Pressing Selim close, he feinted quickly twice, and catching the other off guard he brought his sword down on the stranger's with a crash. There was a flash of sparks, a sharp ring of metal on stones, and of the weapon naught was left but a silver hilt.

"Yield," said Aymer sternly, presenting his point at the man's throat. "It is your last chance."

"I yield," said the other, hurling the bladeless hilt to the ground. "And may the Devil get the rogue that forged this weapon! And now, fair Knight,--for I see that your spurs are golden,--I will avow my destination to be London, and I presume I am at liberty to proceed."

"Nay, I shall have to ask you to bear me company back to Northampton," said De Lacy kindly.

"How so! Am I a prisoner?"

"Only until daybreak."

"It is most unusual--but, so be it." Then he turned to his companion. "Farewell, James," he said, "my misfortune need not affect you. I will join you in London."

De Lacy shook his head. "He came with you, and with you he bides. Giles, see to him."

"Truly, this is a strange proceeding on the King's highway, and with His Majesty but a few miles distant," the other exclaimed with increasing heat.

"Pardieu! how know you of the King's whereabouts?" said De Lacy, scanning the man's face. "I believe you are from Northampton."

A shrug of the shoulders was the only answer.

At that moment the patrol rode up and was about to proceed when Sir Aymer stopped him.

"You know this man?" he demanded.

The soldier came closer; and after a brief glance answered: "He is a squire in the household of Lord Rivers, so please you; I have seen him often."

De Lacy smiled. "So that explains your knowledge of the King. I regret, however, that Rivers' message will not reach Edward to-night. Nathless, I would like to know how you passed the guards thus far."

"This fellow's statement that I am of Lord Rivers' following does not establish that I am from him now," replied the squire. "You, yourself, saw that I struck the highway only at this spot, and that I did not come from the direction of Northampton."

"Yet that proves nothing to my mind, except that you thought to avoid the patrol by a detour and have failed. Come, sir, we will face Northward, if you please; enough time has been wasted in profitless debate."

The squire wheeled his horse to the right, as though to comply; then suddenly driving home the spurs he cleared the road at a bound and dashed back the way he had come.

"After him!" shouted De Lacy; and leaving Dauvrey to guard the other prisoner, he and the patrol sped in pursuit. The squire had acted so quickly that he had obtained a lead of at least a hunted feet and Aymer labored strenuously to overtake him. Being totally ignorant of the country, he could rely only on sight to indicate the course; whereas the other evidently was familiar with the by-paths, and once the first was reached would likely, in the uncertain light, be able to elude him. He swore at himself heartily for his carelessness, and with anger growing hotter at every jump he drew his sword, resolved that there would be no second escape if, when he got within reach, his order to halt were not instantly obeyed. Yet, strive as he might, Selim could not, in that short distance, come up with the big bay ahead; and as the squire entered the heavier timber, he looked back and laughed mockingly. But this act of foolish defiance worked his destruction; for at that very instant, his horse stumbled and plunged forward on his knees, and he, having loosed his thigh grip in turning, was hurled headlong to the ground and rolled over and over by the impetus.

"We will see that you play us no more such tricks," said Aymer. "Bind him with your sword belt."

The patrol bent over and tried to put the strap around the man's arms. The body was limp in his grasp.

"He is unconscious, my lord," he said.

"It may be a sham," said De Lacy, dismounting. . . "Pasque Dieu! your belt will not be needed. The man is dead: his neck is broken. . . It is a graceless thing to do, yet . . . Here, my man, help me carry the body out into the moonlight yonder . . . now, search it for a letter--for a letter, mark you, nothing else."

Kneeling beside it, the soldier did as he was bid, and presently drew forth a bit of parchment. It was without superscription and De Lacy broke the wax.

"As I thought," he muttered, as his eyes fell upon the signature; then, letting the moonlight fall full upon the page, he read:

"Vaughan:

"Buckingham joined Gloucester this evening. Grey and I are prisoners in the inn. Send Edward on to London instantly with Croft. If necessary, use force to keep the King, and then mark well the Dukes. I may not write more; time is precious. I trust in your discretion.

"Rivers."

"It will go ill with the Earl when Richard sees these words," thought De Lacy, as he mounted and returned to the road, where Dauvrey was patiently standing guard over the other prisoner.

"Come, Giles," he said, "secure his bridle rein. We will drop him at the next guard post, and in the morning he can return and bury the squire."

There was the faintest blush of dawn in the eastern sky as De Lacy and Dauvrey crossed the Nene and re-entered Northampton. At the inn all was quiet, and Aymer ascended quickly to Gloucester's room. The Duke was lying on the bed, fully dressed, and the gown that Catesby had placed ready to his hand had not been touched. He greeted the young Knight with a smile and without rising.

"Well, Sir Aymer?" he said.

De Lacy gave him the letter.

"I took it," he explained, "from one of Rivers' squires, midway between the Roman road and the Nene. He had followed by-paths and so avoided the guards."

Walking to the single candle that burnt dimly on the table Richard read the letter carefully.

"You have done good service for England this night," he said. "And now do you retire and rest; I may need you before many hours. But first return to the landlord his keys; they have served their end."

An hour later Northampton had thrown off its calm. A thousand soldiers, retainers of three great nobles, had roused themselves; and to the ordinary bustle of camp life were added the noisy greetings of those who, once comrades, had not seen each other for years; or who, strangers until a few hours aback, were now boon companions. Around the inn, however, there was strict order; but whether disturbed by the general confusion, or because their brains were too busy for slumber, the lords were early astir. Yet, whatever worry there may have been during the night, it was as well veiled now, as they gathered again around the table, as when they laughed and gossiped at the same board the prior evening. And indeed, doubt-less, their minds were actually easier; for Rivers and Grey were believing that their communication had reached Croft; Buckingham was persuaded that at last his day of triumph was come; and Gloucester, with Rivers' fatal letter in his pocket, knew that he had won the first throw in the great game he was playing.

"When does Your Grace desire to resume the journey?" Rivers asked as the breakfast was finished.

"Best start at once.--How say you, Buckingham?" said Richard.

"The Duke of Gloucester commands here," replied Stafford with a courtier's suavity.

"Then let us proceed; it will be more kind to the King in that it will not detain him unduly. . . I presume he will await us at Stoney Stratford?" glancing carelessly at Rivers.

"I so requested by messenger yesterday," the Earl answered.

"You are a model of thoughtfulness, my lord," said Gloucester with one of his strange smiles, as he buckled on his sword and led the way toward the horses.

Two hours after leaving Northampton the cavalcade, now traveling the Roman road, approached the crossing of the Ouse at the boundary of Buckinghamshire. Stoney Stratford lay just south of the river. On the northern bank of the stream Gloucester drew rein and the column halted. A moment before he had been laugh-ing, apparently in the best of humor. Now his face was stern as stone and his voice pitiless as Fate as, turning to the Earl of Rivers who was riding beside him, he said:

"My lord, before we proceed farther, there are a few matters between us that require adjustment."

Rivers' face paled suddenly, and involuntarily he bore so heavily on the bit that his horse reared high. Taken unawares, his usually facile mind was confused by the abruptness of Richard's words and the calm determination plainly foreshadowed in them. Trained by years of experience in a Court where intrigue imbrued the very atmosphere, ordinarily he was equal to any emergency. But all his schemes of the past were as gossamer to the conspiracy in which he was now entangled, and since the previous evening--when the unexpected arrival of Gloucester had hung their whole plot upon his shoulders until he got the King to London--the strain on his nerves had been terrific. He had thought to play the game out in the Capital, not on the lonely bank of a river in distant Northampton; and it is small wonder that under all the circumstances Anthony Woodville fell before Richard Plantagenet, whose equal England had known but twice before, in the first Plantagenet and the first Edward, and knew but twice thereafter, in Oliver Cromwell and William of Orange.

"This is scarce a place for discussion, my Lord Duke," said Rivers, striving to calm his restive horse. "If, as your words imply, there be aught of controversy between us, it were best to settle it in London. Yonder is Stoney Stratford, and it will not profit the King for us to quarrel here."

"Methinks, Sir Earl, that I am quite as capable as you of judging what shall work to Edward's profit," replied Gloucester curtly; "and I choose to settle it here, and not to annoy him with matters too weighty for his young brain."

"It is your own profit and not your King's that you seek," said Rivers. "I decline to hold further discussion or to quarrel with you until I have done my duty to my Sovereign and have seen him safe in London. Then I shall be most willing to meet you, with sword, or axe, or lance--and may God defend the right. Come, Grey, we will ride on alone."

Gloucester had listened with darkening brow, and the gnawing of under lip was ominous; but at the last words he threw his horse in front of the Earl's.

"Ere you depart, my Lord of Scales and Rivers," he said, and smiled peculiarly, "you must hear me out. Of your rash speech I shall make no account; and you know full well that a Prince of England breaks no lance nor crosses sword save on the field of battle, whereon are all men equal. But I fain would ask if you expect to meet Edward the Fifth in yonder town?"

"I have already told you that I dispatched a messenger to detain him until we arrived," retorted the Earl hotly.

"Aye! And later another messenger to hurry him on," said Richard laconically.

"What proof have you for that?" demanded Rivers, reining back.

"This!" replied the Duke sternly, producing the captured letter.

"I see nothing but a bit of parchment; yet well I know that it can be made to tell strange tales for selfish ends."

"It is parchment, unfortunately for you, my lord, and it tells a selfish tale," said

Gloucester calmly. "It is the letter you dispatched last night to Edward's Chamberlain, but which was taken by one of my good Knights, though your Squire died in its defence. You know its contents--and, mayhap, you also begin to know the depth of your folly."

"It is evident that I am in the toils of a plot laid by you and yonder brother-in-law of mine," said the Earl with haughty contempt. "You have entrapped me; and the deepest folly that I know would be to hope for justice in such clutches. I am to be sacrificed because, forsooth, I am dangerous to the conspiracy that you have afoot; and well can I foresee what the conspiracy designs. . . Yet did I flatter you overmuch, my Lord of Buckingham; it is no creature of your brain, this scheme whose end is treason. You are too vain and empty-headed to be of any service except to aid its execution--and then, later, to be the leading figure at your own. Your sires were overmuch Lancastrian for you to be trusted by a son of York--after your usefulness is ended."

Gloucester's stern mouth relaxed in a faint smile, but Buckingham flushed angrily.

"By the Holy Saints!" he broke out, "were it not that the very touch would soil a Stafford's gauntlet, I would lay my hand across your Woodville mouth."

"It is passing strange then, if we be so degraded," said Rivers quickly, "that you should have chosen a Woodville for a wife."

Pushing his horse past Grey, Buckingham leaned forward and would have struck the Earl had not the calm tones of Gloucester stayed him in the very act.

"Hold! Stafford, you forget yourself--and you, Sir Earl, return your dagger."

"He shall answer me for those words," Buckingham exclaimed.

"I am at your service this very instant," returned Rivers, doffing his bonnet and bowing to his charger's neck.

"This very instant be it," cried the Duke, springing down and drawing sword.

Before the last word was spoken, Rivers was off his horse and confronting Stafford with bared weapon. But ere the blades could clash together, Gloucester swung between them and knocked up the Earl's sword with his own, which he had unsheathed with amazing swiftness.

"Cease this foolishness," he said sternly. "Buckingham, you forget yourself. Ratcliffe, arrest the Earl of Rivers and Sir Richard Grey."

The Master of Horse rode forward.

"Your sword, my lord," he said to Rivers.

For a moment the Earl hesitated; then hurled it far out into the river.

"In the name of the King, whose uncle and governor I am, I protest, lord Duke, against this unwarranted and outrageous conduct," he cried.

"And I arrest you in the name of that very King, whose uncle and guardian I am," replied Richard. "Ratcliffe, execute your orders."

"I must request you to accompany me forthwith," said Ratcliffe courteously, to the two noblemen.

Resistance was utterly hopeless, and without a further word the Earl remounted; and Grey taking place beside him they passed slowly toward the rear. Presently, as they neared the end of the long column, a hundred men detached themselves from the line and fell in behind them. Rivers observed it with a smile, half sad, half cynical.

"They honor us, at least, in the size of our guard," he remarked to Grey; then turned to Ratcliffe. "May I inquire our prison, Sir Richard?"

"Certainly, my lord; we ride to Pontefract."

"Whence two of us shall ne'er return," said the Earl, with calm conviction. "May the Good Christ watch over Edward now."

X
THE LADY MARY CHANGES BADGES

Five weeks had expired since the ***coup d'etat*** at Stoney Stratford and Richard was now Lord Protector of the Realm. Before his dominating personality all overt opposition had crumbled, and with Rivers and Grey in prison, the Queen Dowager in sanctuary at Westminster, and Dorset and Edward Woodville fled beyond sea the political horizon seemed clear and bright.

Meanwhile, the Duchess of Gloucester and her Household had come to London and were settled at Crosby Hall in Bishopgate Street. When they neared the Capital, the Duke and a few of his chosen Knights had ridden out into the country to meet them; and Sir Aymer de Lacy had gone gayly and expectantly, thinking much of a certain fair face with ruddy tresses above it. Nor had he been disappointed; and it was her pleasant, half-familiar greeting that lingered in his mind long after the words and sweet smile of the Duchess were forgotten. He had tarried beside the Countess' bridle until the Hall was reached; and as she seemed quite willing for him to be there, he had been blind to the efforts of others to displace him. With Selim she had been openly demonstrative, welcoming him with instant affection and leaning over many times to stroke him softly on the neck or muzzle. Once, as she did it, she shot a roguish smile at his master, and he had nodded and answered that again he was wishing he were a horse--whereupon she deliberately repeated the caress, glancing at him the while, sidelong and banteringly. But when he would have pursued the subject further, she crushed him with a look, and then for the remainder of the ride held him close to commonplaces.

And if De Lacy thought to have again the delightful associations and informal meetings that had obtained at Pontefract, he quickly realized his error. There, the Household was relatively small, and life had run along in easy fashion. He had seen the Countess daily--had walked or ridden with her as his duties permitted, and every evening had attended in the presence chamber and gossiped with her for a while. Those few days of unhampered intimacy had let them know each other better than months of London would have done. Lord Darby had been his only active rival, and even he was not there constantly. But in the Capital it was otherwise. Scores of Knights, young and old, now sought her favor and were ever in attendance. Indeed half the eligible men at Court were her suitors, and the feeling among some of the more impetuous had reached a point where it needed only the flimsiest of excuses for such an exchange of cartels as would keep the lists at Smithfield busy for a week. But through it all, the Countess moved with calm courtesy and serene unconcern. She had her favorites, naturally,--and she made no pretense otherwise,--but that reduced not a whit the fervor of the others. Like the dogs in the dining hall, they took the scraps flung to them, and eagerly awaited more.

And the Lady Mary Percy gibed sweetly at them all, and at the Countess, too; but she gibed most at Sir Aymer de Lacy.

"You are a rare wooer, surely," said she one day, as the Lord of Ware bore the Countess off to his barge for a row on the Thames. "You had your chance at Pontefract and . . . yonder she goes! One would never fancy you were bred in France."

"Nor that you were really a sweet-tempered and charming demoiselle," Sir Aymer answered good-naturedly.

She laughed merrily. "One might think I were jealous of the Countess?"

"Yes . . . or of the Earl of Ware."

"Or of all the others who hang about her," she added.

De Lacy looked down at her with an amused smile.

"Methinks Ware is enough," he said, with calm assertion.

She tossed her head in quick defiance. "Your penetration, Sir Aymer, is extraordinary--when it concerns others," she retorted.

"And when it concerns myself?"

She answered with a shrug.

He went over and leaned on the casement beside her.

"Just how stupid am I?" he asked.

She turned and measured him with slow eyes. "I am not sure it is stupidity," she remarked; "some might call it modesty."

He laughed. "And which does the Lady Mary Percy call it?"

"I can tell you better a year hence."

"Why so long a wait?"

"You will then have won or lost the Countess."

He shook his head dubiously.

"How will that decide the matter?" he asked.

She smiled. "Because only stupidity can lose."

He looked at her curiously and in silence, a quicker beat at his pulse and she read his thoughts.

"Oh, I am betraying no confidences," she said. "Your lady gives none--save possibly to the Duchess. But I have been of the Household with Beatrix for two years and------"

"And . . . what?" he inflected.

"You can guess the rest--if you are not stupid," she said, turning away.

But he stayed her. "My barge is at the landing. Shall we follow . . . the others?" he suggested.

She hesitated--then, catching up a cloak and scarf that lay on a couch, she nodded acquiescence.

"Up stream or down?" he asked, as he handed her in and took place beside her.

"Up," she said.

"Give way," he ordered, and the eight oars that had been raised high in salute dropped as one, and they shot out into the stream.

The Lady Mary settled herself among the cushions, one arm thrown carelessly around the awning post.

"What nonsense it is," she remarked presently.

De Lacy nodded. "Doubtless--but what?"

"This foolish dissimulation we all play at; . . . this assumed indifference which deceives no one. Here are we, barging together on the Thames, when you would rather have the Countess . . . and I would rather have Ware."

"But would they rather have us?"

"I am quite sure she would, and" . . . holding up a hand and slowly flashing the rings . . . "I think he would, too."

"If you happen to know which way they went," De Lacy laughed, "we might follow and suggest an exchange."

She sat up smartly. "Come," said she, "come; if you will venture it with the Countess, I will with Ware."

He smiled. "I thought you gave me a year wherein to prove my stupidity."

"But would it be stupidity--might it not be rare brilliancy--a master stroke?" She flashed the rings again. "Lord Darby would risk it were he in like case."

"Nay, Darby is no fool."

"True enough--yet, neither is he afraid to brave the hazard; he is a hard fighter, in love as well as war."

"I find no fault with him for that," De Lacy answered, "so long as he fight fair."

She gave him a quick glance of interrogation.

"Would you trust him to fight fair?" she asked.

"I usually trust every man of noble birth until experience prove him undeserving."

"And you have had no experience with Darby?"

"No--not yet."

A sly smile crossed her lips and she was about to comment further, when Lord Ware's barge suddenly swung out from behind a large vessel and met them.

"We are going to the Tower," the Countess called. "Will you not meet us there?"

The rowers backed water instantly, and the two boats drifted slowly past each other.

"We will join you very shortly," Lady Mary answered--then smiled at De Lacy.

The Earl of Ware looked curiously at the Countess.

"Now why this sudden notion for the Tower?" he asked, when the barges had drawn apart. "But a moment since and you declined to stop there and preferred to stay afloat."

"A moment since is far aback with a woman," the Countess laughed--"nor had I then seen the Lady Mary."

"Nor the Knight with her," said Ware sententiously.

She made no answer, save to look him in the face with calm composure.

"Who is this De Lacy," the Earl asked with, a supercilious shrug; "one of the new nobility?"

A faint smile came into her eyes.

"New? May be, my lord--the term is but relative--yet *I* would scarce call him so: his ancestor came with Norman William and built Pontefract."

"So . . . one of old Ilbert's stock. Well, even a Ware may not cavil at that blood . . . though it is passing strange I never heard of him until within the week."

"Strange for him or for you?" she asked.

"For me, of course--seeing that he has been so much at Court." The tone was bantering, yet the sarcasm was deliberately veiled.

She turned upon him rather sharply.

"My lord," said she, "if you would criticise Sir Aymer de Lacy, do not, I pray, make me your confidant. He is my good friend."

"And you like him . . . well?" he questioned.

"Aye, that I do," she retorted instantly. "It is a pity his sort are growing scarce."

"His sort!" the Earl inflected. "In family, mean you, or in looks?"

"In manners, mainly."

The Earl shrugged his shoulders. "French training," he drawled. "There never was one came from that Court but caught you all with his bow and talk."

"Perchance, my lord, it has never occurred to you that, save in him she wed, a woman cares only for a man's manners and his speech."

"And what does she care for in him she weds?"

"Ask her whom you wed."

"And what, think you, will the bride of this De Lacy find in him beneath his bow and speech?"

She turned and looked him in the eyes.

"An English gentleman--a trusty Knight," she answered.

He laughed--and now his air was light and merry.

"Believe me, my lady, I have no quarrel with your De Lacy," he said; "I, too, like him well. But I envy him his champion. Marry, how you rapped me with voice and eye. I wonder, would you do the same for me?"

"Yes, for you . . . and the Lady Mary."

"And why the Lady Mary?" he asked, after a pause.

"If you do not know, then there is no 'why,'" said she, facing about and looking up stream. "However, she is coming and, perchance, can answer for herself. Shall I ask her . . . or will you?"

The touching of the boat just inside the St. Thomas Gate saved him an answer. Giving the Countess his hand he aided her to alight, and almost immediately De Lacy's barge ran in; and, he and Lady Mary disembarking, the four sauntered across the vast courtyard toward the royal lodge.

As they turned into one of the shaded walks the Earl of Ware, who chanced to be a pace in advance, suddenly halted and drew aside, his bonnet doffed, his attitude deeply respectful.

"The King!" exclaimed De Lacy, and they all fell back.

A slender, fair-haired boy was coming slowly down the path, one hand on the neck of a huge mastiff, whose great head was almost on a level with his shoulder. His dress was rich, but very simple--black velvet and silk from head to foot, save the jeweled dagger at his hip and the blue ribbon of the Garter about his knee. His bearing was wondrous easy, and there was a calm dignity about him most unusual in one so young. It may have been the innate consciousness of his exalted rank that raised the thirteen-year-old boy to the man, and made his majesty sit so naturally upon him; or it may have been that the resemblance he bore to his imperious father carried with it also that father's haughty spirit; but, whatever it was, there could be no mistaking that Edward the Fifth was a true heir of the Plantagenets, the proudest and bravest family that ever sat a throne.

He was unattended, save by the dog, and as he passed he smiled a courteous greeting.

"God save Your Majesty!" said the two Knights, bowing with bent knee, while the Countess and Lady Mary curtsied low.

He turned slightly and smiled at them again, then proceeded on his way, as unruffled as a man of thrice his age.

"A brave youth," said Sir Aymer de Lacy, gazing after him.

"Aye," the Earl answered, "brave in person and in promise--yet prone to melancholy, it is said; a queer trait in a child."

"Inherited?" De Lacy asked.

Ware shrugged his shoulders. "Doubtless--almost anything could come through Jacquetta of Luxembourg."

Meanwhile the Countess and Lady Mary had gone on together, leaving their escorts to follow, and presently they turned toward the wharf.

"What say you," the Earl asked as they neared the gate, "what say you to--an exchange of companions?"

"I am willing," De Lacy answered instantly, thinking of Lady Mary's words, "and so is------" then he stopped; that was not for him to tell Ware, and doubtless she had been only jesting. "Suppose you suggest it to the Lady Mary," he ended.

The Earl gave him an amused smile. "Suppose you suggest it to the Countess."

Then both laughed.

Ware rubbed his chin thoughtfully. "We might suggest it to them both together," he said.

"How, for instance?"

"Why . . . just intimate casually that . . . that . . . that . . . we would . . . you know."

"No," said Aymer, "I do not."

Ware pondered a space. "We might put them in the wrong boats--by accident, of course."

"And have them get out the instant we get in."

"Then it passes me," said the Earl. "I have supplied the idea; it is for you to execute it."

De Lacy shook his head. "It is too deep for me; had I a week I might contrive a plan."

"I presume we will go back as we came," the other commented. "Marry, what a brave pair we are!"

As they reached the landing, their barges, that lay a little way down stream, swung around and came quickly up to the gate. The Earl's entered first, and as he was about to proffer his hand to the Countess to aid her to embark, the Lady Mary stepped quickly into the boat, and giving him a smile of bewitching invitation sank languidly among the cushions. For an instant he was taken aback; but, with a sharp glance at De Lacy, he sprang aboard, and the oars caught the water.

The Countess watched them as they sped through the gate and away, then turned to De Lacy with a roguish look and eyes half veiled.

"It seems, Sir Aymer, it is for you to take me back to the Hall," she said.

XI
ON CHAPEL GREEN

On the following morning Sir Aymer de Lacy again sought the Tower; but this time he went alone. The hour was early, yet the place was full of life; there was to be a state council at nine, and the nobility were assembling to greet the Lord Protector when he should arrive. For although the young King occupied the royal apartments and was supposed to hold the Court therein, yet, in fact, the real Court was at Crosby Hall, where the Duke resided and whither all those that sought favor or position were, for the nonce, obliged to bend their steps.

Indeed, at this time, Richard was, in all but name, the King of England; and on this very day, ere the hour of noon had passed, was the name also to turn toward him, and through the first blood shed by his new ambition was he to progress to the foot of the throne, the steps of which were to prove so easy to his feet.

Just in front of the Wakefield Tower De Lacy came upon Sir Robert Brackenbury, now Constable of the Fortress, and paused for a word with him. Then sauntering slowly toward the Chapel, he took possession of a bench from which he could observe those who crossed the courtyard between the St. Thomas Gate and the White Tower. A moment later, Sir Ralph de Wilton came swinging along the walk and De Lacy hailed him.

"Tarry with me till the Council has gathered," he said. "Here come their reverences of York and Ely."

Scarcely had the churchmen entered the White Tower, when along the same path came two others, bound also for the council chamber.

The one on the right, the Garter about his knee, with the keen, grey eyes, sharp, clear, Norman features, and well-knit, active frame, was William, Lord Hastings; gallant knight, brave warrior, wise counsellor and chosen friend of the mighty Edward. His long gown and doublet were of brilliant green velvet, with silk trunks and hose to match; his bushy brown hair was perfumed and dressed with exquisite care; from his bonnet of black velvet trailed a long white ostrich plume pinned by three huge rubies; at the richly chased gold belt dangled a dagger, the scabbard and hilt glistening with jewels, and his fingers flashed with many rings. It was the typical costume of a courtier of the Plantagenets--fops in dress and devils in battle.

His companion was utterly dissimilar. His garments were of sober black, without ornament or decoration, and no ring shone on his fingers. His sandy hair was cut rather shorter than was wont, and there was no mark of helmet wear along the brow or temples. His frame was neither active nor powerful, and his walk was sedate, almost to preciseness. His countenance was peculiar, for in it there was both cunning and frankness: cunning in the eyes, frankness in the mouth and chin; a face, withal, that would bear constant watching, and that contained scarce a trace of virility--only a keen selfishness and a crafty faithlessness. And of a verity, if ever a human visage revealed truly the soul within, this one did; for a more scheming sycophant, vacillating knave and despicable traitor than Thomas, Lord Stanley, England had not seen since the villain John died at Newark.

"A powerful pair," said De Wilton, "yet a strange companionship--one rather of accident than design, I fancy. There is little in either to attract the other, nor is it any secret that the Lord Chamberlain does not love the fickle Stanley."

"No more does Stanley love him, nor any living creature, for the matter of that," said Sir Aymer. "It passes me why the Lord Protector trusts him."

"Pardieu!" exclaimed De Wilton, "the Duke may use him; he will never trust him. He knows the truckler of old--the first to greet Warwick when he came to lead Henry from the Tower; the loudest for Edward when Barnet's day was done."

"Well, mark me," said De Lacy, with lowered voice, "yonder false lord will be a troublesome counsellor, even if he be not a faithless baron. I would have none of him."

"***Bon jour, mes amis***!" Hastings called out in hearty greeting. "Has the Protector arrived?"

"No, my lord," returned De Wilton, as he and De Lacy arose; "he was engaged, and may be a trifle late for the council."

"Who has preceded us?" said Stanley; and in contrast to the melodious voice of the Lord Chamberlain his tones were like melting ice.

"Only the Lord Chancellor and the Bishop of Ely."

"Then, Hastings, we shall have time to discuss further the matter I touched on a moment since," said Stanley, making as though to go on.

"As you will," Hastings answered indifferently, and without moving, "but believe me, my lord, it will boot little what may be the record. Eleanor and Katharine Neville were sisters, true enough, but Eleanor is dead and you have wed a second time; while Katharine still chatelaines my castles of Ashby and Calais. The matter has been left to her sweet judgment, and her wish is my decision. It is quite needless to debate the subject further."

Aymer caught the quick look of resentment that flashed through Stanley's eyes, but Hastings missed it, for he had turned and was gazing toward the royal lodge.

And Stanley, with that cool indifference to aught but expediency which characterized his whole life, let the curt speech pass, seemingly unheeded.

In a moment the Lord Chamberlain said courteously, as though regretful for his recent abruptness:

"Well, my lord, shall we proceed? It will be well for the Council to be assembled when Richard comes."

"In truth, yes," said Stanley suavely; and bowing stiffly to the two young

Knights, the traitor of Bosworth linked arms with Hastings and went on toward the White Tower.

"Did you mark that?" De Wilton queried; "and evidently it was a matter of some moment since Hastings has submitted it to his wife."

"There are more than royal prerogatives at issue these days," replied De Lacy, "and private grievance may work deep into the greater game."

"It will be the only way by which the Stanley can be led to bear a part," said De Wilton sententiously. "He savors more of the shops in the Cheap yonder than of Castle or Court."

"And hence the pity that he has such power of rank and wealth behind him with his new Countess, the Beaufort heiress."

"Aye--and what is worse, in her and her son lie the last hope of Lancaster."

"You mean the Earl of Richmond?" said Aymer. "I saw him a year or more ago at the Court of Blois. His appearance gave little promise of kingly blood or spirit."

"Nathless, my good friend, our own Duke of Gloucester would give a few hides of land to have that same Earl safe within these walls. York sits not firm on England's throne while the Tudor lives in freedom."

"It is a shrewd test of Stanley's faith--his step-fathership to this Richmond," De Lacy observed.

"Of a truth, yes; and one that will find him wanting if the trial ever come. Had not His late Majesty died so suddenly, this Margaret would have had a brood of treasons hatched ready for the occasion; and I doubt not that she and her adherents are, even now, deep in plottings with the Welsh and France's King."

"With Stanley's knowledge?"

De Wilton's only answer was a shrug and a jerk of his head toward the river.

"Here are two more of the Council," he remarked; and the Duke of Buckingham came rapidly up the path in company with Lord Lovel.

"Are we late or early?" Buckingham called.

"Late for Stanley and Hastings and their reverences of York and Ely," said Aymer, "but early for the Lord Protector."

"Did the Chamberlain and Stanley come together?" Lovel asked.

"They did, my lord."

"And their humor?"

"Not the most sympathetic. They were not entirely agreed about some matter the Lord Hastings had submitted to his Countess, and that she had decided, seemingly, against Stanley's wishes."

"It is the old matter of the Neville sisters that cropped up even in Bonville's time," said Buckingham. "The more Stanley urges that now, the better it will fit our purpose. Come, let us stimulate the dispute if occasion offer," and with a sarcastic laugh he turned away.

"Methinks, my Lord of Buckingham," observed De Wilton, when he and De Lacy were again alone, "that you will scarce find another Rivers in either Hastings or Stanley. It requires a master hand to play Stoney Stratford twice in six short weeks."

"No need for another seizure, I fancy," said De Lacy. "Richard's power is secure now and the King will be crowned on St. John's Day."

De Wilton looked at him thoughtfully. "It is strange, Sir Aymer, that you, who have lived under The Fell Louis, should not look deeper into the minds of men. St. John's Day is but nine days hence, yet will I wager you ten good rose nobles it brings no coronation with it. I know"--as De Lacy regarded him incredulously--"that the council has so fixed it--that the ceremonies have been arranged--that the provisions for the banquet have been ordered--and that the nobility are gathering from all England, yet none the less will I make the wager."

De Lacy was silent for a bit. Then he spoke:

"It would be foolish to pretend I do not catch your meaning, but I had never faced the matter in that light. In France there may be strife of faction, plottings and intrigues and blood-spilling for position in the State; yet is the Crown ever secure. The struggle is but for place near the Throne, never for the Throne itself. . . Naturally, I appreciate our need for a strong King at this crisis. Edward is but a child, and York's grip on the Crown may grow perilously lax, or even slip entirely. With Gloucester it would be different. His hand is not likely to loosen if once it grasp the sceptre. I shall not take your wager. It would be against my own heart. If Richard's aim is England's Throne, my poor arm is at his service."

"Now are you one after my own soul," exclaimed De Wilton. "Up with the White Boar banner! Hurrah for King Richard the Third!"

"But that I knew Sir Aymer de Lacy and Sir Ralph de Wilton to be loyal subjects of Edward the Fifth, so long as he be King of England, I should be obliged to commit you both to yonder tower," said the stern, calm voice of the Duke of Gloucester behind them.

Both Knights sprang to their feet and uncovered. De Wilton was confused and could make no reply. De Lacy, however, was not so easily disconcerted and, despite the censure in the words, he felt that they were not grave offenders.

"If an honest desire to see the Duke of Gloucester King of England be a crime," he answered, bowing low, "then we both are guilty. Yet plead we in clemency, that we shall follow only where the White Boar leads."

The severe lines of Richard's mouth relaxed a trifle.

"Let me caution you," he said, and the chill was gone from his voice, "talk not treason so publicly; even stones have ears at times. I go now to the Council; await me here or in the inner chapel."

"What think you of it?" asked De Wilton.

"Enough to make me glad I refused your wager; there is something brewing."

"Whatever it be I hope it will come quickly," said Sir Ralph with half a sigh. "This is not like the old days when Edward held his state here. Many is the time I have seen this great place bright with women's faces and ringing with their laughter; the ramparts crowded, and scarce a shady seat but held a fair dame and gallant lover. Where are now the sweet voices and the swishing gowns? Gone--maybe, forever; Elizabeth is in sanctuary a mile up yonder stream, and Edward is too young to mate at present."

"Perchance the Duchess of Gloucester may come here and revive it all."

De Wilton shook his head. "Richard seems to have small love for this old pile of stone; and besides he ceases to be Lord Protector when the King is crowned."

"In truth!" exclaimed De Lacy. "What then will he be?"

"Duke of Gloucester and uncle to His Majesty."

The two men looked at each other and smiled.

Neither had observed an elderly Knight in dusty riding dress and long boots hurrying down the courtyard, until he had passed them; then De Lacy sprang up and hastened after.

"Sir John de Bury," he called; "stop and speak to a friend."

The other whirled around.

"De Lacy!" he exclaimed; "by St. Luke, I am overjoyed to see you, I seek the Duke--get me an audience at once."

"Come," said Aymer, and they hastened to the White Tower.

Just as they reached the upper landing the door of the great council chamber opened and Gloucester came out, followed by Buckingham.

"Ha, De Bury! what brings you in such haste?" Richard demanded. "What is amiss in the North?"

"It may be much and it may be little, so please you," said Sir John, removing his bonnet and bowing slightly.

"Follow me," said the Duke, and descending to the second floor they entered the small room next the chapel, leaving De Lacy on guard without.

Slowly the minutes passed. Once Aymer heard Buckingham's voice raised as though in sharp argument. Then it ceased abruptly, and he knew that Richard had silenced him. A little later Stafford laughed, and this time was joined by De Bury. At length, the door opened and Gloucester called him:

"Summon twenty of the guard," he said. "Lead them hither yourself."

At the outer door De Lacy came upon Raynor Royk.

"Twenty of the guard instantly," he ordered.

From across the courtyard De Wilton had seen Aymer, and he was already sauntering toward him. De Lacy motioned for him to make haste. "It has come," he said, as De Wilton joined him.

"Oh, has it! Well, it took you long enough to find it, surely. And may I ask, what has come?"

"The next move in the Duke's game."

"In sooth! When--what--how?"

"Now, my dear Sir Ralph. The how is yonder with Raynor Royk. If you wish to know the what, come with me."

Up the stairway Royk led his men, following close after the two Knights. On the second landing the Protector was waiting.

"Now, attend," he said to De Lacy. "I return to the Council. You will bring the men up very quietly and post them without. The instant I strike on the table, fling open the door and arrest every man. Do you yourself stand in the passage and stop any that would escape. Let none use weapon unless necessary . . . but if an axe were to fall by accident upon either Stanley or Ely, no punishment would follow," and he smiled significantly.

"I think I understand," said De Lacy; and Richard, carelessly brushing a bit of dust from his black doublet, turned away.

Raynor Royk chuckled when he learned the orders.

"I will attend to Stanley myself," he said. "My axe arm at times has an ugly habit of sudden weakness when the weapon is swung high."

De Lacy nodded. "Get yourself into position," he replied shortly; for, of a truth, he little liked the business. Yet there might be no delay, and he followed after the soldiers with De Wilton at his side.

Raynor massed his men before the door and he himself was close against it with his hand upon the latch. From within came numerous voices; presently these were silent and the Protector spoke in angry tones, though what he said De Lacy could not distinguish. Then a single voice replied, and De Wilton had scarce time to whisper, "Hastings," when the signal came.

With a crash, Raynor Royk hurled back the heavy door, and the soldiers rushed in.

Around the long table in the center of the apartment were gathered the members of the Council, and at its foot stood the Duke of Gloucester, one hand upon his dagger, the other pointing at the Lord Chamberlain. In an instant Hastings was seized by two of the soldiers, and all was wild confusion.

Lord Stanley, divining some sinister design as Raynor Royk sprang toward him with upraised weapon, sought safety in a sudden and inglorious dive under the table. Yet quick as he was, the old retainer was quicker. His heavy axe came down with a sweep, and never more would the fickle Stanley have played the dastard had not a carved chair arm stayed, for an instant, the weapon's fall. Ere it had shorn its way through the oak, Stanley was safe from death, though the edge scraped his head glancingly, sending the blood flying and leaving him unconscious on the floor.

The Bishop of Ely escaped the axe aimed at him by a hurried retreat to the rear of the room out of the general melee; for he was shrewd enough instantly to comprehend that, while there might be fatal danger to him in the crowd, there was but little when he stood aloof: God's Bishops were not wont to be murdered deliberately in public. Yet it did not save him from arrest, for Raynor glanced at the Protector, and reading the order in his face stalked back and clapping Morton on the shoulder said gruffly: "Come, Lord Bishop."

The whole affair was over almost as quickly as begun, and the Duke of Gloucester never so much as changed position during the tumult, save to lower the hand that had menaced Hastings. Then, when all the counsellors were crowded together and surrounded by the soldiers, he spoke quietly, addressing Raynor Royk:

"Commit the Archbishop of York, the Bishop of Ely, and Lord Stanley to the Garden Tower. See that Stanley's hurts be dressed. Release the others, save the traitor Hastings. Him conduct to the Chapel Green, and let his head be stricken from his fell carcass without delay, save for absolution if he so desire it. . . Gentlemen, attend me."

Adjusting his cloak the Protector quitted the apartment and in silence descended to the courtyard. There he drew his arm within Stafford's, and dismissing the others proceeded slowly toward the royal lodge at the southeast angle of the fortress.

"Verily will this day live in England's history," said De Wilton. "Stoney Stratford was but a game of marteaux beside it."

"But when ends it?" said De Lacy solemnly.

"Yonder, on the throne in Westminster," De Wilton replied, almost in a whisper.

"Nay, I mean the final end. Methinks I hear the rattle of armor and the splintering of spears."

At that moment the file of soldiers emerged from the White Tower with Lord Hastings in their midst, walking with the same grace and ease of carriage that always distinguished him, his face calm and serene. As his eyes fell upon the two younger Knights, who were moving slowly toward the river gate, he said a word to Raynor Royk, and the column halted. Raising his voice, that had rung over so many stricken fields, leading the very flower of York's chivalry, he called:

"Be Lacy! De Wilton! . . . Will you not," as they hurried to him, "by your oath of pity and humility, accompany me to the block? It is hard enough, God knows, that one who has both rank and blood should die without trial or legal judgment; yet that none but hirelings should be with me at the end is inhuman beyond measure. Look at yonder sycophants, who but an hour ago hung upon my slightest gesture, now hurrying from me as though I had the plague."

"Whatever we can do, my lord," said De Lacy, "pray command. I would we had power to stay your doom."

Hastings smiled sadly. "I shall not detain you long. Lead on, my man."

It was but a step to the Chapel, and seeing that neither block nor headsman was in waiting he shrugged his shoulders and laughed sarcastically:

"Not honored even by the usual participants," he remarked. "Yon log of timber and a common axe must serve the purpose. A strange undoing for one who has ridden boot to boot with Edward . . . a Lord Chamberlain and Captain of Calais."

"My Lord of Hastings!" said Raynor Royk, with doffed bonnet and in a voice so changed from its usual gruffness that De Lacy and De Wilton both marked it with surprise, "it grieves me ill that I, who have followed the Sable Maunch so oft in battle, should lead you to your death. Yet I may not shirk my duty, as you, great warrior as you are, well know. But if there be aught I can do to aid you, that touches not mine honor (for, my lord, we have what we call honor as well as those who wear the yellow spurs), speak but the word."

Hastings stepped forward and placed his hand upon the old retainer's shoulder. "My good fellow," he said gravely, "there are many with golden spurs who are far less worthy to wear them than are you. Not always does honor, nay nor chivalry either, dwell beneath the banner or pennon of the Knight. Permit me a word apart with these kind friends."

For answer, Raynor Royk gave a sharp order and the soldiers drew out of earshot.

"Need I say to you, Sir Aymer de Lacy, and you, Sir Ralph de Wilton," said Hastings, "how deeply I appreciate your great kindness in coming with me here. Place yourselves in my position and you will know the comfort you have given me. It would be foolish to say I am willing to die; I love life as well as any man; yet bear me witness that I meet my doom as becomes a Peer of England. I have but two requests to make of you, my friends--for though you both are of Gloucester's Household, yet have you been friends to me this day, as Knight to Knight, for you owe me no obligation. I ask that when yonder deed be done you recall to the Lord Protector his brother Edward's dying wish that I might lie by his side in Windsor Chapel. And lastly, I pray you bear to my sweet Countess the assurance of my endless love and adoration. Give her this ring and (pressing it to his lips) say that it bears my dying kiss. Tell her"--and his voice broke, and for the first time in this man's life tears started to his eyes and trickled down his ruddy cheeks--"tell her that my last thought was of her . . . tell her that I wish not Heaven save it bring her dear face to me." He mastered his emotion. "Farewell, my friends," extending his hands, and they silently grasped them, "may God, in His Providence, grant you a kinder death than mine."

Then with placid face and voice he turned to Raynor Royk, who stood leaning on his axe in evident distress of mind.

"I am at your service, my good man," he said. "Dispatch the business quickly and do not, I pray you, bungle it at the stroke."

Removing his handsome cloak, he opened his doublet at the neck, and with quiet dignity walked to the piece of heavy timber that had been used in repaving the Chapel only the previous day, and which lay across the green. Raynor Royk made a motion, and a tall soldier stepped forth. Hastings knelt as the man stopped beside him and drew back his doublet, baring his neck for the blow.

"Strike true, fellow," he said, and calmly placed his head upon the timber's end.

XII
THE KING'S WORD

From this moment Gloucester moved with no uncertain nor halting steps toward the object of his ambition. With the death of Hastings was removed the only man in England who might have blocked his purpose through either power or ability; and he and Buckingham were left free to play out to its end the wonderful game that won a kingdom without a single disturbance or the drawing of a sword. The moves followed one another in bewildering rapidity, yet with such consummate skill, that when in the great chamber of Baynard's Castle the final offer of the Crown was made, and the Lord Protector with seeming diffidence accepted it on Stafford's urging, it appeared but a natural consequence of spontaneous events, brought about only by the force of circumstances and through no deliberate human agency.

In some of these events Sir Aymer de Lacy was an actor, while in others he was but a spectator or bore no part at all. From the grim death-scene in the Tower he had gone back to Crosby Hall and a long talk with Sir John de Bury, wherein he learned what had brought the old Knight so hastily to London and the Lord Chamberlain to the block; and which, ere nightfall, was to send Sir Ralph de Wilton galloping back to Pontefract, bearing an order constituting the Earl of Northumberland Lord High Steward, and directing the trial of Rivers, Grey and Vaughan for the same crime that had proven Hastings' doom: conspiracy against the Lord Protector. He had chanced to ride by St. Paul's Cross while Dr. Shaw was in the midst of his sermon on "Bastard slips shall not take deep root." He had gone with Buckingham to the Guild Hall two days later; had listened with strong approval to the speech wherein Stafford boldly advocated the setting aside of the young Edward in favor of his uncle; and had lent his own voice to the cry: "King Richard! King Richard!" He had witnessed the tender at Baynard's Castle and the halting acceptance by the Duke--had heard the heralds proclaim the new King in the streets of London--and had seen him ascend the marble seat at Westminster and begin the reign that promised so bright a future. He had ridden in the cavalcade that accompanied the King from the Tower on the Saturday preceding the formal coronation, and had formed one of the throng that participated in the gorgeous ceremony of that July Sunday, when all the power of England's nobility passed from the Palace to the Abbey to honor him who was to be the last of his Line.

Never for generations was England to see such a gathering of her Peers and Barons and Churchmen as walked in that procession. There, was the huge Northumberland, fresh from Pontefract--where but a week aback he had sent Rivers and his friends to the headsman--now bearing Mercy's pointless sword; Stanley (his peace made by empty words) with the Mace; Suffolk with the Sceptre; Norfolk, Earl Marshal of the Realm, with the Crown; and Richard himself, in purple gown and crimson surcoat; the Bishop of Durham on his right and the Bishop of Bath on his left; and behind him, bearing his train, the Duke of Buckingham. . . And then the Queen's attendants: Huntington with her Sceptre; Lisle with the Rod and Dove; Wiltshire with her Crown. She, herself, paler than pearls and fragile as Venetian glass, yet calm and self-contained, moved slowly in the heavy royal robes; and after her walked Margaret, Countess of Richmond and mother of him who next would wear the crown, the usurping Tudor.

And then the throne was reached--the music swelled in solemn chorus--the aged Primate raised the crown and placed it on Richard Plantagenet's head--the "Te Deum" rolled out in thunderous tones--and a new King reigned in England.

It was in the late afternoon of the following day that De Lacy, strolling along Bishopgate Street, chanced upon Sir John de Bury near the White Hart Inn, the newest and most popular hostelry in London.

"By St. Luke," Sir John exclaimed, "you are a welcome sight. Come and drink a measure of Burgundy, and I will tell you a bit of news."

They pushed their way through the motley throng in the main room and, coming upon the landlord, were conducted with many bows and smiles to a retired corner and in a moment the wine was set before them. Sir John lifted high the vessel and watched the heavy liquid fall. Then taking a sip he let it run slowly down his throat.

"Not bad, by half," he said, smacking his lips with the air of a connoisseur, and drained his cup at a draught. "What think you of the Coronation?"

"It was a noble spectacle, and a proper act for England."

"Aye, it was--yet I would that Hastings and not Stanley had borne the Mace."

"And that Stanley had been sent in Hastings' place to Chapel Green?" De Lacy asked.

"By St. Luke, yes!" said Sir John instantly; then he leaned over and put his hand on Aymer's shoulder--"and truly, it was a gallant thing you and De Wilton did that mournful morning. Has Gloucester--the King, I mean--said aught to you of it, or has it not reached his ears?"

De Lacy laughed. "He knew it ere he left the Tower, but he found no fault with us."

"And if I know Richard, he liked you both the better for it. . . Here, fellow, another measure of wine, and see that it be of the same barrel. . . These rogues need watching else will they serve poorer stuff the second time, as you have likely noticed."

"Human nature, and innkeepers' nature in particular, does not change between Dover and Calais; yet they would hardly do us the discourtesy to think that our heads muddled so easily."

"Nay, lad, I was but following my motto that it is better to warn before the fight than after."

"Did you warn before the fight in Yorkshire?"

"By St. Luke! there was the fitting moment for the motto, but the villains would give me no breathing space to speak. And that reminds me: do you recall the smooth-tongued Abbot of Kirkstall?"

"In truth, I do," said Aymer. "The most inquisitive monk I have chanced upon in many a day."

"Well, the notion grips me hard that the Abbot Aldam could tell some tales about that little incident, and violate no secret of confessional either. There have been strange rumors lately touching his Abbey and the style of servitors it employs at times."

"Then we at least decreased their numbers--but one escaped, if I remember rightly," Aymer replied.

"Aye--one; but it is enough. Some day I may chance upon him and then . . . I shall know the story."

"Can you recognize the rogue?"

"Instantly. I marked him well, for I had wounded him in the face by a thrust he turned but half aside. A short, thick-set, red-haired knave, with a nose as flat as a sword blade."

"I shall not forget," said Aymer, "and mayhap I may find the story for you. But it occurs to me you spoke of a bit of news."

"By St. Luke, yes! I nigh forgot it, yet it would have mattered little. It is only that I ride North two days hence."

"To Craigston Castle?"

"The same, unless I meet with misadventure on the way."

"In the guise of a flat-nosed, red-haired knave," said Aymer with a laugh.

"A pleasant misadventure, truly! Though, were there any likelihood of that, you would best accompany me and save me from the rogue a second time."

"Nay, my lord, an old bird is not caught twice in the same snare. I scarce fancy you will be surprised a second time, or that he will again venture voluntarily within your reach."

"Then you may not be persuaded to go with me?"

De Lacy shook his head. "I fear I am not open to persuasion; I could not leave the Court at present."

"It is a pity," said Sir John, as he flung the score on the table and arose, "for I had thought the Countess of Clare might like to have you with us. But of course, if the King cannot spare you, there is an end to the matter."

De Lacy looked at the old Knight quizzically for an instant and then laughed frankly.

"It was not fairly done, Sir John," he said; "you caught me foul--you asked first, and reasoned only after I was helpless."

"Well, there is no crime in reconsidering. Will you come?"

"If the King will grant me leave, I shall fare with you."

"With me or with the Countess?" Sir John laughed.

Upon leaving De Bury, Sir Aymer de Lacy bent his steps to Baynard Castle, where the King had come that evening.

At the main door he encountered the Duke of Buckingham in company with Sir William Stanley and was passing them with a courteous salutation when Stafford caught his arm.

"Here, De Lacy," he exclaimed--and Aymer saw he was excited and angry, "you know all the facts! Tell Sir William who is most responsible for the crowning of Gloucester . . . who sent him message to Pontefract . . . who joined him at Northampton . . . who has done all the open work here in London?"

"Nay, Stafford," broke in Stanley, "be not so wrathful. Doubtless His Majesty will be most fair and liberal in the matter. Give him time to feel his crown."

"Time!" retorted the other. "Time! He has had time and to spare. Am I not co-heir to De Bohun through Aleanore, Hereford's daughter, and will Richard of Gloucester think to retake what Henry of Monmouth abjured? By the Lord Omnipotent, let him dare it!"--and with a fiercely menacing gesture he stalked into the courtyard, and springing to horse rode noisily away followed by his attendants.

"His Grace appears a trifle annoyed," said De Lacy.

Sir William Stanley shrugged his shoulders. "It would seem so; yet it were unwise to parade it. However, Buckingham was ever hasty of temper."

"Nathless, the question was embarrassing and I would not care to answer it before a Stanley," Aymer reflected, as he ascended the stairs to the presence chamber.

Baynard Castle, though large and roomy for a nobleman's town residence, was not suited to the needs of a monarch, and as the Court was about to move from Westminster to Windsor, Richard had brought only a few of his favorite Knights and personal attendants with him for the short time he intended to tarry in London. When De Lacy entered the Hall, Richard was not in presence, and lounging at ease on the numerous bancals were some of the minor officers of the Household. He made his way by them to join a group that was gathered about the Duke of Norfolk, when immediately there was a touch upon his arm, and a page summoned him to the King.

Richard was standing at an open window that overlooked the courtyard. He turned as De Lacy entered and demanded abruptly:

"What said Buckingham and Stanley yonder?"

Aymer was too used, by this time, to Richard's ways to be surprised, and he repeated the conversation as accurately as his memory held it and without comment.

The King listened with half-closed eyes, an inscrutable smile upon his lips.

"It may happen, De Lacy," he said, "that there will come a time when you must choose between Henry Stafford and Richard Plantagenet."

"Not so, Sire," Aymer replied. "As against Your Majesty there can never be a choice for me."

Richard looked him straight in the eyes. "I believe it," he said. "I would there were more De Lacys."

Aymer bowed low. "Your Majesty is very gracious; and it encourages me to prefer a request."

"Say on, sir," the King said kindly.

"I would ask a few weeks' leave from Court."

"Wherefore?"

"To accompany Sir John de Bury to Craigston; and to stop at my own castle of Gaillard on my return."

Richard laughed lightly. "It is granted, and may success attend you," he said. "And by St. Paul! if you win the Countess you shall wed her, else I am not King of

England."

De Lacy blushed like a girl, and the King laughed more heartily.

"Methinks Sir John is friendly to you," he added, "and in that you are very fortunate. But you have rivals in plenty, so watch them carefully. Remember, I do not make the match, but should you two wish it, none shall make it otherwise."

"Perchance some day I may remind Your Majesty of those words," said De Lacy.

"And shall find me ready to fulfill them, though I bring an army at my back. . . If need be, you are now excused from attendance until you return, but report to me to-morrow night; I may have some service for you on the journey. . . Announce me."

Swinging back the door, Aymer lifted the arras.

"The King!" he heralded.

Instantly quiet reigned and every one sprang to his feet and uncovered.

"Be seated, gentlemen," said the King. . . "Ah! Norfolk, a word with you," he said, and led the way to a large window in a far corner of the apartment.

"Well, Howard," said he, "the break with Stafford nears--though it comes quicker than I had thought. Were you here when he left me?"

"In sooth, yes, and he was wildly angry. He overtook the younger Stanley at yonder door and his words were high enough to carry back, though not distinguishable."

"I know their import. De Lacy met him in the courtyard, and was appealed to to tell who made Gloucester King."

"The man is a fool or crazy," the Duke exclaimed; "and thrice so to make a Stanley his confidant. Methought he would have got a little wisdom lately by association with Your Majesty."

"Nay, Stafford has no statecraft in him and can learn none."

"Yet it would seem he deems himself a second Kingmaker," the Earl Marshal remarked sententiously.

"Let him beware then lest he meet a Warwick's death--or one less noble."

"But, Sire, do you trust entirely this De Lacy if Buckingham grow discontent? Was he not first vouched for by him?"

"Did you ever hear of a De Lacy untrue to England's King?"

"By the Rood, no! they were ever stanch for him who wore the crown--even as Howard has been."

"And I trust De Lacy as I trust Howard," with the winning smile he could use so well when he wished.

The old Peer bent knee and made to kiss the royal hand.

"Not so, John," said Richard, raising him; "let that go save where ceremony demand it. Your honest grip makes faith enough for Gloucester."

After some serious consultation Norfolk took his leave, and Richard, passing on to his apartments and to the window that overlooked the courtyard, watched him ride off to his own abode. Then with serious face he turned away.

"Norfolk and Surrey are trustworthy," he said half aloud, "but who else of the Peers? . . . By St. Paul! it would seem well to finish Edward's business of snuffing out the old Nobility. Yet I have no Teuton and Tewkesbury to work an opportunity, nor are the Yorkists united behind me. . . It is a hard problem; and the way through is far from clear. . . Buckingham--the Stanleys--Northumberland--all their friends--I trust them not . . . yet must favor them with power that ere long may work my ruin. . . It has become fashionable in England it would seem, since the Second Richard's time, to crown a new King ere the old one died. It was so with him of Bordeaux--of Windsor--and my own dear nephew--and pardieu! it may be the same with me. Yet, no! By St. Paul, no! If that time ever come, there shall be a change in the fashion: when the new King feels his crown, Richard of Gloucester will be dead."

XIII
AT ROYAL WINDSOR

But the following day brought a change of plans. The King had held council with himself during the night; and in the morning there went forth the word that in late July he would make a royal progress through his realm, and in the ancient town of York be crowned a second time. Of this purpose Richard had promptly informed the Queen at Westminster; and the same messenger who bore her answer bore also a letter from the Countess of Clare to Sir John de Bury, advising him that she would not go North, as had been intended, but would wait and attend Her Majesty; explaining that not only could she thus make the long journey with no trouble to him and with more comfort to herself, but also that she was moved by the express desire of the Queen, who was loath to lose her.

Sir John straightway sought the castle, and De Lacy had small trouble in persuading him to remain and ride back to Yorkshire with the King. That evening Aymer informed His Majesty that, on account of the new orders, he would not relinquish for the present his duties as Knight of the Body, and Richard smiled comprehendingly, but made no comment.

Three days later the Court moved to Windsor. On the morning after the arrival there, as De Lacy rounded the front of St. George's Chapel, he came upon the Queen, attended only by the Countess of Clare. He uncovered, and with a deep obeisance was passing on when the former addressed him.

"Sir Aymer," she said, and he halted and bowed low again, "methought you had left us for distant Yorkshire. We are glad the information was not sound.--Are we not, Beatrix?" with a sly glance at her companion.

"Whatever pleases you pleases me," the Countess answered with a frank smile.

"And do you know, Sir Aymer," said the Queen, who was in a happy mood, "that the Countess of Clare had also proposed leaving us for Craigston Castle . . . and, indeed, upon the very morning you had fixed to go?"

"What rare fortune to have met her on the way," said Aymer.

"Greater fortune, think you, than to be with her here at Windsor?"

The Countess looked at her mistress in blank surprise.

"Could there be greater fortune than to be where Your Majesty is in presence?" Aymer asked.

"Where she is in presence at this particular moment, you mean?" taking Beatrix's hand.

"Your Majesty is hardly fair to Sir Aymer or to me," said the Countess quickly. "You draw his scanty compliments from him like an arrow from a wound--hurting him all the while."

The Queen laughed. "If all Sir Aymer's wounds hurt him no more, he is likely to know little pain."

"I know he is French-bred and a courtier," Beatrix answered.

"As you told me once before in Pontefract," De Lacy observed.

"And as I am very apt to tell you again when you are presumptuous and flattering."

"Henceforth I shall be neither."

"Charming, Sir Aymer, charming . . . if you could."

"I can."

"Till you meet another woman."

"It is not in the other woman that my danger lies."

Beatrix frowned, and the Queen laughed.

"The Countess seems to know your failings, Sir Aymer," she said, "and may be this is a good time for you to know them, too. Nay, Beatrix, you need not accompany me. . . I am going to the Chapel. Do you take Sir Aymer in hand and bring him out of his French habits, since you do not like them. For my part, I think them very charming."

"Surely she loves you," said De Lacy, when the Queen had gone.

The Countess gave him her shoulder.

"She takes a queer way to show it then," she retorted, her foot beating a tattoo on the stones.

He smothered a laugh. "Shall we walk?" he asked.

He got a shrug and a louder tattoo.

"Since the Queen has left me to your tender mercies," she said coldly, "I am at your service."

They walked in silence; he smiling; she stern-eyed and face straight to the fore.

"Does it occur to you, my lady," he said after a while, "that you are a bit unjust?"

The small head lifted higher . . . then presently, with rising inflection: "Unjust--to whom?"

"To the Queen."

"I am sorry."

"And unjust to me also."

No answer--only a faint toss of the ruddy tresses.

"And to me also," he repeated.

She surveyed him ignoringly--and turned away, eyebrows lifted.

De Lacy smiled and waited.

Presently she gave him a quick, sidelong glance. He was gazing idly toward the river. . . Again she looked . . . and again--each time a trifle more deliberately. . . . Finally she faced him.

"You are unusually disagreeable to-day," she said.

"I am sorry," he answered instantly. "I do not wish to be."

It was so contrary to what she had expected that she halted in sheer surprise.

"I wonder," she said musingly. . . "I wonder . . ." then she laughed forgivingly. "Come, let us cease this constant banter. We have been at it ever since we met, and it profits nothing to our friendship."

"With all my heart," he exclaimed, taking her hand and pressing it with light fingers.

She drew it away sharply.

"Do you think that a fitting way to begin?"

"Your pardon," he said softly; "I fear I did not think."

She looked at him with quick scrutiny.

"We islanders are not given to impulse, Sir Aymer, and do not trust it deeply. I forgive you--but . . . not again."

"By St. Denis! I seem to blunder always," he said sadly. "I please you in nothing and am ever at fault."

"You are unjust to yourself," she protested. "You please me in much, and . . . you ought to know it;" then she blushed. . . "Let us go on the terrace," and hurried across. . . "Now talk to me . . . not about me," she said rather curtly, as she sat down.

De Lacy was growing used to these swift shifts of humor, these flashes of tenderness, veering instantly to aloofness, and then back to a half-confidential camaraderie, that was alluringly delicious, yet irritatingly unsatisfying. At first he had tried to force the situation to his own liking,--to break through her moods and effect an atmosphere more equable,--but she soon had taught him the folly of it, and never failed to punish when he forgot. This time she, herself, had broken through a bit, but that would only make his punishment the heavier.

At first the conversation was aimless and disconnected. De Lacy let it drift and the Countess was rather distrait and steered it uncertainly. Presently she took a grip upon herself, and, before he realized it, he was telling her of the French Court; of Louis the King, whom men called "The Fell," but who was, he said, the ablest of the Valois, and would do much for France--though not by the means then deemed most honorable,--being far ahead of his Age. He spoke of the brave, dead St. Pol, the Constable--after Dunois, the greatest since Du Guesclin's time. He told her of their palaces . . . of the life of their women, though he touched but lightly upon its loose gayety . . . of the cities . . . of the great domains whereon the noble had the "right of high justice, the middle and the low," and indeed up until very lately had done his own sweet will toward aught but the King, and in many cases toward the King himself. . . And at length he mentioned having seen and met Henry Tudor, Earl of Richmond, at the Court of Blois. Concerning him the Countess asked many questions, and Aymer answered them as best he could. He had not given the Earl much thought, nor had he offered him any attentions, for he was regarded as little more than adventurer--though one with strangely plenty of money; and who was tolerated by the crafty Louis only because he might be useful some time to play against the Yorkist King of England.

"Methinks there is more in the Tudor than you credit," said the Countess. "I have heard much of him, and from one who knows him well--or did a few years since. He is not a brave Knight or skilled warrior may be, but he has a certain shrewdness and determination which would make him a formidable rival for the Crown, if he were able to muster a following or had an opportunity to arouse any enthusiasm for his cause."

"And from what wise person did you learn all this?" De Lacy asked with an amused smile.

"From the Countess of Northumberland."

"And whence comes her knowledge?"

"If you were not new to England you would not ask," said she. "Henry Tudor was for years a prisoner of state in her father's castle of Pembroke. She knows him from daily companionship and should be competent to judge. Indeed, as the Lady Maude Herbert, it is said she was betrothed to him."

"Why did she marry Percy?"

"That, I can only guess. Her father fell at Edgecote; there were six other sisters . . . and the great Earl came a-wooing. Besides, Richmond was in exile, had lost his patrimony and a price was on his head."

"And she never loved him?" De Lacy asked.

"Nay, that I do not know; but she was very young, and if she did it was not likely a lasting passion. She seems happy enough as chatelaine of Topcliffe."

"Doubtless--yet, nevertheless, there is another woman in England than Stanley's Countess who may be dangerous to Richard if Henry Tudor ever seek an issue with him."

"You mean the Countess of Northumberland?"

"Aye. Percy wields huge power. He and the Stanleys together could well-nigh topple the throne. Lord Stanley no man trusts--and it was a Percy whose treason sent the Second Richard to his doom."

"Richard of Bordeaux was not Richard of Gloucester," she argued.

"In truth, no, but the conditions then were far more favorable to the King. Believe me, wore I the Crown, these two women would give me more concern than all the nobles in my kingdom."

"What would you do if you *were* King?" she asked, smiling.

De Lacy held up his hands. "Do! When I cannot control even one woman, I would make a merry mess with two and a kingdom besides."

Just then a horn spoke merrily from the courtyard and De Lacy sprang up.

"Richard is for a ride in Windsor forest and I must away," he said. "I would that you went, too."

"We do go," she said. "Let us haste or I shall be late to horse."

"May I ride with you?" he asked.

She nodded. "For a little way."

"Why not all the way?" he persisted.

"Because the King would object"--it was the flash of tenderness now.

"Nay, he would be quite satisfied," De Lacy answered unthinkingly.

She stopped short.

"Indeed!" she exclaimed frigidly; "well, I would not;" and turning abruptly, she entered a private passage and disappeared.

"Now the Devil take my foolish tongue," Aymer muttered, as the door clanged behind her. . . Then the horn rang out again, and in vast disgust and anger he hurried to his room and into riding dress.

But his haste made him awkward and he lost precious moments; and when at length he rushed down the stairs and into the courtyard it was to see Lord Darby swing the Countess of Clare into saddle and dash off beside her.

De Lacy swore such a string of good round French oaths that the silent Giles Dauvrey was so startled from his wonted equanimity that for the moment he forgot to mount and follow, but stood watching his master in serious wonder, as Selim raced toward the gate.

However, anger would not mend the matter and good humor might, so he put on a smiling front. And when he presently neared the Countess and Lord Darby he reined close beside her and cantered by with bonnet doffed.

"I shall claim your promise presently," he said, his eyes seeking her face--though he doubted much if she would give it to him.

But her humor had veered again, and she answered with such a bewitching smile he was utterly bewildered, and for a time Selim went whither and how he listed.

"May I ask what is the promise?" said Lord Darby.

The Countess raised her eyebrows in annoyed surprise.

"I promised to ride with him this morning."

"The promise is cancelled now."

"And why, my lord?"

"He was a sluggard at the start."

She bent forward and put aright a bit of Wilda's mane.

"Nay, sir, why should you wish him punished," said she lightly, "since it gives you a little of my society?"

He leaned suddenly over and laid his hand upon her arm.

"Will you not give it to me until the end of life?" he asked earnestly.

She gazed at him a moment in startled surprise--then laughed merrily.

"You said that with delightful promptness, my lord," she exclaimed. "Practice makes one proficient, surely."

A cold light settled in Darby's eyes, and he straightened in the saddle and faced to the front.

"If a man be a gallant once, need that condemn his words to disbelief forever?" he asked. . . "May not even the most confirmed trifler have, some time, an honest passion?"

"Doubtless, yes," she said, with a shrug of the shapely shoulders. . . "Only . . ."

"Only . . . only what?"

"Only that it is very rare and its proof requires strong demonstration and long service."

"And I am ready to do both," he said eagerly.

"Then, one day, my lord, you will bring great joy to some loving heart," she replied, looking him calmly in the eyes.

An awkward silence followed--that was not broken until Sir Aymer came galloping back. With a familiarly courteous salute he swung Selim around; and Lord Darby, seizing the opportunity, bowed low to the Countess, and with a menacing glare at De Lacy--who met it with a careless smile--he spurred away.

The Countess had observed Darby's look and she followed him with a frown . . . and De Lacy wisely kept silent.

"I am glad you came," she said presently--then pulled Wilda to a walk. "Let us loiter; since we are late it is small matter when we reach the rendezvous."

"Why reach it at all?" he asked.

She hesitated.

"Why not ride?" he persisted.

She looked at the horses thoughtfully . . . then shook her head. "I would far rather ride," she said, "but the Queen expects me; duty calls."

"St. Denis! I had quite forgot--duty calls me, too."

But they did not take the horses from their walk, and it was far after time when they reached the wide open space in the forest, where the party had assembled.

Upon one side were pitched three large silk pavilions; the center one of red and blue--the colors of the Kingdom; the others, gold and blue--the colors of the House of York. In front and for a wide space around on the soft turf were spread the thick carpets of the far East. Before the tents paced two archers of the guard; and stationed at close intervals around the clearing were a goodly force of those veterans, all of whom had been among the personal retainers of Richard when he was Duke of Gloucester.

Not over two score of the Court had been bidden, and these were clustered before the royal pavilion when De Lacy and the Countess rode up. A volley of chaff greeted them as he lifted her from the saddle. One suggested that they had lost their way . . . another that it was a shame to bring in horses so utterly exhausted . . . another that they must have stumbled on the Court by accident . . . another that there was powder on De Lacy's sleeve. . . And so it went; until Beatrix, in sheer desperation, gathered her skirts about her and fled into the tent.

The Queen was alone, resting on a couch in the inner apartment; but she had heard the noisy greetings outside and had wondered who were the victims. Beatrix's entrance and snapping eyes told her; and she met her with a smile of sympathy.

"Do not mind them, dear," she said. "They mean nothing and you have beard a dozen others treated so, under similar circumstances."

"I know . . . I know . . . Your Majesty," she replied, with nervous energy . . . "but it was most annoying . . . and with Sir Aymer."

"I doubt not he would give much to know that fact," said the Queen with an amused smile.

"It is because I fear he does know it that I am so vexed. By my faith, I have made a merry mess of it all through this morning."

"The merriest mess and the best you could make, my dear girl," motioning her to a place on the couch, "would be to marry Sir Aymer de Lacy."

The Countess gave a look of startled surprise--then dropped her head.

"And methinks," Anne went on, watching her closely, "that you are of the same mind. Take your Queen's word, aye, and your King's as well--for Richard has spoken of it--and quarter the red chevrons with the silver stag."

The Countess was slowly tracing figures on the carpet with her riding whip; and her mistress pressed on:

"You surely cannot hesitate from doubt of his affection. In a thousand ways he shows you that. And certes you have had enough of suitors to be able to weigh very scrupulously the faith they bring. He loves you honestly. He is your equal in birth; and though his English title be inferior to yours, he is a Count in France. Why not, my dear Beatrix, be . . . kind to him?" and she put her arm about her.

"You are an earnest pleader, my dear mistress," said the Countess, still busy with the carpet . . . "and, may be, not without cause. . . Sir Aymer is all you aver . . . a braver Knight or truer heart I never knew. . . And it would be false modesty to pretend I think he does not love me. I did doubt it until lately, but the doubt has gone now. Were I as sure of myself as I am of him, I would hold him off not a moment longer--he might speak when he chose . . . and the quickest would not be too quick for me . . . Indeed, sometimes I long for him with eager heart; yet, when he comes, I grow weak in resolution and from very timidity give him only chilly words."

The Queen drew her a little closer. "I understand, dear," she said. "It was so with me when my own dear lord came wooing."

"And how did you . . . change?" Beatrix asked, and blushed winsomely.

And Anne blushed, too. "Nay, I do not know. . . One day my heart met his words and all was peace and happiness."

The Countess sighed. "I wish it might be so with me," she said, and tears were in her voice; "for lately I have grown very lonely--and after you, this man comforts me the most."

"My sweet Beatrix," said the Queen, "Sir Aymer has you safe enough," and she put both arms around her and kissed her cheek.

And so, a moment later, the King found them; and with a smile, half sympathy and half amusement, he said:

"Methinks, my dear, you and the Countess are wasting sadly your favors on each other. And I am acquainted with many a gallant Knight--but one especial-- who would give his quarterings to be prisoner to her as you are at this moment."

Beatrix's cheeks and brow went rosy and in sharp embarrassment she hid her face upon the Queen's shoulder.

"Pardieu, my dear," said Richard, "I did not mean to distress you--yet since I have said it, let me say a little more. As the Queen likes you, so like I De Lacy, and I have given him these words: 'I make not the match, but if you two wish it, none shall make it otherwise.' And I give them now to you also. Nay, thank me not," as she arose and curtsied low; "and while the match would please us well, yet it is our pleasure to follow your desires. All we need is to know them, and that in your own good time." And Richard took her hand and kissed it; then flung aside the curtains and went out as abruptly as he had entered.

XIV
THE QUEEN OF ARCHERY

As the King appeared before the pavilion, a bugle rang out, the soldiers presented halberds, and all talk ceased sharply.

"My good friends," said he, "I have brought you here to-day to test your skill with a weapon that once made an English army the most feared in all the world. In a word, I am curious to know how steadily you can draw the cord and lay your bodies to the bow. Yonder are the butts, and here the staves and the draw line. It is but a poor one hundred paces to the nearest clout; and as that will be too beggarly a distance for you, my lords, you shall use the second. The first has been placed for the fair dames who are to shoot with you, if they will."

And taking the hand of the Queen, who had come forth with the Countess of Clare and was standing beside him, he led the way to the near end of the clearing where, on a rustic table built of boughs, were piled an assortment of yew staves and arrows of seasoned ash, with cords of deer hide, wrist gloves, baldrics, and all the paraphernalia essential to the archer's outfit.

"Let the lots be drawn," he commanded; and a page came forward with the disc-bag.

As soon as De Lacy saw that Beatrix would participate in the contest, he chose with much care a stave best adapted for her wrist, and picking out a string to correspond and three grey-goose-feather shafts of a proper length and thickness, he brought them to her.

"Do you not shoot?" she asked.

"Yes--but with small hope. The French do not run to the long bow, and while once I could ring the blanc I am sadly out of practice."

"Ring it now . . . you can," she said softly.

He looked at her hesitatingly. "Tell me," he said, coming a bit nearer; "tell me . . . will you be sorry if I fail?"

But the old habit held her and she veered off. "Assuredly . . . it would be poor friendship if I were not." . . . A bowstring twanged and the crowd applauded.

"Come," she exclaimed, "the match has begun."

"And is this my answer?" he asked.

"Yes, Sir Insistent . . . until the ride back," and left him.

The luck of the discs had made the Countess of Clare the last to shoot. When she came forward to the line the butt was dotted over with the feathered shafts; but the white eye that looked out from their midst was still unharmed, though the Duchess of Buckingham and Lady Clifton had grazed its edge. Beatrix had slipped the arrows through her girdle, and plucking out one she fitted it to the string with easy grace. Then without pausing to measure the distance she raised the bow, and drawing with the swift but steady motion of the right wrist got only by hard practice, and seemingly without taking aim, she sped the shaft toward the mark.

"Bravo!" exclaimed the King, as it quivered in the white.

Before the word had died, the second arrow rested beside it; and even as it struck, the string twanged again and the third joined the others in the blanc.

"My dear Countess," said Richard, "I did not know we entertained another Monarch. Behold the Queen of Archery! Hail and welcome to our Kingdom and our Court! . . . Gentlemen, have you no knee for Her Majesty?"

Beatrix blushed and curtsied in return, then quickly withdrew to the side of the Queen.

"Methinks, my lords," Richard said, "you have got a hard score to best. However, it is but two hundred yards to your target; so let it be the notch to the string, the string to the ear, and the shaft in the white clout yonder."

As the King had said, the distance was short for rovers. In all regular contests the mark was never under two hundred and twenty paces, and in many districts it was nearer four hundred. Nevertheless, to strike an object, even at two hundred, that seemed no larger than one's hand is no easy task; and yet, as one after another took his turn, the clout was pierced repeatedly; once by some, and twice by others; but only the Duke of Buckingham and Sir Aymer de Lacy struck it thrice. It chanced, however, that one of the latter's arrows landed directly in the center, on the pin that held the cloth, and this gave him the prize.

"For one who is half a Frenchman, Sir Aymer, you handle a long bow most amazing well," the King remarked. . . "Pardieu! what say you to a match between the victors?"

A murmur of approval greeted the suggestion.

"May it please you, my liege," said De Lacy, "permit me now to yield. I am no match for the Queen of Archery."

"We will not excuse you . . . nor, I fancy, will the Countess," turning toward her.

"If Sir Aymer de Lacy will engage to shoot his best and show no favor, I shall not refuse the trial," she replied, coming forward.

"By St. Paul!" Richard exclaimed. "I will answer for that . . . here is the prize," and deftly plucking the lace kerchief from her hand he passed it to a page. "Substitute this for the clout in the far target," he said.

De Lacy thought she would refuse the contest; but to his surprise she smiled--though with rather indifferent hauteur.

"It is hardly fitting, Sire," she said, choosing an arrow, "that I should both contribute the prize and contest for it."

Then Sir Aymer spoke, bowing low: "May it please Your Majesty, I am your leal subject, yet I shall not shoot at yonder mark unless the Countess of Clare consent."

She gave him a grateful look.

"I thank you, Sir Aymer, for the courtesy," she said. . . "Shoot and welcome;" and she stepped to the draw line.

It may have been that she was careless, or that the scene had made her nervous, for while her first two arrows struck the blanc truly as before, the third went a finger's length above it. With a shrug she turned away, and loosing the string leaned on the long stave, waiting.

De Lacy had purposed letting her defeat him by a margin so slender as not to seem intentional, but catching the dark eyes of the King fixed on him with sharp significance, he understood that he was to win if he could. So he drew with care, and pierced the kerchief thrice.

De Lacy received the bit of lace from the page and proffered it to the Countess.

"It is quite destroyed," he said. "I am sorry."

She laughed lightly. "You owe me no apologies, and need feel no regret. You won it honestly--and I accept it now as a gift; a guerdon of your prowess and your courtesy."

He bowed; and as his glance sought the King, the latter nodded, ever so lightly, in approval.

An hour later, after the repast was served, the trumpet gave the signal for departure. As De Lacy stepped forward to hold the stirrup, Richard waved him aside, and putting one hand on his horse's wither, vaulted easily into place.

"Look to the ladies!" he called; "and do you, Sir Aymer, escort the Countess of Clare. It is meet that the King of the Bow should attend upon his Queen."

Then dropping his tones, so that they were audible only to De Lacy, he said with a familiar earnestness: "And if you do not turn the kerchief to advantage, you deserve no further aid."

Reining over beside the Queen, he motioned for the others to follow and dashed off toward Windsor. In a trice they were gone, and, save for the servants, the Countess and De Lacy were alone.

She was standing beside Wilda waiting to be put up, and when Aymer tried to apologize for the delay, she stopped him.

"It was no fault of yours," she said--then added archly, head turned half aside: "and you must blame Richard Plantagenet for being left with me."

"Blame him?" he exclaimed, lifting her slowly--very slowly--into saddle. . . "Blame him! . . . Do you think I call it so?" and fell to arranging her skirt, and lingering over it so plainly that the Countess smiled in unreserved amusement. Yet she did not hurry him. And when he had dallied as long as he thought he dared, he stole a quick glance upward--and she let him see the smile.

"Am I very clumsy?" he asked, swinging up on Selim.

She waited until they had left the clearing and the grooms behind them and were among the great tall trees:

"Surely not . . . only very careful," she said teasingly.

He was puzzled at this new mood that had come with the archery and still tarried--this careless gayety under circumstances which, hitherto, would have made her severe and distant. He was so used to being frowned upon, reproved, and held at the point that he was quite blind to the change it signaled. He bent his eyes on his horse's mane. He thought of the King's words as to the kerchief and longed for a bit of his astute penetration and wonderful tact, that he might solve this provoking riddle beside him and lead up to what was beating so fiercely in his breast. In his perplexity he looked appealingly toward her.

She was watching him with the same amused smile she had worn since the fixing of the skirt; and was guessing, with womanly intuition, what was passing in his mind.

"And forsooth, Sir King of the Bow," she said--and the smile rippled into a laugh--"are you so puffed up by your victory that you will not deign to address me, but must needs hold yourself aloof, even when there is none to see your condescension! . . . Perchance even to ride beside me will compromise your dignity. Proceed. . . Proceed. . . I can follow; or wait for the grooms or the scullions with the victual carts."

And this only increased De Lacy's amazement and indecision.

"Why do you treat me so?" he demanded.

"Do you not like my present mood?" she asked. "Yea, verily, that I do! but it is so novel I am bewildered. . . My brain is whirling. . . You are like a German escutcheon: hard to read aright."

"Then why try the task?"

"I prefer the task," he answered. "It may be difficult, yet it has its compensations."

"You flatterer," she exclaimed; and for an instant the smile became almost tender.

"Pardieu! . . . You grow more inexplicable still. . . Yesterday I would have been rated sharply for such words and called presumptuous and kindred names."

"And what of to-day . . . if that were yesterday?"

"To-day! . . . To-day! . . . It has been the mirror of all the yesterdays since the happy one that gave me first sight of you at Pontefract; . . . and the later one when, ere I rode back to London, I begged a favor--the kerchief you had dropped by accident--and was denied." . . . He drew Selim nearer. . . "To-day I again secured your kerchief; and though I wished to keep it sorely as I wished before to keep the other, yet like it, too, I could only give it back. And now, even as I begged before, I beg again for the favor. Will you not grant it?"

The smile faded and her face went serious.

"Do you not forget the words of that first refusal," she asked, "that 'Beatrix de Beaumont grants neither gage nor favor until she plights her troth'?"

"Nay, I have not forgotten"--and with sudden hope that made his throat thicken and his fingers chill he reached over and took her hand.

She did not withdraw it nor reprove him. Instead, she fastened her eyes on his face as though to read his very heart and soul. Unconsciously they had checked their horses. Then she blushed, and averting her eyes in confusion strove to release her hand. But De Lacy pressed on, though his heart beat fast and his head throbbed. Leaning across, he put his arm about her waist and drew her--struggling gently--toward him.

"And the kerchief, dear one?" he whispered.

"Nay, Aymer, you surely do not wish it now," she answered brokenly.

"Now, more than any earthly gift or Heavenly grace. . . Give it to me, sweetheart."

She had ceased to resist and his face was getting perilously near her own.

Suddenly, and with a smile De Lacy never forgot, she drew forth the bit of torn lace. "Here, take it, dear," she said.

"And you with it, sweetheart?" he cried.

"Unto death, my lord," she answered; and once more the blushes came.

She tried to hide her face in her hands, but with a joyous laugh Aymer lifted her from the saddle and swung her across and into his strong arms.

XV
THE FROWN OF FATE

It was the Countess' wish that the betrothal should remain secret for the present, and therefore none but Their Majesties and Sir John de Bury were acquainted with it. The old Knight, when approached by De Lacy on the subject, had clapped him heartily on the shoulder.

"Take her, lad," he exclaimed; "and be worthy, even as I think you will. The King, himself, has spoken in your behalf . . . to say naught of the maid herself. But by St. Luke! this fortune will bring its drag. The Countess has had too many suitors for the favored one to escape unhated. Nay, do not shrug your shoulders . . . or, at least, there is no harm in shrugging if your wit be keen, your dagger ever ready, and your arm strong. Remember, De Lacy, that you are a stranger, high in favor with the King, and that Beatrix has broad acres as well as a fair face."

"And also that there is a certain, flat-nosed, red-haired knave at large, who, perchance, may honor me, even as he did you."

"Spare him, lad, spare him for me! . . . Yet if he should come under your sword, put a bit more force in the blow for my sake."

"Trust me for that. . . I shall split him six inches deeper--and tell him why as I do it."

"It will make me still more your debtor. By the Holy Evangels! if I were assured the Abbot Aldam of Kirkstall had aught to do with that attack upon me, I would harry his worthless old mummery shop so clean a mouse would starve in it."

"Hark you, Sir John," said Aymer, "I may resign the Flat-Nose to you, but I shall claim a hand in that harrying business if the time ever ripen."

"Sorry the day for the Cistercian when we batter down his gates," the old Knight laughed, yet with a menacing ring in his words.

"Sorry, indeed, for those on the other side of the gates," came a voice from behind the arras, and the King parted the hangings. . . . "Though may I ask whose gates are in to be battered and for what purpose?"

"The gates of Kirkstall Abbey, under certain conditions, so please Your Majesty," said De Bury.

Richard elevated his eyebrows ever so slightly.

"And the conditions?" he asked.

"Proof that the Abbot Aldam was concerned in a recent murderous assault upon me, or that he harbors a certain flat-nosed ruffian who led it," Sir John replied.

"Methinks you told me of this matter at the time," addressing De Lacy.

"Yes, my liege,--at Leicester."

Richard nodded. "Perchance, Sir John, you may solve the riddle some day, and by way of Kirkstall: though it were not best to work sacrilege. Mother Church is holy with us yet awhile, and must needs be handled tenderly. Nathless, there is no hurt in keeping a close watch upon the Cistercian."

"And if it should be that he plots treason against the King of England?" De Bury queried.

Richard smiled and shrugged his shoulders.

"In that event," he said, "there will be a new mitre to fit at Kirkstall. . . And mon Dieu! John, how would you like to wear it?"

De Bury raised his hands in horrified negation. "Now God forefend that I, in my old age, should come to that. Better take De Lacy; he is young and blithesome."

"By St. Paul! John, best not tell your niece you sought to turn De Lacy monk!" . . . then went on: "Two days hence we fare Northward, but without Her Majesty, who will join us later . . . at Warwick likely. To you, Sir John, I give command of her escort . . . De Lacy, you will ride with me. But of this, more anon," and he moved away--then stopped and said sternly: "Sir Aymer, go to the Queen and say to her it is my command that, until we depart, you walk with the Countess of Clare on the terrace, or ride with her, or do whatever you two may wish." And then he laughed.

On the following Thursday, being the thirteenth of July, Richard departed from Windsor, and behind him rode the most imposing and gorgeous cavalcade that ever accompanied a King of England in a peaceful progress through his realm. There, gleamed the silver bend of Howard on its ground of gules; the red chevron of Stafford in its golden field; the golden fess of De la Pole amid the leopard faces; the three gold stagheads of Stanley on the azure bend; the gold bend of Bolton, Lord of Scrope; the gold and red bars of Lovell; the red lion of De Lisle ramping on its field of gold; the sable bend engrailed of Ratcliffe; the red fess and triple torteaux of D'Evereux, Lord Ferrers of Chartley; the sable twin lions of Catesby; the golden chevron of Hungerford; the red engrailed cross and sable water bougets of Bourchier; and a score of others equally prominent and powerful. And with every Baron were his particular retainers; but varying in number up to the three hundred that wore the Stafford Knot and ruffled themselves as scarce second even to the veterans of the King himself.

Richard was mounted on "White Surray," the famous war horse that he rode first in the Scottish War, and was to ride for the last time in the furious charge across Redmore Plain on that fatal August morning when the Plantagenet Line died, even as it had lived and ruled--hauberk on back and sword in hand. He wore no armor, but in his rich doublet and super-tunic of dark blue velvet with the baudikin stripes on the sleeve, he made as handsome and gallant a figure as one was wont to see, even in those days of chivalry. And no reign, since his protonymic predecessor's, gave promise of a brighter future. The people had accepted him without a murmur of dissatisfaction, well pleased that there was to be no occasion for the riot of factions and favorites that a child King always engenders. England had known Richard of Gloucester, even since his boyhood, as a strong man among strong men--a puissant knight, an unbeaten general, a wise counsellor, a brilliant administrator; in all things able, resourceful, proficient; combining, as it were, in the last of the Angevines, all the keen statesmanship, stern will, and fiery dash of the great House that had ruled England for three hundred turbulent years.

Since the evening in London when Buckingham had quitted the castle in anger at the denial of the De Bohun inheritance, the matter had not been mentioned between them; nor did the Duke know that Richard had ever heard of his outburst. Yet it is sure that from that moment they had distrusted each other, though they varied not a jot their former bearing. Stafford remained at Court in constant attendance, and the King continued to grant him substantial favors and honors, and this day, as they rode side by side toward Reading (as well as until Buckingham turned aside at Gloucester for his demesne of Brecknock), the most astute observer could not have detected in the frank cordiality of their manner, the faintest trace of unfriendliness on the part of either.

The King had thrown aside his haughty reserve, and laughed and chatted gayly with those about him. Toward the inhabitants, who were gathered in crowds along the highways, he was very gracious, doffing bonnet to the curtsies of the women, and acknowledging with a gracious sweep of his arm and hand the respectful salutations of the men. And many were the enthusiastic cries of "God save the King!" or "God save Your Majesty!" or "God save King Richard!" And they came from the solitary individual as well as from the multitude; from the laborers in the country as well as from the tradesmen and artificers in the hamlets and small towns.

It was near evening on the twelfth day after leaving Windsor that the tall towers of Warwick Castle loomed in the distance, the giant "Caesar" rising high above its huge brothers, the "Gateway" and the "Grey," and casting its grim shadow far across the country-side. During much of this day's journey Richard had been very quiet, riding with his head sunk on his breast; and observing this, his attendants, save only the particular Knight of the Body on duty, gradually drew further behind so that their talk would not annoy him. At intervals he summoned one or more of them, but after a short time his interest waned, his abstraction returned, and like discreet courtiers, they quickly dropped again to the rear. As they neared the fortress he roused himself, and when the bombard on the wall roared out the royal salute he waved his suite to him. At the same time Sir William Catesby, who had gone on in advance from Worcester the previous day, came galloping to meet them with Sir James Gascoyne, the Constable of the Castle.

Richard supped alone that evening; and then for a while he paced the floor in meditation, pausing finally at the open window. Presently he struck the bell.

"Who waits?" he asked.

"Sir Aymer de Lacy and Sir Ralph de Wilton," replied the page.

"De Lacy," he said. . . "Come hither," as Aymer entered; "a crowded courtyard always entertains me. . . Sometimes much may be learned from it; and this is very active now. Have you ever seen one so bright and busy?"

"But once before in England, Sire."

"Where?"

"At Pontefract! the night I first met the Duke of Gloucester."

"Aye, that may be true--it was crowded in those days. . . Pardieu! it is scarce three months since then--and yet . . . Holy Paul, what, changes!" He half closed his eyes in retrospection. . . "It is marvellous what memory can show us in an instant," he said, and turning sharply from the casement struck the bell again. . . "Summon the Lord Steward," he ordered . . . then, to De Lacy, when the page had gone: "And do you attend to what is said and pay no regard to Stanley's glances of uneasiness. . . You understand?"

De Lacy bowed. "I do, and with profound satisfaction."

"Why satisfaction?"

"That Your Majesty does not trust him."

Richard smiled grimly. "Trust him or his brother William? Rather look for faith and honesty in the Fiend himself. Nathless, I may not slight them--yet awhile. It is watch and wait--now. And a trying task truly, for they are the shrewdest brained in the land."

"Save the King of England," Aymer added.

"Save none, as you some day may see."

"God forbid!" De Lacy exclaimed earnestly.

But Richard only shrugged his shoulders. "Nay, what boots it? As great Coeur-de-Lion said: 'From the Devil we Plantagenets all come, and to the Devil shall we all go.'"

"Then Your Majesty will never be quit of the Stanleys."

"It would seem so," with a short laugh; "yet it is the live Stanley that worries me now."

"The Lord Stanley awaits Your Majesty's pleasure," said the page, stepping within the arras.

"Admit him," the King ordered, choosing a place where his own face would be in the shadow and the other's in the glare. . . "And would it were my pleasure, rather than my expediency, that awaited him," he added in an undertone.

Stanley came forward in his precise and cautious way and bent knee to the King.

"Be seated, my lord," said Richard cordially. "I wish your advice upon a most important matter, if you can spare me a little of your time."

The Lord Steward bowed. "My time belongs to you, Sire," he said suavely; "though I fear my poor advice can aid but little your own keen judgment; yet it is flattering to be asked it."

Richard made a gesture of dissent. "I did not summon you for flattery," he said; "if I did not value your discretion you would not be here."

"Then I trust your gracious confidence may not be misplaced."

"I am about to test it. . . Tell me, my lord, what is the gravest state problem that confronts me now?"

The Lord Steward's crafty blue eyes shot a sharp glance at the King, but Richard's black ones met it half way and drove it back in quick retreat. Now, Stanley had one weakness. He was vain of his astuteness and ever ready to display it; and he thought he had discerned instantly what was in the King's mind.

"Your Majesty means the two Princes--Edward's sons," he said.

Richard's face showed blank surprise.

"Nay, my lord, I mean nothing in particular," he said. "I sought only what, in your opinion, was my chief embarrassment and peril. . . And you answer: the young Princes. . . By St. Paul! you may be right--give me your reasons."

Stanley saw his blunder and grew hot with rage. He had been outwitted; and now, as between him and the King, he must ever bear the burden of having first suggested Edward's sons as a menace to the State. The trap was so easy; and yet he had never seen it until it had caught him tight. And between his anger and the strange influence which Richard exercised over all men when in his presence, he blundered again--and worse than before.

"When, since time began," he asked, "has a new King had peace or comfort while his supplanted predecessor lived to breed revolt?"

Richard seized the opening instantly.

"Great St. George! You do not urge the Princes' death?" he exclaimed.

And Stanley floundered deeper.

"Holy Mother, Sire, do not misunderstand me," he answered. "I urge nothing. But the problem, as I see it, is, not why to act, but how to refrain."

"Yet Parliament has declared them bastards and so never eligible to the crown," Richard objected.

But Stanley had gone too far now to retreat and he pressed on, knowing that he, himself, was incurring little or no danger by the advice. Richard alone would be responsible if he acted upon it, and all the open shame would fall upon him.

"The Beauforts were bastards," he answered, "and Parliament specifically refused them the royal dignity; yet who, to-day, is Lancaster's chief and claimant for your Crown but the heir of those same Beauforts? Pardieu! Sire, you need not me to tell you that Parliament belongs to him whose writ summons it."

"I would never countenance it," the King answered; "and it would surely destroy me if I did."

Stanley smiled shrewdly. "Did the Fourth Henry sit less easy on the throne when the deposed Richard died suddenly at Pontefract? . . . Did John tyrannize the less because of Arthur's cruel taking off?"

The King arose and paced the floor, looking straight before him. Stanley watched him furtively, trying vainly to read behind the mask of that passionless face.

"Tell me, my lord," said Richard presently, halting beside him and putting a hand on his shoulder, "if you were King of England, what would you do with the Princes?"

Stanley evaded the direct question. "Your Majesty is King of England, and I can never be aught but a subject--how can I know what a King would do?"

Richard nodded. "That is but fair, my lord," he said. "To decide as King one must be King. Yet I would gather from our talk that you deem the . . . removal . . . most essential--is it not so?"

Pushed into the corner, the shifty Baron hesitated and sought to evade again. But he managed badly, for now the King's eyes were hard upon his face.

"Of a truth, Sire," he replied, "our talk this night has convinced me it would be most expedient for Your Majesty."

Richard's lips softened into the very faintest smile.

"Our talk------!" he began.

Then suddenly Stanley started up and pointed to the window.

"Who is yonder listener?" he exclaimed.

Richard turned quickly, following the gesture.

"Are your eyes failing?" he asked. "It is De Lacy--he is on duty to-night."

"Did you know he was there?"

"Most assuredly, my lord."

Stanley stared at the King in amazed silence, and despite his careful dissimulation the indignation blazed in his eyes.

"If Your Majesty deem it wise to discuss such matters before a simple attendant," he said, "it is not for me to criticise . . . yet, methinks, if it be not risky, it is at least unusual."

"Never fear, Lord Steward; I will answer for my Body-Knight," Richard responded.

During the colloquy, De Lacy had been leaning on the window edge, watching idly the courtyard below, but paying strict attention to all that was said behind him. Now he came forward and bent knee to Richard.

"My King's confidence," he said, "makes contemptible the insinuations of the fickle Stanley."

"How now, Sir------" Stanley began angrily; but Richard silenced him with an imperious gesture.

"Hold, my Lord Steward," he said sternly, "no words betwixt you two. And hark you both, no renewal of this hereafter. You are each acquittanced of the other now."

De Lacy drew himself up stiffly and saluted.

"The King commands," he said.

"And you, my lord?" asked Richard, eyeing Stanley.

"Pardieu! Sire, I have no quarrel with Sir Aymer," he answered, and affably extended his hand.

Just then there came loud voices from the outer room, followed immediately by the entrance of the page.

"May it please Your Majesty," the boy said, as the King's curt nod gave him leave to speak, "Sir Robert Brackenbury craves instant audience on business of state."

"Admit him!"

The next moment the old Knight strode into the room, spurs jangling and boots and doublet soiled by travel.

"Welcome, Robert," said Richard, giving him his hand. "What brings you in such haste?"

"Matters which are for your ears alone, Sire," said the Constable of the Tower, with the abruptness of a favored counsellor.

The King walked to a distant window.

"Might the two-faced Lord Steward hear us?" Brackenbury asked.

"No danger, speak--what is amiss in London?"

"Enough and to spare. Edward's sons are dead."

Even Richard's wonderful self-control was unequal to such news, and he started back.

"Holy Paul!" he exclaimed, under his breath; then stood with bent head. . . "How happened it?"

"No one knows, certainly. As you expressly ordered, either the lieutenant or myself regularly locked their apartments at sundown and opened them at dawn. Two nights since I, myself, turned key upon them. In the morning I found them dead--in each breast a grievous wound--Edward's bloody dagger on the floor."

"And your view of it?"

"That Edward killed Richard and himself. He had lately been oppressed with heavy melancholy."

The King shook his head. "Yes, that is doubtless the solution, yet scant cre-

dence will be given it. To the Kingdom it will be murder foul. . . Yet, pardieu! who
else know it?"

"None but my lieutenant."

"And his discretion?"

"Beyond suspicion. He has forgotten it long since."

Richard called De Lacy to him. "Let Suffolk, Lovel, Ratcliffe, D'Evereux and
Catesby be summoned instantly," he ordered.

"My friends," said he, when the last of them had come, "I have sore need of
your wisdom and counsel. Hark to the mournful tidings Sir Robert Brackenbury
brings."

Bluntly and simply the old Knight told the story. When he ended there was
deep concern on every face and all eyes turned toward the King.

"You perceive, my lords, the gravity of the situation," said Richard. "What shall
be done?"

None answered.

"Come, sirs; it is here and we must face it. What say you, Stanley?"

The Lord Steward swept the circle with a keen glance.

"Your Majesty has put a direful question and given us scant time for thought,"
he replied. "Yet but two courses seem possible: either to proclaim the Princes dead
by natural causes and give them public burial; or to conceal the death, and by letting the world fancy them life prisoners so forget them. Each has its advantage; but
on the whole, the latter may be better. Nathless, this much is self-evident--the true
tale dare not be told. Daggers, blood, and death are inexplicable when Kings' sons
are the victims, save on one hypothesis."

One after another endorsed these words, until finally it came back to the King
for decision.

For a long while he sat silent, staring into vacancy. Through the open windows
floated the noises of the courtyard--the neigh of a horse, the call of a soldier, the
rattle of steel on stone; from the anteroom came the hum of voices, the tramp of
a foot, the echo of a laugh. But within, no one spoke nor even stirred. Not a man
there but understood the fatefulness of the moment and the tremendous consequences of the decision, which, once made, might never be amended. At length he
spoke.

"It is an ill-fated event and leaves a dismal prospect," he said very quietly. "Sooner or later my nephews' death will be laid on me. To proclaim them dead would be to declare me guilty now. To conceal their death will be simply to postpone that guilt a time--a very little time, it may be. Curiosity will arise over their prolonged disappearance . . . then will come suspicion . . . and at length suspicion will become accepted fact. . . So, my lords, their blood will be put on me--either now or in the future. That is my only choice--now or the future--. . . and I choose the future. We will not announce the death; and the bodies shall be buried privately and in an unknown spot. To you, Sir Robert Brackenbury, I commit the task, trusting you fully. . . And, my lords, from this moment henceforth, let this council and its sad subject be forgotten utterly. . . Only I ask that when, in after days, you hear Richard Plantagenet accused of this deed, you will defend him or his memory. . . And now, good night."

One by one they came forward, bent knee and kissed his hand; then quietly withdrew, leaving him and De Lacy alone together.

"And yet, forsooth," he exclaimed, "Stanley advised that the Princes be removed! By St. Paul! if he sought to persuade me to my injury, the Fates have subserved his wishes well. Him I can baffle, but under their frown the strongest monarch fails."

XVI
THE FLAT-NOSE REAPPEARS

It was September, and Their Majesties had come to Pontefract with the immediate Household for a brief rest after the labors and fatigues of the summer, and which had culminated in the festivities and ceremonies at York. In the room where Sir Aymer de Lacy first saw Richard of Gloucester, the King and Queen were alone together. Evening had fallen, but the brilliancy of a full moon in a cloudless sky had prolonged the day. Through the open windows came the freshness of the woods and hills, and the candles flickered and flamed in coquetry with the gentle breeze.

"Come, Anne, let us walk. It is too fine an evening to spend indoors," Richard said, laying aside the papers he had been examining.

She answered with the sweet smile that was always on her lips for him, and arm in arm they passed out upon the ramparts.

The main body of the soldiery were quartered in the town below the hill, and the castle was very quiet, save only for the tramp of the guards on the wall, the rattle of their weapons, and an occasional burst of laughter from the great hall. The peace and calm appealed to the Queen, and she sighed.

"How so, sweetheart," said Richard; "what troubles you?"

"I was thinking how much preferable Pontefract is to London."

The King laughed. "I believe you would rather be Duchess than Queen."

"Aye, Richard, much rather, much rather," she replied instantly.

He put his hand on her fair hair and stroked it softly. "Nay, dear, the wearisome work is over now, I trust. Henceforth it will be pleasanter . . . Pardieu! was there ever another woman, I wonder, who needed encouragement to wear a crown?"

"A Neville once refused one," she replied.

"True, indeed; and gave it back to the miserable Henry. . . You resemble your great father in many ways--and may our own dear son be like you both."

"You are very good to me, Richard," she said, taking his hand.

"But much short of what you deserve, dear one."

Suddenly a bugle rang loudly from before the barbican, followed in a moment by the rattle of the drawbridge and the clatter of hoofs on the planks.

"It is Beatrix and Sir John returning from their ride," the Queen said.

"It was not De Bury's call," he answered.

"Why, it is Sir Aymer de Lacy!" she exclaimed, as a pair of horsemen cantered across the inner bailey.

Richard nodded. "And a day earlier than I anticipated . . . but he has a good excuse."

"And a bit of disappointment also, that Beatrix is not here to greet him."

"He can spare her until he has supped, I fancy."

"She would not be pleased to think so."

"A woman wants a man to think of naught but her," he smiled.

"Yes, she does--and even though she know it to be futile . . . it is foolish, doubt-less."

"It is more than foolish; it is unfortunate. It annoys the man and grieves the woman."

"Nay, Richard, you look at it with a man's view only."

"And you, my dear?"

"I?--with the proper view, of course."

The King laughed aloud; and as De Lacy, who had just dismounted before the keep, recognized the voice and glanced up, Richard leaned over the parapet and beckoned to him.

"We are glad to see you," he said, as the Knight presently bent knee and kissed the Queen's hand.

"Yes, Sir Aymer, you are always welcome," she added.

"Your Majesties overwhelm me."

"Well, if our greeting overwhelm you," the King remarked, "the Countess of Clare's wilt likely end your life."

"I am very anxious to risk it, Sire," De Lacy answered quickly.

"Beatrix has left the castle," said Richard.

"Gone!" Aymer exclaimed.

"Oh . . . only for a ride."

"A ride--at night?"

"Surely--why not--on a fine night and with a gallant escort?"

"Nay, Richard," the Queen broke in, "do not distress him. Sir Aymer, Beatrix is with her uncle, and as they have been absent since before vespers, they must soon return."

De Lacy's face cleared so quickly that Richard smiled.

"A bad case, truly," he commented, putting his arm about the Queen. "Has the lady the disease so deep?"

"I would not tell you even if I knew," she answered.

"Nay, I only jested. . . But seriously, De Lacy, why should the wedding be delayed . . . why not have the ceremony here at Pontefract before we go South-ward?"

"That it has not already taken place is no fault of mine------"

"It is, sir; you should have won the Countess to consent," the King interrupt-ed.

"Her wish runs with mine."

"Then what ails the matter? . . . Not De Bury surely?"

"Sir John is as willing as we. It is the behest of the dead Earl that bars."

"Beatrix's father?"

"Yes; she promised him she would not wed before her twenty-fifth birthday."

"Peste! A senseless thing to exact; she was little more than child. As King I can absolve her from it."

"I fear that would not help the matter, Sire; Beatrix regards it as sacred--it was given at the Earl's deathbed."

Richard made a gesture of annoyance. "Does no consideration lift the obligation from her?" he demanded.

"Naught, as she views it now, but a question of life, honor, or imperative necessity."

"Now may the Devil fly away with such foolishness! Wherefore shall the dead rule the living? . . . How old is the Countess?"

"She was four and twenty last month."

"Great St. George! You have a wait, indeed; and ample time to pray for the imperative necessity. Meanwhile, best continue to keep the betrothal secret. It will likely save you both some embarrassment and considerable gossip at the long delay."

Just then another bugle blared from the barbican.

"Sir John and Beatrix!" the Queen exclaimed.

Richard shook his head.

"It was Ratcliffe's call," he said.

A moment later the Master of Horse came at full gallop across the courtyard.

Jumping from saddle and letting his horse run loose to be caught by the grooms, he sprang up the steps. In the anteroom the page met him with the information that Their Majesties were on the wall and were not to be disturbed. But at the first word, Ratcliffe dashed into the King's chamber and thence to the ramparts. Richard saw him coming and went quickly to meet him.

"What is it?" he demanded.

"Where is De Bury?" Ratcliffe asked.

"Gone for a ride with the Countess."

"I feared it. I found his horse at the foot of the hill, trotting toward the castle from the West. There is blood on the saddle cloth, and the rein is cut in twain at the bit."

"Foul work!" the King exclaimed. "Send an order to the camp for a hundred men to scour the country toward the Aire, and let another fifty muster before the barbican at daybreak; then come to me." . . . and turning, he sauntered back to the Queen. "Come, my dear, let us go in," he said, putting his arm through hers, "I must take up some matters that Ratcliffe has brought. And do you remain, De Lacy; perchance you can aid me."

"Will you be occupied very late?" she asked, as he held back the arras.

"Only a short time, my dear. I will come to you presently," and himself closed the door behind her.

"Are you very weary?" he asked De Lacy.

"Fit for any service Your Majesty may wish."

"It will be your own service."

"Mine! Mine! . . . You cannot mean----" taking a step forward.

"Steady, man, steady! I mean only that Sir John's riderless horse has just been found near the castle, with severed rein and bloody saddle."

De Lacy passed his hand across his forehead.

"And Beatrix?" he asked huskily.

The King shook his head.

Again Aymer passed his hand across his eyes; his brain was working very slowly how.

"You have given orders?" he asked.

"One hundred men-at-arms are seeking for a clue. Fifty others will await you at the barbican at daybreak."

"Meanwhile I, too, will seek," and he sprang toward the door--and into Ratcliffe's arms.

"Stay, Sir Aymer," said the King; "it would do no good for you to search at night--you may go far astray. All that can be done till daybreak the scouts will do. . . You gave the orders, Ratcliffe?"

"I did, and venture to amplify them by sending twenty men along the North road as far as the Aire for any trace of Sir John or of the fight--for, of course, there was a fight."

"And a passing hard one ere De Bury was unhorsed," said Richard.

"The remaining eighty," Ratcliffe continued, "I divided into bands of ten and five, bidding them follow every cross-road or bridle-path, and inquire for information from every traveler and at every habitation. The instant aught is discovered you will be advised."

The King turned to De Lacy. "You rescued Sir John when he was attacked last April near his own castle; might this be the same band?"

Aymer shook his head. "We killed all of them but one."

"True, I remember now. . . The flat-nosed one alone escaped. . . Did De Bury ever speak to you of enemies in these parts?"

"Never directly; though, as you know, he seemed to dislike the Abbot of Kirkstall and suspected him of being, at least, party to the other attack."

"Well, we must wait for even a plausible solution until we have a few facts. Yet I would wager much it is an abduction--and God grant it be so. . . Of course, it may be the villains did not molest the Countess. In that case, find Sir John and you find her, too."

"The chance is slight," De Lacy said quickly, "yet I shall ride rapidly back for a few miles and, perchance, it may be so. If I be not here by daybreak, Sire, I will join the men en route."

"It will be a relief for you to be on the move," said Richard kindly; "but return here for your escort. We may have clues then; and if the Countess has been abducted, she is quite as likely to be carried South as North."

"I shall be here at daybreak," Aymer answered. He saddled Selim with his own hand, and with Dauvrey beside him hurried away. They rode in silence with eyes alert, scanning sharply the ground on both sides of the road that lay like a silver stream before them. A mile from the castle a soldier rode out from the shadow and reined across the track, his casquetel and drawn sword glistening in the moonlight.

"Hold!" he ordered.

"Yorkshire!" said De Lacy . . . "Any news?" he demanded, as they swept by.

"None, my lord."

At the first cross-road two horsemen barred the way. Aymer paused to question them, but learning nothing, the pace was resumed. Another mile was passed, and they had tarried a moment to breathe and water the horses at a rivulet that gurgled across the road, when Selim suddenly threw up his head.

"Some one comes!" said De Lacy . . . "it is news . . . he rides furiously; he must be stopped."

They drew out into the middle of the track and waited. Presently a running horse shot into view ahead, and the rider, seeing the two in front, shouted the royal messenger's call: "Way! In the King's name! Way!"

"Stay, Allen," Giles Dauvrey cried, recognizing him. "What word?"

"Sir John has been found," the man answered, drawing up short.

"Dead?" Aymer demanded.

"No, my lord, not yet."

"And the Countess of Clare?"

"Gone, my lord; no trace."

"God in Heaven! . . . Where Is Sir John?"

"Half a league further on."

"Tell the King I have gone thither," Aymer called over his shoulder as he raced away.

In a patch of moonlight, fifty feet or so in from the road, lay Sir John de Bury, his eyes closed, his face upturned, motionless--to all appearances a corpse. De Lacy sprang down and knelt beside him.

"He is not dead, my lord," said a soldier.

Aymer laid back the doublet and shirt, wet and heavy with blood that had come from a deep wound in the right breast, and was still oozing slowly. The heart was beating, but very faintly, and forcing the set jaws apart with his dagger, he poured a measure of cordial down Sir John's throat.

"May it please you, sir," said one of the men, "we have arranged a litter of boughs, and if you think it good we will bear him back to the castle."

"It can do him no harm," De Lacy answered. . . "How say you, Giles?"

"With even step it will not hurt him," the squire replied.

Lifting the old Knight carefully they placed him on the litter and Aymer wrapped his own cloak around him, then nodded to the soldiers to proceed.

"Go slowly," he ordered, "a jolt may end his life. Watch his heart closely; if it grow weaker, use the cordial," and he handed them the flask.

"The fight was not at this place," said Dauvrey after a moment's examination of the ground; "there are no mingling hoof marks. De Bury likely fell from the saddle here and the horse kept on to the castle; his tracks point thither."

"Let us follow the back track," De Lacy exclaimed.

For a score of paces it led them, slowly and laboriously, into the dark forest, and then vanished, and though they searched in all directions, no further trace was found. It was a fruitless quest; and at length the squire persuaded his master to abandon it and await the coming of the dawn.

Reluctantly De Lacy remounted and they rode slowly back to Pontefract. The soldiers bearing Sir John de Bury had reached there some time before, and he lay on the couch in his own room. There was no material change in his condition, though under the candle-light there was less of the ghastly pallor of death in the face; and about the ears were evidences that the blood was beginning to circulate more strongly. The King's own physician, Antonio Carcea--an Italian--sat beside him with his hand on the pulse and, ever and anon, bent to listen to the respiration.

At Be Lacy's entrance he glanced up with a frown which faded when he saw who it was.

"He will live, Signor," he said in Italian. "He has not yet come to consciousness, but it is only a matter of a little while."

"Will he speak by daybreak?" De Lacy asked.

"Most likely, Signor."

"Summon me on the instant, and may the Good God aid you."

Going to his quarters and waving Dauvrey aside when he would have relieved him of his doublet, Aymer threw himself upon the bed. He had ridden far that day, and with the coming of the sun would begin what promised to be a labor long and arduous. He could not sleep--and his closed eyes but made the fancies of his brain more active and the visions of his love, abducted and in hideous peril, more real and agonizing. Yet to serve her he must needs be strong and so he tried to compose himself and rest his body. There was scanty time until morning; but an hour of quiet now might breed a day of vigor in the future.

Presently there came a sharp knock and Ratcliffe entered.

"Lie still," he said, as De Lacy would have risen. "I know you found no trace of the Countess else you would not be here. Yet, perchance, Sir John may speak or some of the scouts return with a clue. If not, the sunlight, doubtless, will reveal what the night has hidden. The King has retired, but he bade me say to you not to depart without word with him. Meanwhile if any of the scouts come in they are to report to you."

Slowly the minutes dragged themselves out. The shadows lengthened more and more as the moon went to its rest behind the distant Craven hills. Then of a sudden, light and shadow mingled and all was dark. Presently a cock crowed; and the sound seemed loud as a roar of a bombard. Again the cock crowed, and from the retainers' houses another and another answered, until the shrill cry ran along the outer bailey and across the wall and on down the hill to the village, growing fainter and fainter until, at the last, it was like a far distant echo, more memory than reality.

De Lacy turned his head toward the window, hoping for some sign of day, but the East was black. With an impatient sigh he lay back. Was ever man so sorely tried--so cruelly used--so choked by horrors of the probable! Then came a troubled slumber--a tossing and a waking--that was ended by a quick step in the corridor, and with a bound he reached the door and flung it open.

"Sir John------" the page began, but got no farther--De Lacy was gone.

Sir John de Bury lay as when Aymer left him, but the color was coming back to his face and his eyes were open, and he smiled very faintly in greeting.

"He may speak?" De Lacy asked.

"A few words, Signor," the Italian answered.

Just then the King entered hastily, a long gown about him. Sir John tried to raise his hand in salute, but Richard quickly caught the weak fingers.

"Nay, nay, my friend," he said; "another time for that." . . . Then to Carcea: "Has he spoken?"

"Not yet, Sire; and if it please Your Majesty, it would be well to ask the questions so that they can be answered by a motion of the head. The patient's strength will permit few words."

"Do you understand, John?" Richard asked.

De Bury smiled faintly and indicated that he did.

"Were you attacked?" the King went on.

"Yes," said the nod.

"By highwaymen?"

A pause, and then--"No."

"By men hired for the purpose?"

"Yes," readily.

"Do you know by whom?"

Another pause; then--"No."

"You have suspicion?"

"Yes," quickly.

"More of that in a moment; first, tell me, did they carry off the Countess?"

"Yes," and the old eyes glowed fiercely.

"Was she hurt in the struggle?"

"No."

"Were you attacked in the main road?"

"No."

"On a by-track?"

"Yes."

"North of the main road?"

"Yes."

"Near the main road?"

"Yes."

"Two leagues from here?"

"Yes," after a slight pause.

"More than two?"

"No."

"Oh! the path to the Hermit's Cell?"

"Yes," quickly.

"How long after you left Pontefract--two hours?"

"Yes," readily.

"Can you show the number of your assailants on your fingers?"

The right hand opened and closed twice.

"Ten, mean you?" the King exclaimed.

"Yes," instantly.

"Pardieu! did you recognize any of them?"

"One," said the raised finger.

"Can you whisper his name?" and the King bent low over the bed.

Sir John's lips twitched. He labored hard to speak, but the strength was wanting; no sound came; the tongue refused to move. A spasm of disappointment passed over his face. Then suddenly he fixed his eyes meaningly upon De Lacy, and Richard understood.

"Does Sir Aymer know this fellow?" he asked.

"Yes," was the instant answer.

"Has he been about the Court?"

"No."

"St. Denis!" exclaimed De Lacy, "was it Flat-Nose?"

"Yes! Yes!" eagerly.

"One more question," said the King: "Can you suggest whither they carried the Countess?"

Again the eyes turned to De Lacy.

"Kirkstall Abbey?" Aymer asked.

"Yes," but the hesitating nod signified it was only a suspicion.

"We will leave you now, old friend," said Richard. "Be not concerned. Ample precautions were taken hours ago to trace the Countess; and De Lacy with fifty horsemen rides in pursuit at daybreak--as soon as trail can be followed. The quest ends only when she is found and saved. Come, Sir Aymer, morning dawns and a word with you before you mount. Hark! your troopers muster now within the camp."

XVII
IN PURSUIT

"It is meagre information, yet enough to make a start on," the King said when they had left the room. "Perchance ere you reach the spot, you will gather more from the scouts who should be coming in. Yet it is most improbable that the villains took the main roads with the Countess. They will travel by secluded paths and through the forests; and if their destination be distant, they will not trust the highways inside a day's ride of Pontefract. Therefore, go slowly until the trail be plain. Then--well, I need not tell you what to do then."

"By St. Denis, no, Sire! My sword arm knows how to slay."

"Would that I could go with you," Richard said, his ardor for adventure and danger working strong. "Yet the King may not, and I do not care to assume disguise just now. Some day . . . Peste! Some day must care for itself and wait." . . . He drew a ring from his finger. "Here, De Lacy," he said, "this bit of gold, bearing my arms and the Boar, may prove of use. Show it, and your least word will be obeyed--send it to me, and, if need be, an army brings it back. Guard it well; there are but four others in the Kingdom. . . Nay--no thanks; Richard trusts few--them he trusts to the end. Use the ring without stint when necessary; but hark you, beware the friends of Buckingham. There is mischief afoot and, maybe, treason brewing at Brecknock."

"And Your Majesty does naught to stem it?" De Lacy exclaimed.

A cold smile crossed the King's face.

"Not yet," he answered. . . "And further, if your course should lie near Kirkstall, best be mindful of the Abbot. There may be some basis for De Bury's notion. And now, away.--You have the Queen's prayers, the Ring of the Boar and your own good sword. You must needs prevail."

As De Lacy and Dauvrey emerged from the shadow of the barbican a bugle spoke and Raynor Royk rode forward and saluted.

"Are you ready?" De Lacy demanded, running his eye along the line.

"Yes, my lord."

"Forward, then;" and at a trot he led the way.

"You know our mission?" he asked.

"Yes, my lord."

"And the men, also?"

"I ventured to tell them."

"It may be heavy duty and full of danger."

The old warrior drew himself up sharply. "Your lordship does not doubt me?"

"Nay, Raynor, never you. I only want your vouchment for the soldiers."

"Many would give their lives for you, Sir Aymer; all would die for the Countess of Clare."

"And you all may be afforded the opportunity ere the quest be ended," said De Lacy grimly. "We take the path to the Hermit's Cell; see that I do not miss it. Furthermore, you know this country intimately, so do not hesitate to advise me at any time."

Raynor Royk dropped back to resume his place; then quickly turned: "Two horsemen gallop after us, my lord."

De Lacy reined around and raised his arm for the column to halt.

"They wear armor," said he, "but I discern no jupon."

Raynor Royk shook his head. "The corselets shine plain, but methinks it is Sir Ralph de Wilton in front."

"Aye, it is Sir Ralph!" Dauvrey exclaimed, "or I know not a man's seat in saddle."

De Lacy rode back to greet him.

"Did you come from London at that pace, Ralph?" he asked as they met.

"Nay, only from Pontefract to overtake you."

"You have news of the Countess?"

"Alas, no. I reached Pontefract town from London last night, but too late to report at the castle before morning. . . Now, His Majesty can wait until we have found Beatrix. I ride with you, my friend."

De Lacy put out his hand and De Wilton reached over and took it; and in the firm grip of their fingers was the confession of the one and the sympathetic appreciation of the other.

"We will save her, never fear," Sir Ralph said. Then his eyes fell on the ring. "By St. George, The Boar! I salute you--for even though you are not the King, still are you almost as powerful. Whoever wears that ring has all but the title--aye, and more--he has the King's enemies as well as his own."

"And me a stranger!" De Lacy observed tersely.

"Aye, and what with that, and the Ring, and the Countess, your life is not worth a third that mine is."

"It is worth absolutely nothing to me unless Beatrix be found alive."

"Pardieu! her life is in no danger. At the most, she will be held only for ransom."

"Heaven grant it! though I fear the plot is more deeply laid."

"In that case, my dear De Lacy, when she is rescued let the Church work quickly its sacrament upon you; there will be less temptation then to carry her off."

"Yonder, my lord, lies the way to the Hermit's Cell," came the voice of Raynor Royk.

Under the oaks and beeches whose gnarled and twisted arms overlapped the path the column bent its course; and as it wound along the narrow way, the shafts of sunlight, breaking through the leaves, rippled over the steel casquetels and trappings until it was as if a rivulet had suddenly gushed forth and was flowing down this forest by-path.

The Hermit's Cell was tenantless. The door had rotted from its fastenings and lay athwart the entrance. The roof was fallen in. Mould and rank vegetation choked the place. Long since had its holy denizen come to the dark River and been lost in the Mists.

A little way beyond the hut was where Sir John and the Countess had been attacked. There could be no missing it, for the turf on both sides of the path was torn and the bushes were crushed and broken. A brief inspection proved that the Countess had been the quarry, for the assailants had not cared enough about De Bury to pursue him. They had gone Northward, as the hoof marks showed, and springing back into saddle, De Lacy hurried on. A quarter of a mile beyond, the tracks turned abruptly and struck off through the forest. At length the trees grew thinner, and presently the highway lay before them, and the trail ended--nor could they find it again.

"We will on to Kirkstall and its crafty Abbot," De Lacy exclaimed.

"Surely you do not think he knows of this affair?" De Wilton asked.

"When it comes to priests in general and abbots in particular, I never think," Aymer answered. "It is their game, and few can play it with them and have a chance to win. I prefer to fight them with my own weapons," jerking his head toward the fifty men-at-arms. "If the Abbot know aught of this business, it will do no hurt to let him see these honest followers of His Majesty. It may loose his tongue."

"It will take more than steel coats to make Aldam speak, if he be minded otherwise," said De Wilton.

"Doubtless; but while we hold converse with him, Raynor Royk shall have the premises spied over."

When they reached Kirkstall no porter was in the lodge, but the gates were open wide, and halting the column, the two Knights with their squires rode into the courtyard. At the further end of the quadrangle a dozen horsemen were drawn up, and their leader, his foot in stirrup ready to mount, was having a last word with the Abbot.

Hearing their approach they turned quickly.

"Darby!" exclaimed De Wilton. "Now what brings him here so early in the day?"

"Penance and absolution likely," De Lacy answered scornfully.

"Well, I trust he has got them and feels more easy with the world."

"My lord Abbot," said Aymer, as they dismounted, "I am a trespasser a second time, and an ill-timed one I fear, for which I beg your kind indulgence--and Lord Darby's," and he bowed to the latter.

"Nay, Sir Aymer de Lacy, you interrupt nothing," Darby responded; "I was but making my adieu before pushing on to Pontefract."

"And Sir Aymer knows he is ever welcome at Kirkstall, both on his own account and because he is of the Household of the royal Richard," the Abbot answered easily; "and I trust His Majesty and his gracious consort are in the best of health."

"We left them at daybreak much distressed over a most dastardly outrage perpetrated upon the Countess of Clare and Sir John de Bury," said Aymer abruptly, watching the monk's face--but all he saw there was blank amazement.

"Holy Mother! my son, what do you mean?" he cried.

"That they were set upon last evening near the Hermit's Cell by a band of cutthroats; Sir John all but murdered, and the Countess carried off."

The Cistercian raised his arms in horrified surprise.

"Incroyable! Incroyable!" he exclaimed.

And Lord Darby began to swear copiously in French.

"What were the facts, and what has been done for rescue?" the Abbot asked.

Briefly De Lacy told of the riderless horse and the finding of Sir John de Bury. Of the story revealed by De Bury's finger and head in answer to the King's questioning and the fact that a hundred men-at-arms had been searching the country since the late evening of yesterday, and particularly as to Flat-Nose having led the assailants, he was most careful to say not a word.

When he had finished, Lord Darby went off again in a storm of fierce imprecation; this time, however, in good Anglo-Saxon. And the Abbot was seemingly so stunned by Aymer's recital that he did not note the irreverence of his lordship, who was let free to curse away to his heart's content until brought up by De Wilton.

"Take a fresh start, Darby; you are repeating yourself. Change off again into French."

Darby turned upon the young Knight with a gesture of sharp surprise.

"None but a weakling could hear Sir Aymer's tale without a rush of hot resentment," he exclaimed.

"By the Rood! I observed only a rush of oaths," Sir Ralph laughed.

Darby's quick anger flamed up; and jerking off his riding gauntlet he flung it at De Wilton's face. But the Abbot dexterously caught the glove.

"For shame, Lord Darby, for shame!" he said, "that you, a man in life's full prime, should so far forget your knighthood over a bit of innocent banter. Nor may you, Sir Ralph de Wilton, accept the gage. This is holy ground; dedicated to the worship of the Humble One; and I charge you both, by your vows of humility, to let this matter end here and not to carry it beyond yonder gates. Have I your promise, my lord?"

"If Sir Ralph de Wilton be willing, I am content. Doubtless I was hasty," Darby answered with well-assumed frankness, his passion quickly curbed.

"And you, Sir Ralph?" the Abbot queried.

"Am content, even as Lord Darby. I have no cause for quarrel," De Wilton replied indifferently.

Darby bowed curtly in acknowledgment; then sprang into saddle.

"I shall gallop straight to Pontefract;"--addressing De Lacy--"I may aid in the search. Have you any message for the King?"

"Only that you left us at Kirkstall."

Darby gave him a quick, searching look. "It is a very meagre report."

De Lacy smiled. "There has naught happened since we crossed the Aire; and what was discovered between the Castle and the river has already been communicated to the King."

The Abbot watched Darby pass the gate. "His lordship would have liked much to know what you found at the Hermit's Cell and in the forest," he remarked.

"Doubtless, though it was little enough," said Aymer. "However, it is but a few leagues to Pontefract and there he will learn all the news of the Court."

"True, my son; yet, to an ardent lover and one not without hope of acceptance if rumor speak correctly, it would have been a satisfaction to know if you have anything that gives clue to the Countess or her captors."

De Lacy shrugged his shoulders. "Small comfort would I give him, then."

"Peste! my son, I am very stupid. I quite forgot that there are others than Darby who can see the attractions of the Lady of Clare. And of a surety will she be grateful to him who rescues her."

De Lacy made a gesture of dissent.

"It is scarce honorable, this motive you ascribe to me, my lord Abbot," he said curtly.

"Honor and expediency go not always hand in hand," the priest answered with a half suppressed sneer; then without giving time for retort, he changed his tones to grave courtesy. "But I am remiss, my lord, I have not yet done you the civility of inquiring how we of Kirkstall can serve you."

"Not at all, I fear; at least upon the matter that brought us here; it is evident you can give us no information as to the Countess."

"Alas! no, my son. Would to Heaven I could! . . . Have you then lost all trace of her?"

"Aye, a league south of the Aire."

"I will summon the brother who was on duty last night at the outer lodge; maybe he noted something that will aid you."

But Father Ambrose had not seen a single way-farer; though as he had dozed several times during the night he thought a few persons might have passed quietly, and not aroused him.

"You doze!" exclaimed the Abbot in sarcastic displeasure and eyeing the good monk's ample girth and heavy, jowly face. "Your doze would need a pole-axe to awaken. An army could have marched by with trumpets sounding and you never lift an eye. Other duty shall be given you and a more slender brother assigned to the night watch. You may go. . . By my faith, sirs, I wonder if you soldiers have as much trouble with your subordinates as we churchmen have with ours."

"We, at least, can deal out heavier discipline when occasion demand it," De Wilton answered.

"Aye! you men of war tread not after the Merciful One," the Abbot said.

De Lacy laughed shortly. "Mercy is but relative, and methinks, you ecclesiastics are no slower in your judgments than are we. The punishments differ only in kind."

"But our discipline is a step toward Holiness and Christ, my son."

"And ours a leap toward Sin and Satan, think you? Nathless, am I quite as willing to take my chance of Heaven in a coat of mail as in the priestly gown."

The Abbot's eyes snapped with irritation, but his speech was easy and pacific. "You are young, my son; perchance, when you have more grey hairs there will be a change in your views. Meanwhile you and Sir Ralph need refreshment, to say naught of the good squires and the horses."

De Lacy hesitated. They had already tarried overlong, under the circumstances, but perchance Raynor Royk had not yet completed his scrutiny of the Abbey. There was need that this should be thoroughly done, yet so carefully, withal, as not to arouse suspicion. If Aldam were to imagine he and his were mistrusted it would make him an enemy if innocent, and a doubly armed foe if guilty. The doubt, however, was solved by the entrance of a strange horseman into the courtyard. A faint frown crossed the Abbot's face as he saw him, and De Lacy instantly decided to remain. Evidently the newcomer was either unwelcome or inopportune; and if it were because of their presence, then undoubtedly here was their place.

"We will accept with thanks, your reverence," he said.

Aldam smiled suavely; then went forward to greet the new guest.

"It is Sir Christopher Urswicke--the priest Knight--the confessor of Margaret of Richmond," De Wilton whispered.

"A bit far out of his demesne, methinks," De Lacy muttered.

"Aye! too far to be passed over without report to His Majesty. Where Urswicke goes his mistress sends him--and lately she has but one object in life: to make her son the King of England."

"And like enough will succeed only in making him shorter by a head," De Lacy responded.

Meanwhile Urswicke had greeted the Abbot and dismounting had turned his horse over to his two attendants--who were neither squires nor yet ordinary servants, and who doubtless could either fight or pray as occasion demanded. Their dress partook of the style of their master, who wore the ordinary riding costume of a Knight, even to the golden spurs; the only marks of his clerical calling being his short cropped hair and the string of beads about his neck with the pendant crucifix. His frame was angular and above the ordinary height. His face was long and narrow, with a hawk-like nose, pointed chin, thin, straight lips, prominent cheek bones and deep-set grey eyes that glittered and chilled like those of a snake. He swept the others from helm to spur with a single glance, and Aymer saw his eyes fasten for an instant on the Ring of the Boar.

But if Urswicke's countenance were forbidding, not so was his voice. Its clear, sweet tones were in such sharp contrast to the fell face that De Lacy was startled into showing his surprise. And the priest noticed it, as he had many times before in others, and smiled in indifferent contempt.

During the refection, that was served immediately, Urswicke was most amiable and paid particular attention to De Lacy and De Wilton. By most astute and careful conversation he sought to draw from them information as to the King's programme during the Autumn; how long he would remain at Pontefract, and whither his course when he left there. Yet with all the art of an adept, he risked no direct question and displayed no particular interest in these matters, when by his very manoeuvring they were touched upon. But De Wilton had been bred in the atmosphere of Gloucester's household and De Lacy had been trained by years of service amid Italian and French plotters; and they both quickly discerned that the Abbot and the Priest-Knight were working together, and they only smiled and played them off against each other; and at the end of the meal, what the two had learned of Richard's intentions was likely to be of scant profit to either Henry Tudor or his scheming mother.

"What a precious pair of priestly scoundrels!" De Wilton exclaimed, when he and De Lacy had mounted and were trotting toward the gate.

"They will be the first knocked on the head if Raynor Royk has located the Countess," said Aymer.

"By the saintly Benedict! why not do the knocking now and then hear Raynor's report?" De Wilton laughed.

"It would give me great pleasure and doubtless be altogether proper as a matter of abstract justice; but I fear rather impolitic. Best wait for Royk."

But Royk's search was barren; and so the Abbot Aldam and Sir Christopher Urswicke were left to their plotting, while Sir Aymer De Lacy and Sir Ralph De Wilton rode Westward, seeking vainly for a clue to the lost Lady of Clare.

XVIII
THE HOUSE IN SHEFFIELD

Three weeks later, toward evening, Sir Aymer de Lacy with a dozen weary and travel-stained men-at-arms rode into Sheffield and drew up before the Inn of the Red Lion. In fog and rain and sunshine, by day and by night, they had kept to the search, and all in vain.

The morning after leaving Kirkstall Abbey, De Lacy and De Wilton had separated. It was useless to hold so many men together when there was no immediate prospect of a fight or even a hard stern chase; and there would be much more profit in dividing them into small bodies and so spreading over a wider stretch of country. De Wilton with half of the force turned Northward to cover the section beyond the Wharfe, while De Lacy with the others kept on toward Lancaster; and these he further divided and subdivided until there was scarce a hamlet or bridle-path in the West Riding that had not been visited.

As the days passed with no fortune for him, and no word from the King of success elsewhere, he went from fierce anger to stern determination and from headlong haste to dogged persistency. He had refused to entertain for an instant the notion that the Countess of Clare was dead, though he knew that such had become the prevailing view at Court, and that even Richard himself was growing fearful lest murder had followed the abduction.

To the hasty and obsequious greetings of the landlord De Lacy gave only a short nod and ordered lodging for himself and men. Choosing a small table in the farthest corner and in the shadow of the big chimney, he slowly sipped his wine. There were eight others in the room, but Flat-Nose was not of them. Three were merchants, traveling in company, possibly for protection on the road, and en route doubtless to York and its busy marts. They were gathered about an abundant meal spread at one end of the large table and were talking loudly of their business. At the other end of the board, their heads close together in subdued and earnest converse, were two Benedictines in the black tunic and gown of the Order. De Lacy had early learned on the Continent that a traveling monk usually meant mischief afoot for some one; and as from their manner of talk they evidently had not been journeying together, but were just met, and possibly by prearrangement, it would be well he thought to keep them under a temporary surveillance. Over near the window in the rear of the room were two lusty-looking men-at-arms, each with a big mug of ale at his elbow; and as they wore no badge of service, they also would bear watching. The eighth and last was of De Lacy's own rank, but older by at least ten years; and he stared across with such persistence that Aymer grew annoyed and drew back into the shadow.

Until the night when he had lost his betrothed, Aymer de Lacy had been genial, frank and open-hearted; taking life as it came, meeting man against man in the open, searching not into the dark. But the outrage at the Hermit's Cell, and the days of distress which followed had worked a change. He was growing cold and stern and distrustful; cautious of speech; reserved and distant in manner; seeking always for a clue behind even the most friendly face or cordial greeting; and holding every stranger under the ban of suspicion.

At length having long since finished his wine, he was about to rap on the table for the landlord when the front door opened and a young girl glided into the room. She wore the fancy dress of the tymbestere, a red bodice slashed and spangled, and a red skirt that came midway between the knee and the ground, disclosing a pair of trim and shapely ankles and small feet. But as if to compensate for this display, her face was hidden by a black mask through which the eyes shone and smiled, but which effectively concealed her other features.

Pausing an instant, until satisfied she was observed by all, she began a slow and stately dance, timing her steps to the soft jingle of her tambourine. The girl had a lithe gracefulness and stately bearing unusual in those of her class--whose exhibitions were rather of the fast and furious kind with a liberal display of their forms--and when with a last low curtsy she ended, there was plenty of applause from all save the two monks. They eyed her with a displeasure they took no trouble to conceal; and when she tripped lightly over to them and extended her tambourine for an offering they drew back sourly.

"Avaunt, foul baggage!" the elder exclaimed. "Have you no shame to ply your lewd vocation before a priest of God? Verily, you do well to hide your face behind a mask."

The girl drew back timidly, and with never a word in reply passed on to the two men-at-arms. Here she got a different sort of greeting.

"Do not fret your pretty eyes over that pair of hypocrites in black, yonder," one of them exclaimed loudly and speaking directly at the Benedictines; "they are holy only in a crowd. If they met you when none else were near, they would tear off each other's gowns to be the first in your favors."

"Right, comrade mine, right!" laughed his companion, bringing his fist down upon the table until the mugs rattled.

The two monks turned upon them.

"You godless men," said one sternly; "it is well you bear no badge of maintenance, else would your lord have chance to work some wholesome discipline upon you."

But the men-at-arms only laughed derisively and made no response.

Meanwhile the damsel had approached the strange Knight and sought a gratuity. With ostentatious display he drew out a quarter noble and dropped it on the tambourine. Then as she curtsied in acknowledgment he leaned forward, and caught her arm.

"Come, little one, show me your face," he said.

With a startled cry the girl sprang back and struggled to get free. But the Knight only smiled and drew her slowly to his knee, shifting his arm to her waist.

"Pardieu! my dear, be not so timid," he scoffed. "Kiss me and I may release you."

For answer she struck at him with the tambourine, cutting his chin with one of the metal discs so that the blood oozed out.

"Little devil!" he muttered; and without more ado bent back her head, whispering something the while.

With a last desperate effort to free herself, which was futile, and with the dark face drawing with mocking slowness toward her own, she realized her utter helplessness and cried appealingly for aid.

In a trice, she was seized and torn away; and between her and her assailant, and facing him, stood Sir Aymer de Lacy, his arms folded and a contemptuous smile upon his lips. The next instant, without a word, the other plucked out his dagger and leaped upon him, aiming a thrust at his neck. By a quick step to the side Aymer avoided the rush, and as the other lurched by he struck him a swinging right arm blow behind the ear that sent him plunging among the rushes on the floor, while the dagger rolled across to the farther wall.

"Bravo! Bravo!" cried the two men-at-arms. "Shall we throw him into the street, my lord?"

He waved them back; and the Knight, who had been slightly dazed, struggled to his feet and looked about him. Then seeing De Lacy, who had resumed his calmly contemptuous attitude, he grasped the situation and a wave of red anger crossed his face. But he was not of the blustering sort, it seemed, and drawing out a handkerchief he proceeded carefully to fleck the dirt and dust from his doublet and hose. When he had removed the last speck, he bowed low.

"Shall we settle this matter with swords or daggers, my lord?" he said, in French.

"I think too much of my good weapons to soil them on one who assuredly has stolen the golden spurs he wears," De Lacy replied scornfully.

"My name is Sir Philebert de Shaunde and my escutcheon quite as ancient as your own," with another bow.

"It is a pity, then, it has fallen upon one who needs more than his own word to sustain the claim."

De Shaunde's face went red again and his voice trembled and was very soft. "His Grace of Buckingham will be my voucher, though it will misdemean him much as against one who has a tymbestere for mistress and is a coward, as well."

De Lacy glanced quickly around the room:

"She is no longer here to feel your insults," he said, "but it is her due that I refute them. I never saw the maid until I saved her from your foul caress. As for my cowardice, good sir, I but protect my knighthood against a caitiff whose very touch is dark pollution."

"I shall proclaim your refusal to accept my defiance before King and Court and let them judge of the quarrel."

"So be it--you will find me known there," Aymer replied curtly; and sauntering back to his table he called for another bottle of wine.

De Shaunde, however, stayed only long enough to give some order to the land-lord, who received it with rather scant courtesy; then with showy indifference, slapping his gauntlets against his leg as he walked, he left the room by the street door just as Giles Dauvrey entered. The squire stood aside to let him pass, then crossed to his master.

"Did you recognize that fellow?" De Lacy queried.

"No, my lord."

"He styles himself 'Sir Philebert de Shaunde.'"

Dauvrey scratched his head. "I am sure I never saw him before."

"Well, it is small matter, but as we may see more of him hereafter it will be wise to keep him in mind"--and he told of the encounter.

"What became of the damsel?" the squire asked.

"She disappeared during the scuffle; but doubtless the landlord can advise you where to find her," De Lacy said good-naturedly.

"A most extraordinary tymbestere who refuses a Knight's caress," Dauvrey ex-plained.

"But would not, you think, refuse a squire's?"

"Nay, my lord, what I think is that she might bear investigation. She is in dis-guise, I will stake my head."

"How does that concern us?"

"Only as every mystery concerns us now. To solve one sometimes solves an-other."

"It is a queer notion, Giles, but it will do no harm to question the host. Mean-while, I will await you without."

Night had fallen and it was very dark save when, at intervals, the narrow cres-cent of the new moon cut through the clouds that were crowding one another in heavy ranks across the sky. Before the inn the street was illumined feebly by the reflection of the torches and candles from within, and at wide intervals along the roadway light shone from the houses. But all this only made more dense and visible the blackness that lay around.

From far up the street came the sound of singing and laughter; and De Lacy, recognizing the voices of some of his own men, envied them their light hearts and freedom from care and sorrow. They lived for the day; the morrow was sufficient when it came.

Presently the squire appeared.

"It is as I suspected," he said. "The girl has never before been seen about the inn or even in the town. He says he knows all the tymbesteres for miles around, but this one is not of them."

"It is a pity we had none to watch her when she left the room," De Lacy replied. "However, I hear our men making merry out yonder, and after going with me to see that they are up to no serious mischief you are at liberty to devote the entire time until the morning in searching for this mysterious maid--though it will be good sleep wasted, I have no doubt."

The two started down the road, keeping well in the centre where the walking was likely to be easiest. There were no side paths and the way was rough and full of holes. Stumbling along in the dark they came, after a little, to a house from the upper story of which a bright light was shining. De Lacy glanced indifferently at the window--then halted short and seizing Dauvrey's arm pointed upward.

Just inside the open casement, and standing so that every line of his face and shoulders was distinctly visible, was the man De Lacy and all the royal commanders of England had been seeking for the last three weeks.

His thick red hair was bare of casquetel and there could be no mistaking that great, flat nose, even if there had not been the bright scar blazed across the face by Sir John de Bury's sword, and the short, thick-set figure to complete the identification.

De Lacy's heart gave a great leap. Was this, then, the end of his chase? Was Beatrix in yonder house? Would he soon hold her in his arms--or was he about to learn that she was lost to him for ever? In the tumultuous rush of feeling his power of quick decision left him for the moment; but Dauvrey's muffled exclamation broke the spell.

"It is he--Flat-Nose!"

"Aye!" De Lacy whispered, drawing the squire aside into the shadow. "He must be seized at once. Summon the men and surround the house. I will remain on guard. Hasten, Giles! In God's name, hasten!"

Dauvrey plunged away into the darkness and Aymer, choosing a position from which he could best watch the window, but at the same time be himself hidden, settled back to his anxious wait.

Flat-Nose was not alone; presently he began to speak to some one behind him, and hoping to overhear the conversation, Aymer worked his way with great care across the road to the house. There were no lights on the lower floor, and the upper story, projecting a foot or more over the street, made him secure from observation.

But the new position was very little better than the other one; and try as he might he could not catch anything but an occasional word which, in itself, had no significance. He began to grow impatient--it seemed most unduly long since Dauvrey had gone.

Then a chair was shoved back in the room above and some one began to move about. Suddenly a head was thrust out and Flat-Nose peered into the darkness.

"God in Heaven! what blackness!" he exclaimed. "The Devil's own night for a ride. . . No danger," he went on, answering some remark from within. "I know every path in Yorkshire."

It was evident he was preparing to depart and De Lacy drew his sword and stood close beside the door. He wished only to disable the fellow; but he would kill him rather than suffer him to escape. Just then, a number of forms came slowly out of the darkness and at a motion from the one in front flitted off toward the rear of the house. It was Dauvrey and the men, at last, and the Knight gave a sigh of relief.

To avoid crossing the zone of light in regaining the place where he had left his master, the squire drew close to the house and so chanced upon him.

"Just in time," De Lacy whispered, "Flat-Nose is going."

An inside door was opened and a heavy step came down the stairs. There was a fumbling with the fastenings of the street door; then it swung back and a man stepped out and shut it behind him.

The next instant two pairs of strong arms closed around him, De Lacy's hand fastened on his throat, he was borne to the ground, and before he could struggle his legs were bound above the knees with Dauvrey's belt. His arms were then quickly secured and a piece of cloth thrust into his mouth as a gag. A low hiss brought the nearest soldier to guard him and De Lacy and the squire cautiously entered the house.

It was darker there even than outside and they listened for a space; but all was quiet. Then working carefully along the wall, they found a door which stood ajar. De Lacy whispered to make a light, and the squire, with as little noise as possible, struck the flint and ignited the bit of candle he always carried in his pouch. As it flamed timidly up they peered about them. The place was empty, save for a table and a few chairs, but on each side was a door and in the rear the stairway to the upper floor. An examination of the remaining two rooms was barren of results; one was the kitchen and the other a sleeping chamber, but the bed had not been disturbed. If the Countess of Clare were in the house she was on the next floor; and, at least, the man who had been with Flat-Nose must be there, so it would be two prisoners instead of one if he were unable to give a good account of himself.

The stairs were old and shaky and creaked and groaned as they cautiously ascended. And the noise was heard; for suddenly the door at the head of the landing swung back--and Flat-Nose himself stood in the opening.

"What is amiss, my lord?" he began--then stopped. "De Lacy!" he cried and springing back hurled the door shut.

The appearance here of the man they thought was lying bound and helpless in the road held both De Lacy and Dauvrey for an instant. Then with sudden fury they flung themselves up the last few steps and against the door. It yielded easily and they rushed into the room--just as Flat-Nose leaped from the window ledge. And the fortune that had befriended him so long still stood true, and a mocking laugh came back, as the darkness wrapped itself about him.

De Lacy put his hand on the casement to follow when Dauvrey seized him from behind.

"To the front, men, and after him!" he shouted through the window. . . "Your pardon, my dear lord," he said with deep respect, "but you could ill afford to take such risk now. Hark, sir, they are already in pursuit."

Sir Aymer nodded. "You are right, Giles. It would have gained naught but perchance a broken bone. He has escaped this time--on such a night an army would be lost. . . But who, in the Fiend's name, is the fellow we have below?"

Seizing the burning candle from the table, they hurried out, and bending over De Lacy flashed the light across the prisoner's face--and started back in vast amaze.

"Holy St. Denis! Lord Darby!"

For a space he stood looking down upon him; then motioning toward the house he went within, and behind him Dauvrey and the guard bore the captive--and none too easy were their hands.

In the front room De Lacy put down the candle.

"Release him," he ordered. . . "So, sir, you search for the Countess of Clare in company with her abductor. Truly, it is wondrous strange you have not found her. Tell me, my lord, might it be that though we missed the servant we got the master?"

"What I can tell you, my French upstart," Darby retorted, "is that this night's work will bring you heavy punishment."

"Forsooth! From whom?"

"From me perchance; from the King surely."

De Lacy laughed disdainfully. "You always were a braggart, I have heard; yet you will need all your wits to save your own head when arraigned before him."

"Arraigned! Save my head! These are queer expressions for such as you to use to a Peer of England."

"No more queer than for a Peer of England to be an abductor of women."

"You are still pleased to speak in riddles," Darby answered with a shrug.

"Pardieu! it will be a riddle for which you have a shrewd answer ready for His Majesty."

"Methinks you have lost what little sense ever had and are not responsible," said Darby; "therefore I have the pleasure of wishing you a very good night," and he turned toward the door.

De Lacy laughed scornfully.

"Not so fast, my lord," he said. "You will have to bear with my poor company for a space. The King is at Lincoln."

"What has that to do with me? . . . Stand aside, fellow," as Dauvrey barred the way.

For answer the squire drew dagger and the man-at-arms laid a heavy hand on Darby's shoulder. It was useless to try bare fists against such odds and he wheeled about.

"What means this fresh outrage?" he demanded.

"It means that you are my prisoner."

"Your prisoner! And wherefore?"

"As the abductor of the Countess of Clare."

Darby held up his hands in amazement. "Are you clean daft?" he exclaimed.

"It is useless, my lord, longer to play the innocent," said Aymer. "Either confess what has been done with the Countess or to the King you go straightway."

Darby shrugged his shoulders. "Since you have the rogues to obey you and I have not the information you desire, it must be to the King," he said. "And the more haste you use to reach him the quicker will come my time to even scores with you," and he sat down and began to brush the dirt from his garments.

De Lacy eyed him in stern silence, his resentment growing fiercer as he held it in restraint; while the squire, in equal anger, kept shooting his dagger back and forth in its sheath as if impatient to use it. And but for the sake of the information Darby could furnish as to Beatrix, the dagger might have been suffered to do its work and De Lacy raise no hand to stay it. Nay, rather, would he have stood by and watched it strike home with grim satisfaction.

Presently Darby had finished with his clothes and glancing up met De Lacy's eyes. A taunting smile came to his lips and he began to whistle softly to himself. It was De Lacy who spoke first.

"I should like to know," said he, "how one of your craftiness could be so stupid as to carry off the Countess of Clare? What possible profit could you think to gain?"

Darby did not answer at once. When he did, it was with a sneer.

"Methinks, good sir," he said, "you are too stupid to appreciate that you have, yourself, unwittingly advanced the best proof of my innocence. Fools, you know, sometimes speak truth."

"Aye, but even a fool would know that Flat-Nose and you were together in yonder upper room. Can you explain that, my dear lord?"

Darby laughed. "Naught easier, Sir Frenchman, if His Majesty deem it necessary. You will pardon me, however, if I keep you waiting until then."

"So be it. We start for Lincoln at daybreak. Have I your word to ride quietly and attempt no escape, rescue or no rescue?"

"And if I refuse the word?"

"Then shall you go bound hand and foot and strapped to saddle."

"Pasque Dieu! It would be most uncomfortable riding, so I pass my word," Darby replied carelessly. "But, understand me, it is no acknowledgment of your authority either to demand it or to receive it."

"As to that I am answerable to the King, not to you," said De Lacy. "And further, Sir Abductor, if you violate your word--which, indeed, I trust but lightly--you will have an arrow through your carcass ere you have gone two paces. I wish you good-night," and leaving Dauvrey in command he returned to the Red Lion.

XIX
BACK TO THE KING

The door of the Inn was barred, and with the hilt of his dagger De Lacy pounded sharply. It was the host, himself, who admitted him, and as he passed in the man touched his arm.

"May I have a word with you, my lord?" he whispered, and led the way into a small room in the rear. Closing the door very easily he laid his ear against it, and then seeming satisfied came close over.

"You are from the Court, my lord?" he said softly.

"I am of the Court, but not directly from it."

"Then you do not know if His Majesty fear an uprising in the South?"

De Lacy was instantly interested, though he answered indifferently enough. "Uprising! Not likely. Who is so far done with life as to meditate such folly?"

"That I think I know, sir; and it is hatching as sure as Dunstan's a saint."

"Which is anything but sure, my man. Come to the facts."

"Do you recall the two monks and the Knight you punished because of the tymbestere."

De Lacy nodded.

"After your lordship went out the Knight returned and the three held conference together. I myself served them with wine and heard some of their talk--only a chance word, sir; and they were most suspicious. They spoke of ships and troops, but I could not gain the sense of it. Once they let fall the word 'Richmond' and tried to catch it back ere it were out. Then they went above to the monks' room. Your worship's room is next to it------"

"Good, I will go up," Aymer interrupted.

The landlord stopped him. "It will be too late, sir. They have gone."

"Diable!" De Lacy exclaimed. "Why did you not try to hear the rest of their talk?"

The man smiled shrewdly. "I did my best, sir. There is a spot where the wall in your lordship's room is very thin. I listened there, and though I caught a sentence only now and then, yet I made it that the Earl of Richmond is to land in England with an army on the eighteenth of this present month. The Knight--De Shaunde, methinks they called him--comes from the Duke of Buckingham, and the two monks from Lord Stanley. Stanley declined to fall in with the proposals of Buckingham and sent him warning to withdraw from the conspiracy at once, for he was about to advise the King of Richmond's coming. So much I gathered, sir, from their conversation, though I cannot repeat their words."

"How long have they been gone?"

"Some little time, sir. They rode Southward together."

De Lacy strode to the front door and flung it open. A gust of wind and rain drove through, extinguishing the torch and blowing the smouldering fire on the hearth into a flame. Without was a sea of darkness which made pursuit impossible and hopeless. Clearly there was naught to be done till daybreak, and with an imprecation he turned away.

Verily, this night was full of surprises. First, Flat-Nose . . . then, Darby . . . and now a rebellion, with Buckingham traitor and Stanley true. Matters were getting complicated and required some consideration. Of course, his first duty was to the King; to warn him of this invasion by Richmond and the insurrection in the South. It superseded even his obligation to the Countess; and with the dogged faith and discipline of a soldier he accepted the situation and prepared to act accordingly.

Haste was essential; and as two could make more speed to Lincoln than a dozen, the question was whether to go himself or to dispatch trusty messengers. Each course had its advantages and defects. If he went, he would be obliged to leave Lord

Darby behind and trust Dauvrey to bring him to the King. Not to go, would be to seem lax in Richard's service, and possibly to miss the opening moves in the campaign, which must necessarily begin instantly and hurry Southward, and in which he would perforce be obliged to take part the moment he did arrive. For well he foresaw that Richard would have no time to devote to the Countess' affairs at such a crisis. The business of the individual, however much a favorite, must needs give place to a struggle for a Kingdom and a Crown.

Yet he was loath to let Darby out of his own grasp and, for an instant, he was minded to stake all on one throw. He was firmly persuaded that Darby could disclose the Countess' whereabouts, if she were still of this world. Why not put him to the torture and wring the truth from him? Success would excuse, nay, approve such measures. . . But to fail! Mon Dieu! No; decidedly, no! It would be folly pure and childish. Only the long strain and his stress of feeling would have suggested it. Then he thought of sending Darby to Pontefract and, on the authority of the King's ring, place him in confinement there until a more favorable period. But this, too, was dismissed, and he came back to the original problem: whether himself to hurry to Lincoln or to send a message.

There was but one wise choice, however, as he had appreciated all along, though he had fought against it; and now he took it but with sore reluctance. Wrapping his cloak about him, he motioned for the landlord to unbar the door and plunged out into the storm. In the face of the gale and pounding rain, through mud and water, he presently regained the house where he had left his men.

Drawing the squire aside he related the host's story and his own purpose of hastening on to warn the King. To Dauvrey he gave command of the party and full instructions as to the custody of the prisoner and the course to pursue when Lincoln was, reached. Then directing that one of the men be sent to the inn at daybreak to attend him, he returned once more to his lodgings and retired.

Morning brought no change in the weather; and when he rode off, at the first touch of light, the rain was still falling with a monotonous regularity that gave small hope for betterment.

Save a shirt of Italian steel, worn beneath his doublet, De Lacy was without armor, only a thick cloak being thrown over his ordinary clothes. It was a long ride to Lincoln ere nightfall, even in the best of weather; but to make it now was possible only with the very lightest weight in the saddle and good horse-flesh between the knees. No one horse--not even Selim--could do the journey over such roads without a rest, so he left him for Dauvrey to bring; depending upon being able to requisition fresh mounts from the royal post that had been established lately along this highway. Nor was he disappointed. The Boar and his own name, for he was known now throughout England as one high in the Household, got him quick service and hearty attention, and he made the best speed possible under the circumstances; though it was often poor enough to cause him to grit his teeth in helpless despair and anxiety. League after league was done no faster than a walk; the horse, at every step, sinking into the mud far above fetlock, and coming to the relief station completely exhausted. And all the day the rain poured down without cessation, and the roads grew heavier and more impassable until they were little else than running streams of dirty water pierced, here and there, by the crest of a hill that poked its head out like a submerged mountain.

But through it all, with head bent low on his breast, and bonnet pulled far down over his eyes, De Lacy forged ahead, tarrying only long enough at the stations to change mounts.

At mid-day half the distance had been covered, and as evening drew near they crossed the Trent and, presently, were out of Yorkshire. Then as night closed about them, the lights of Lincoln glimmered faint in the fore, and shaking up the tired horses they hastened on. And at last the castle was reached; the guards at the outer gate, recognizing the King's Body-Knight, saluted and fell back; and with a sigh of relief, De Lacy swung down from his saddle, the long ride over at last.

Just within the corridor he came upon Sir Ralph de Wilton, who started forward in surprise:

"By all the Saints! De Lacy! . . . But are you drowned or in the flesh?"

"Both, methinks. Where are my quarters--or have none been assigned me?"

"Your room is next mine. Come, I will show the way; for by my faith, you need a change of raiment; you are mud and water from bonnet to spur. What in the Devil's name sent you traveling on such a night?"

"The King's business, Ralph; ask me no more at present. . . His Majesty is in the castle?"

"Aye! and in the best of fettle," De Wilton answered good-naturedly. "Here are your quarters; and that they are saved for you shows your position in the Court. The place is crowded to the roof."

"I fancy I can thank you rather than my position--at any rate, Ralph, squire me out of these clothes; they cling like Satan's chains."

"I would I could cast those same chains off as easily," De Wilton replied, as he unlaced the rain-soaked doublet and flung it on the couch. "Tell me, Aymer, did you find aught of . . . of her?"

"No and yes," De Lacy answered, after a silence, "I did not find the Countess nor any trace of her, but I saw Flat-Nose."

"The Devil! . . . And took him?"

De Lacy shook his head.

"Killed him?"

"Nor that, either--he escaped me."

"Damnation! . . . However it is better than that he die with tale untold."

"That is my only consolation. Yet I shall kill him whene'er the chance be given, tale or no tale."

"Where did you see the knave?"

"At Sheffield--and with whom, think you?"

"This whole matter has been so mysterious I cannot even guess," said De Wilton.

"And wide would you go of the clout if you did," De Lacy replied, as he flung a short gown about his shoulders and turned toward the door. "It was Lord Darby."

"Darby! Darby! . . . Mon Dieu, man! are you quite sure?"

Aymer laughed shortly.

"Methinks I am quite sure," he said. "And now I must away to the King."

"So you have come back to us at last," said Richard graciously, as De Lacy bent knee; "but I fear me, without your lady."

"Aye, Sire, without her. It is your business that has brought me."

"Pardieu!" the King exclaimed; "we gave you leave indefinite. Until you were willing to abandon the search you need not have returned."

"Your Majesty misunderstands. No vain notion of being needed here has brought me; but danger to your crown and life--Buckingham is traitor--Richmond lands this day week as King."

"So! St. Paul! So!" Richard muttered, gnawing at his lower lip. "At last . . . at last . . . and earlier by six months than I had thought. . . Yet, better so; it will be ended all the sooner. . . Where did you get this news and how?"

"At Sheffield, last night."

"Last night!--When did you leave Sheffield?"

"At daybreak. The rain and darkness delayed me until then."

"By St. George! plead no excuse. It was an amazing ride in such weather."

"I made bold to use the post horses; but it was heavy labor even for them."

"And for you as well, my good De Lacy. This King thanks you--perchance the next one will not," and he laughed queerly.

"It is this King I serve; not the next one."

"I believe you," said Richard, putting his hand on Aymer's shoulder. "Now let me hear the story."

And De Lacy told it in the fewest words he could; making no mention of Flat-Nose or Darby.

For a while Richard sat quiet, pulling at his chin.

"What a miserable scoundrel Stanley is," he said presently. "He refuses Stafford because he scents failure ahead; and is ready to make capital of a trusting friend by betraying him to his doom. For well he sees that Buckingham has gone too far to recede. I would he had stood with them,--his own scheming Countess and Buckingham. Then I could have wiped all of them out at one blow." He struck the bell. "Summon the Master of Horse," he ordered.

"Ratcliffe," he said, when the latter entered, "Buckingham revolts on the eighteenth; Richmond lands in England that same day. Dispatch instantly to the Lord Chancellor for the great seal, and have commissions of array drawn. Let messengers start with the sun to all the royal domains and summon hither every man who can wield a sword or draw a bow. What's the weather?"

"There is no improvement, my liege."

"It will, of a surety, have rained itself out by morning. For it to continue means a slow muster, and the time is all too short as it is," the King said meditatively. "And hark you, further," he broke out suddenly, "let word go to Lord Stanley at Lathom, this night yet, of this matter, bidding him instantly gather his retainers and report at Nottingham."

Ratcliffe hurried away, to return almost instantly with a packet which he gave the King.

"From Stanley," he said. "It arrived but this moment."

Richard flashed a smile across to De Lacy.

"He moves quickly, by St. Paul!" . . . then with a touch of sarcasm: "Hold a bit, Ratcliffe; perchance our news may be a trifle old in Lathom." He broke the seals and spread the parchment under the candles on the table. It ran:

"To Our Sovereign Lord the King:

"It has come to us that Henry Tudor, styled Earl of Richmond, intends to sail with an army from St. Malo, on the twelfth day coming of the present month, and will adventure to land at the town of Plymouth on the sixth day thereafter, there and then to proclaim himself King. According, will we muster instantly our Strength and proceed, with all dispatch, to meet Your Majesty at Nottingham, or wheresoever it may be we are commanded.

"Written with humble allegiance and great haste at our Castle of Lathom, this tenth day of October.

"Stanley."

"It will be unnecessary to advise the Lord Stanley--he has already learned of the matter," said Richard--and Ratcliffe hurried away. He passed the letter to De Lacy. "Read it. . . Now you see the depth and foresight of this man. But for your chance discovery and furious ride he would have been the first to warn me of this danger. Note his shrewdness: he does not mention Buckingham, but only the Tudor, his own step-son; and hence the greater will seem his loyalty. And by St. Paul! he bests me. I must accept his message at its seeming value; for he will now follow it by prompt action. Yet his motive is as plain as God's sun: he would hasten Buckingham to the block, and himself to his dead friend's offices. Well, so be it. When I can read his purposes I hold him half disarmed. He shall be Constable of England--have the title without its dangerous powers. The higher he go the further the fall when he stumble," and the dagger went down into its sheath with a click. . . "Pardieu, De Lacy! it would seem that you are ever getting into my confidences. But then neither do you like the Stanley."

"So little, Sire, that I shall hope to see that stumble."

"It will be a passing grateful sight to many another also, I warrant." Then with one of those quick shifts of thought characteristic of his active mind: "Did you find naught of the Countess of Clare in all these weeks?"

"I came upon a clue last night," De Lacy answered.

"And let it slip to hasten hither?"

"Not exactly; the clue will follow me here."

"Follow you? Explain."

"I found Flat-Nose in Sheffield."

"And caught him?"

"Alas! no; he escaped in the darkness, but we captured his companion. He is the clue that follows."

"Was there anything about him to show what lord he serves?"

"He serves Your Majesty."

"What, sir!--Serves me?"

Aymer bowed. "It is Lord Darby."

The King raised his eyebrows and fell to stroking his chin again; then arose and began to pace the room.

"Pardieu, man! but you have brought a budget of surprises," he said. "Are you sure it was Flat-Nose? You have never seen him."

"He fit Sir John de Bury's words as the glove the hand--my squire was as convinced as myself."

"Give me the full details."

The King listened with a frown, but at the end he made no comment.

"Let Lord Darby be brought before me as soon as he arrives," he said simply. "Meanwhile you are excused from attendance till the morrow. Good night. . . By St. Paul! this Darby business is untimely," he soliloquized. "He has some strength in Yorkshire, and it will be unwise to estrange it at this crisis. Yet appearances are dark against him, and if he have no adequate explanation he dies. . . But if he have a good defence, why not accept it for the nonce? And then, after Buckingham has shot his foolish bolt, look deeper into the matter. . . Now as to this rebellion," resuming his walk back and forth, "it will require six days for the seal to come from London. Therefore to-morrow shall the Commissioners go North and East with an order under my own seal, and the formal authority can follow after them--they can levy in the interval and muster later." Pausing at the window he swung back the casement. "Parbleu! how it rains . . . it will flood every river in England . . . and it will fight for us. I will destroy the bridges of the Severn; Buckingham will be unable to pass; his juncture with Richmond and the Southern rebels will be prevented--and I can mass my strength and cut them up in detail."

Then with his own hand he wrote the orders to Sir Thomas Vaughan, Rice ap Thomas, and others of the royal captains and trusty Yorkist adherents in Wales and Shropshire; and lastly he indited a proclamation, wherein Henry Stafford was declared a traitor, and a reward of a thousand pounds put upon his head. These finished, and confided to Ratcliffe for forwarding, Richard sought the Queen's apartments and remained in converse with her for an hour, but said never a word of the occurrences of the evening lest they disturb her night's repose. It would be time enough in the morning for her to begin again the old fear for her lord's life--for his crown she cared not a whit.

XX
IN ABEYANCE

And on the morrow there was great stir and rustle and preparation. Those lords and barons in attendance at Court who were from the vicinity went off to gather their following; and those from distant parts of the Kingdom sent commands to their constables or stewards to hasten hither their very last retainer and every man available for service with the King.

About noon Richard called his principal officers together in council to consider who were liable to join with Buckingham in the revolt. That he had confederates of power and prestige was certain enough; for despite his oft-repeated boast that as many wore the Stafford Knot as had once displayed the Bear and Ragged-Staff of the King-Maker, and reckless as he was, yet it was not likely he would attempt to measure himself against the King--and that King the great Gloucester--without substantial assistance and cooperation of others of the Nobility. Nor was it easy to fix upon these confederates. The old, pronounced Lancastrian lords were either dead or in exile, and there was little else than general family relationship or former family affiliation, that could guide the judgment. And the session was long and tiresome and not particularly satisfactory, for of all the names gone over, only the Marquis of Dorset and the Courtneys of Exeter seemed likely traitors, and yet it was very certain there must be many more.

As De Lacy passed into the antechamber Lord Darby came forward and confronted him.

"I have come as I gave parole," he said haughtily. "It is now withdrawn, and I demand that you straightway prefer your charge."

"So be it," said De Lacy, and bowed him into the presence of the King.

Richard eyed Darby with searching sternness, as he bent knee before him, nor did he extend his hand for the usual kiss; and his voice was coldly judicial as without pause or preliminary he began:

"We are informed, Lord Darby, of the happenings last night in the town of Sheffield. You have demanded to be brought before the King and have refused explanation to another. Such is your warrant and privilege as a Peer of England. You are accused by Sir Aymer de Lacy with being concerned in the abduction of the Countess of Clare. What have you to answer?"

"That I am not guilty, Sire; and I defy the foreign upstart who brings the accusation."

The King frowned. "Be so good, my lord, as to answer our questions without recriminations," he said sharply. "Then, being innocent, will you explain how it was that you were in conference with the fellow known as 'Flat-Nose,' who was the leader of the abductors?"

Lord Darby smiled blandly.

"Naught easier, my liege. The fellow who was with me at the house in Sheffield, last night, was not that villain but my own chief man-at-arms."

"Has he not a flat nose and------" De Lacy broke in; but Richard silenced him with a gesture.

"Describe this retainer of yours," he ordered.

"He is stout of build and medium in height; his hair is red, his face broad, and he has a heavy nose, so broken by a sword hilt that it might, indeed, be termed flat," Darby answered.

"How long has he been in your service?"

"For years, Sire--at least a dozen."

"Where was he on the day and evening of the abduction?"

"The day, in the evening of which I understand the Countess disappeared," Darby began with easy confidence, "I rode from my castle of Roxford in early morning, en route for Pontefract and the Court. This under officer of mine, Simon Gorges by name, who has, it seems, been taken for the villain called Flat-Nose, was left at the castle, where he remained in command until my return some seven days thereafter. I myself lodged at the Abbey of Kirkstall, that night, and was making my adieu to the Abbot, the next morning, when this . . . this . . . Knight"--indicating De Lacy by a motion of his thumb--"arrived with news of the outrage. Then I hastened to Pontefract and joined in the search, as Your Majesty knows."

"You have been most detailed as to your own movements at that time, but very meagre as to those of your servant," the King remarked dryly. "You left him, you say, at your castle on the morning of the abduction, and found him there, a week later, on your return. Bethink you that is any proof he remained there in your absence?"

"It is very true there is a wide break in my own observation," Darby answered with instant frankness; "yet I know absolutely that he was not beyond my own domain during my absence. It is some queer resemblance betwixt him and this Flat-Nose. And by my faith, Sire, broken noses and red hair are not such a rarity that Simon Gorges should be the only one to possess them."

"That may be; but they are enough, in this instance, to put that same Simon Gorges on suspicion, and quite to justify Sir Aymer de Lacy in arresting you and carrying you hither; and particularly when you scorned to offer him any explanation. For you must know, my lord, he wears the Ring of the Boar, and what he does is in my name."

"Perchance, I was hasty, Sire, but I did not know of the Ring; it was never shown me. And poor indeed were the manhood that would not resent the manner of my seizure--the gyves and arrogant address of your Body-Knight."

"Will Your Majesty ask Lord Darby," Sir Aymer exclaimed, "why this flat-nosed Simon Gorges, as quickly as he saw me, sprang from the window crying: 'De Lacy! De Lacy!' and fled into the darkness? If he be innocent, wherefore such action?"

"You hear, my lord?" said Richard. "Can you explain?"

"That I cannot," Darby replied. "Perchance, Gorges has had trouble some time with Sir Aymer de Lacy or his household; though, of course, of that I know nothing. But I do know, Sire, that not I nor mine, with my knowledge, had aught to do with the outrage upon De Bury and the Countess. It would be most humiliating to have been under even an instant's suspicion of such a crime, but to be arrested and arraigned before one's King. . . Bah! it is deeper degradation than words can sound," and he folded his arms and stared, vacantly and with drawn face, straight before him.

"It is the misfortune of a red-haired, flat-nosed servant, my lord," said Richard; "best give him his quittance and a new master. Meanwhile, be not so downcast.--I accept your explanation."

Lord Darby dropped upon his knee, and now the King gave him his hand.

"We will put your gratitude and allegiance to the proof," he said, fixing Darby's eyes with his own and holding them. "The Duke of Buckingham and the Tudor Henry rise in rebellion seven days hence. We need an army within that time. Go, collect your retainers, and join me without an hour's delay."

"Your Majesty is very gracious to make but my liege service the earnest of my faith and word. I ride for Roxford this instant," and with a graceful salute to the King, and a sneering smile at De Lacy he left the apartment.

Richard's quick change--after his searching questions and stern front--in suddenly accepting Darby's assertion of innocence and dismissing him with honor, came to De Lacy like a blow in the face. Had he been within reach when Darby flaunted him, not even the royal presence would have held his arm. As it was, with a stiff bow he was withdrawing, when Richard laughed.

"Are you displeased, Sir Aymer?" he said kindly.

"It is not for me to question the conduct of the King," De Lacy answered respectfully.

"You are surprised, then?"

"Marry, yes! Sire; that I am."

"Only because you have never had to study men to use them. It is not Richard Plantagenet's wont to discuss his decisions with another; yet in this instance, because you are led by no whit of selfishness but solely by love for your betrothed, I will make exception. Surely, you saw there was no evidence sufficient to condemn Darby. If you had ever seen this Flat-Nose it would have been another matter. But resemblances are not conclusive; and in the face of his explanation and absolute denial, the case against him fell for want of proof. Mark me, I do not say that he is innocent; and when the struggle with Buckingham is over we will go deeper into this mystery."

"Then Your Majesty has not sacrificed the Countess of Clare for Lord Darby's retainers?" De Lacy asked pointedly.

Richard smiled good naturedly.

"It is a just question, Sir Aymer," he said; "yet be assured I have no thought to sacrifice Beatrix. At this exigency, I have not an instant to devote to aught but this insurrection. I do not fear Darby--though he would desert to the rebels without hesitation if he thought it would advantage him--but Stanley's course will be his also--it will prove to him there is no hope for the Tudor. Furthermore, assuming that this Gorges is Flat-Nose, he has warned those in charge of the Countess--if, as God grant, she be alive--and to imprison or to kill Darby would be simply to hang more awful peril over her, and aid not a jot the finding of her prison. As it is, Darby must bring this Simon Gorges with him, or raise fresh suspicion by leaving him behind. Yet he has two chances to escape even if he be guilty. Sir John de Bury is still ill at Pontefract, and as he alone knows Flat-Nose, Darby may confidently produce Gorges; and then have him removed by a chance arrow or sword thrust during the coming campaign. The other chance hangs upon the triumph of Buckingham and Darby's desertion to him at the critical instant. In such event, he can frankly acknowledge the abducting of the Countess without fear of punishment and force her to wed him. The Tudor would be glad enough to pay the debt so cheaply."

"Perchance Darby may force the fellow to confess that he alone is guilty," De Lacy suggested.

"A man is not so ready to condemn himself to death," Richard answered; "and to confess would necessitate all the details, and in the maze Darby could not escape ensnarement."

"Might it not have been well, Sire, to detain him and dispatch a force to search Roxford? Many a time were we near it, but then, alas, no suspicion rested upon him."

The King shook his head. "That might have been proper a fortnight since, but it is so no longer. Every soldier is needed with the army now, and it would require a goodly force to reduce Roxford, if you were met with a lifted bridge; though me-thinks you would be received most courteously--and find your quarry flown; if she was there, Flat-Nose has removed her since the adventure at Sheffield."

"Your Majesty is right," said Aymer; "I crave pardon for my ungrateful doubt."

"Nay, nay, I do not blame you. Only remember, De Lacy, that Richard the King is not Richard the man. The man sympathizes with you and trusts you; but he must be the King to do you service and aid your quest. . . Nay, do not thank me. When we have crushed Stafford and Tudor, rescued Beatrix, and you are Earl of Clare, it will be time enough for gratefulness."

XXI
BUCKINGHAM'S REVENGE

Three weeks from that day Richard Plantagenet, with his army, lay at Salis-bury; the rebellion of Buckingham wholly quelled and the leaders fugitives with a price upon their heads.

The conspirators had perfected well their plans and at the same hour threw off the mask. On the morning of the eighteenth, Sir Thomas St. Leger--the King's own brother-in-law--the Marquis of Dorset, and the two Courtneys, proclaimed Henry Tudor in Exeter; Sir John Cheney raised the standard of revolt in Wiltshire; Sir William Norris and Sir William Stoner in Berkshire, and Sir John Browne, of Bletchworth, and Sir John Fogge in Kent. Buckingham with all his force marched from Brecknock and set out, by way of Weobley and through the forest of Dean, to Gloucester, there to cross the Severn. That it was his purpose to throw himself in Richard's path, and risk a battle without waiting for a juncture with his confed-erates, is altogether likely. Stafford was ever rash and foolish; and never more so, indeed, than in this present enterprise.

But whatever his intention may have been, it was thwarted by the visitation of a power more potent than all the hosts of the King. Nature, herself, frowned upon him and his schemes and swept them all to ruin in the rush of angry waters. The rain that began the day Sir Aymer De Lacy made his forced ride from Sheffield to Lincoln had continued with but indifferent diminution for the whole of the following week. As a result, the greatest flood the West of England ever knew poured down through the Severn and its tributaries, destroying fords and bridges, overwhelming hamlets and villages, and drowning scores upon scores of the inhabitants. In the face of this hostile manifestation of Providence, which washed out ardor and bred disaffection and something of superstitious terror, as it held them fast behind the impassable river, Buckingham's followers began to waver; then to drop away; and finally, when it became known that his very castle of Brecknock had been seized by Sir Thomas Vaughan, and that almost before he was out of sight of its towers, they forsook him forthwith, as rats a sinking ship.

All these matters came to the King by messengers from time to time; for he had paid no heed to Buckingham, but had hurried Southward, gathering his forces as he went. His strategy was to throw himself between Stafford and his confederates; cut the latter up in detail; and then hurl himself upon the Earl of Richmond at the quickest possible moment. But as the royal army advanced into the disaffected districts, the revolt faded away like fog before the sun; and without striking a blow or laying lance in rest, it marched into Salisbury. And thus it was that when the Tudor arrived off Plymouth, he found no greeting but an adverse wind and a hostile populace. So he wore ship and turned back to Brittany, making no effort to aid those who had proclaimed him at risk of life and fortune. But such was ever Henry's way.

In these days of strain and striving Sir Aymer de Lacy had few hours of leisure. He who was of the Third Richard's household must needs keep pace with a master in whose slender body was concentrated the energy of many men, and who in times of war never rested nor grew tired.

The Darby episode had been whispered through the Court; and speculation was rife as to the truth of the accusation. Nor was it set at rest when he overtook the array without the flat-nosed Simon Gorges among his retainers. The King, however, seemed to treat him as though the matter were ended; and the courtiers, noting it, were quick to trim to the royal wind.

Yet on the very night of Darby's arrival, had Richard held council with De Lacy, and secret instruction had gone forth to keep him under constant surveillance and on no account whatever to permit him to separate from the army.

"It is suspicious, this course of his," the King said; "but for the present, it will profit nothing to tax him with it. Let him think himself trusted; and perchance the doings of the next few weeks may disclose something that will clear our path of doubt and show the truth. If not, then shall this Gorges be brought before Sir John de Bury and in our presence, though we ride to Pontefract for the purpose. Meanwhile, do you avoid his lordship, and permit no brawling between his retainers and your own. Ratcliffe shall caution him, also, and most peremptorily in this particular. Later, if he be acquittanced of the crime, you may settle the quarrel as you see fit."

And while there had been sore provocations on both sides, for each went as near the line of open rupture as he dared, yet when Salisbury was reached, the command had not been disregarded; though it was very evident to the Household, and perchance to Richard, too--for he missed little that went on about him--that at the first skirmish with the rebels, a certain private feud would be worked out to a conclusion wherein but one of the participants would be left to couch lance for the King.

On this Sunday morning, De Lacy was crossing the courtyard of the Blue Boar Inn when he was attracted by a shouting and evident excitement toward the North gate of the town, and which grew rapidly nearer. Then up the street, at a quick trot, came a clump of spears followed by a mass of soldiers, camp followers and citizens on a run. All were brought up sharply by the guards, stationed a hundred yards or so beyond the royal lodgings; but after a short parley, the horsemen were permitted to pass. The device on the banneret was new to Aymer, and, knowing it belonged to none of those now with the army, and curious as to what could have attracted the rabble, he waited.

Before the inn, from which floated the royal standard, they drew up, and the leader, an elderly Knight of heavy countenance and rotund frame who carried his visor up, dismounted, and, saluting Sir Aymer de Lacy, whose handsome dress evidenced his condition and rank, demanded instant audience with the King.

"His Majesty has but lately returned from Mass," said De Lacy; "but if your business be of immediate importance, I will announce you."

The other laughed swaggeringly.

"I am Sir Thomas Mitten, Sheriff of Shropshire," he said; "and methinks my business is of most immediate importance, good sir, seeing that I bring with me the traitor, Henry Stafford."

"St. Denis! Buckingham a prisoner!" De Lacy exclaimed.

"Yonder--among my men. Think you not I shall be welcome?"

For answer, De Lacy turned on his heel, and, leaving the Sheriff to find his way to the King the best he could, strode over to the horsemen. Motioning them peremptorily aside, he extended his hand to the tall, ruddy-haired man in the stained and torn velvet.

"Believe me, Stafford," he said, "it is a sad day to me that sees you here. I hoped you had escaped."

A spasm of anger swept over the Duke's face; then he smiled and seizing De Lacy's fingers gripped them hard.

"But for treachery and ingratitude baser than Hell's deepest damned you would not see me here," he said. "And it is a brave and noble heart that beneath the Plantagenet's very eye dares show open friendship for the traitor Buckingham. God knows it is sweet after my life lately; yet be advised, De Lacy, it is dangerous to your standing and, mayhap, your liberty as well; best pass me by on the other side."

Aymer made a gesture of dissent. "The King trusts me," he said. "He will not doubt my faith."

Stafford laughed sarcastically. "Pardieu! has the Devil turned saint that Gloucester has come to trust a mortal man! At least, I shall soon see if it has changed his fierce spirit, for here is Ratcliffe to lead me to the Presence. . . Does our Cousin of England desire our company, Sir Richard? If so, we are quite ready to embrace him."

But Ratcliffe was not one to do his present duty with levity on his tongue, and he bowed with stiff formality.

"Will you come with me, my lord?" he said.

"*Au revoir*, De Lacy," smiled the Duke. "Now, to brave the Boar in his lair and see him show his tusks."

And with an air of easy indifference, this man, for whom the world had held such vast possibilities if he had but known how to attain them, went to meet his doom. For that his life was forfeited Stafford well knew; he had been taken in arms against the King and death would be his portion.

Yet the judgment came with a stern swiftness that startled the entire Court; and within the very hour that Shropshire's Sheriff entered Salisbury, was the scaffold for the execution being put in place in the courtyard of the inn.

From the window of the room in which he was confined, Buckingham idly watched the work; and as he stood there, the King and the Duke of Norfolk came forth with a few attendants and rode gayly away.

A scowl of darkest hatred distorted his face, and he shook his fist at Richard--then laughed; and the laugh grew into a sneer, that after the features were composed again still lingered about the mouth.

"It was well for the Plantagenet he did not grant the interview," he muttered; "else------" From within his doublet, he took a long silver comb, such as men used to dress their flowing hair and of which, naturally, he had not been deprived, and touching a secret spring, drew from the heavy rim a slender dagger.

"It is a pretty bit of Italian craft and methinks would have cut sure and deep," he mused. He felt the blade and tested its temper by bending it nigh double . . . "Why should I not cheat yonder scaffold and scorn the tyrant to the end?" . . . then with calm determination returned it to its sheath. "It would give them cause to dub me coward, and to say I would have weakened at the final moment. A Stafford dare not risk it."

He turned again to the window--and started forward with surprise. "Darby! By all the devils in Hell! Here, with the King. . . The false-hearted scoundrel! With him, at least, I can square off."

He struck the door sharply; it opened and Raynor Royk stepped within and saluted.

"Will you deliver a message for me?" Buckingham asked, offering him a rose-noble.

The old soldier drew back.

"I am not for sale, Sir Duke," he said. "What is the message?"

"For Sir Aymer de Lacy, my good fellow. Tell him I pray a moment's conversation on a matter of grave importance."

Without a word Royk faced about and went pounding down the passage.

Presently a light, quick step came springing up the stairway, and De Lacy entered and closed the door behind him.

"You sent for me?" he said.

"Aye, Sir Aymer, and I thank you for the coming. Tell me, when did Lord Darby join the King?"

"About a week since; though he left us at Lincoln on the seventeenth to gather his retainers."

"Bah! I might have known it!" the Duke exclaimed. "It was he, then, that betrayed our plans to Richard. God in Heaven, that I might have him by the throat!" and he clinched his hands in fury.

"Was Darby forewarned of your revolt?" De Lacy asked.

"Forewarned! Forewarned! The dog helped me arrange and mature it. He swore he hated Richard."

"Doubtless he did--and does so still, it was not he who betrayed you."

Stafford stared incredulously.

"Then how, in Satan's name, comes he here now?" he demanded.

"I can answer that better after I know his part with you--may I send for Ratcliffe?"

"As you wish," was the reply.

That the Master of Horse was surprised at the summons was very evident; and he turned to De Lacy questioningly.

"The Duke has certain information touching Lord Darby which must be confided to some one else than me," Sir Aymer explained.

Ratcliffe nodded. "Since your quarrel with Lord Darby such a course were very wise."

"I know nothing of Darby's quarrel with Sir Aymer de Lacy," said Stafford, "but I have seen him here and have learned that he joined Richard at Lincoln, the day prior to that set for the revolt, so I denounce him as a double traitor--traitor to the King, forsworn to me. It was he--he and that hawk-faced priest Morton--who, ere we left Windsor and on all the march to Gloucester, urged and persuaded me to turn against the King. He visited me at Brecknock to arrange details; was there only four days before he deserted me at Lincoln. It was he who was to lead the rising in West Yorkshire. The only reward he asked was my promise for the new King that he be permitted to marry the Countess of Clare."

"The Countess of Clare!" De Lacy exclaimed.

"Yes--she of the ruddy locks and handsome face and figure. He said they loved each other, but that Richard had laughed at their affection and their prayers and had bade her prepare to marry another. Consequently, to avoid all danger of her being forced into the nuptials before the revolt, they had arranged that she be abducted by some of his men, and then lie concealed in his castle until after Richard were deposed. And it seems they did effect their plan--at least, so he told me the last time he came to Brecknock. But methinks he is no better off now, so far as the Countess is concerned."

"Rather the worse off, I fancy," said Ratcliffe. "Two months since, with the King's approbation, the Countess of Clare became the affianced bride of Sir Aymer de Lacy; and Lord Darby's tale, as to her love for himself and Richard's treatment of them, is pure falsehood."

The Duke looked at him in sharp surprise; then shrugged his shoulders.

"Pasque Dieu! I have been an easy dupe," he said. "A child in intrigue should have picked the flaw though he were half asleep. Yet it was a pretty enough story--a loving lady, a frowning King, a false abduction. . . And all a lie."

"All but the abduction--that is true enough," said Ratcliffe.

Buckingham frowned slightly. "I do not follow you, my lord. Methought you said the Countess was betrothed to Sir Aymer."

"And so she is--yet she has been abducted, none the less, these four weeks back, and no trace of her been found. Now, however, you have furnished the clue."

"Nay, simply confirmed the one we had," exclaimed Sir Aymer de Lacy, who from sheer fury had been too choked to speak; "and I have done with waiting--already two weeks have been wasted. If the King want me let him send to Roxford Castle."--His hand was on the door when Ratcliffe seized his arm.

"Compose yourself, De Lacy," he said kindly yet sternly. "Have you learned Richard so little as to think that even we of the Ring dare disobey him?"

"Nor forget, Sir Aymer," added the Duke quickly, "it will be my word against Lord Darby's; and I am a condemned traitor. . . Yet, stay a moment, there is one other knows it. The Abbot of Kirkstall Abbey was in Darby's secret and engaged to aid his scheme."

De Lacy, who was handling his drawn dagger, suddenly sent it deep into the table beside him.

"We seem to have been a pair of fools, Stafford!" he exclaimed. "The very morning after the Countess disappeared I found those two villains together at the Abbey yet suspected them not at all." He drew out the dagger, then plunged it in again. "Well, so be it. I shall wait until the King has heard your story. Then I go North--with his permission, if may be; without it if I must."

"It will be a triple pleasure," said the Duke, "to revenge myself on Darby and do some service to the Countess and to you."

"With your permission, my lord," Ratcliffe observed, "Kendale will take down your statement and you may sign it. . . His Majesty will not return till vespers."

The Duke laughed shortly. "Ere which time I shall be sped, you mean. Well, summon Kendale, and that promptly, for methinks yon scaffold is about ready for its office."

Word for word the King's secretary reduced the narrative.

"Read it," the Duke commanded when it was done. . . "Is that sufficiently definite and accurate? . . . Then let me sign it."

With a labored flourish he attached his name and sealed it with his ring. Ratcliffe and Kendale duly attested it; and sealing it again over the outside edge he handed it to De Lacy:

"When Darby stands against you," he said, "strike one blow for the dead Buckingham. . . Nay, man, take it not so to heart; it is a hazard we all must play some time. And who knows, forsooth, but that in the cast I win a fairer land than this I leave behind?"

"Aye, perchance it is we who lose," said Ratcliffe thoughtfully.

"God grant it be so," De Lacy added.

"Amen!" the Duke rejoined. "For then some day you, too, shall win."

From below came the measured tramp of men; and though the window was closed, the murmurings and mutterings of the crowd grow noticeably louder. The pounding of hammers had ceased and in its place were the gruff commands as the soldiers forced the rabble back from the scaffold; followed presently by the ring of grounded halberds.

The Duke of Buckingham walked to the window and opening the casement looked for a moment into the courtyard. Then as the tread of the guard sounded on the stairs, he turned away and, shaking the dust from his cloak, flung it about his shoulders.

"Lead on, my man, I am ready," he said indifferently, as Raynor Royk, death warrant in hand, stepped within. "No need to read it; I know its message. . . Will you bear me company, good sirs?" he asked rather as one who invites than requests. "I promise I shall not detain you long."

For answer, both Ratcliffe and De Lacy sprang forward and offered him their arms. The Duke shook his head.

"You are most fair and courteous, but I must walk alone--to be supported would give ground for evil tongues to slur upon my courage. Your simple presence will be sustenance enough."

As the procession of death came out into the courtyard, the crowd that swayed and surged behind the men-at-arms, went quiet . . . a murmur gathered, that swelled louder and still louder, until the proud figure of Buckingham stepped upon the scaffold--then it ceased abruptly, and a heavy stillness came. And beside the block, in black shirt and hose and leaning on the long shaft of the huge axe, stood the masked headsman, motionless and grim.

For a space Stafford glanced carelessly over the crowd; then lifted his eyes toward the blue above him, as though fain to see the bourne whither he was bound. And standing so, suddenly a smile of rarest beauty broke upon his face, as if, in truth, a flash of immortal vision had been vouchsafed of the Land beyond the sky.

Even the stern, prosaic Ratcliffe saw it thus; and in awed tones whispered to De Lacy, "He has had that sight of Heaven which is said comes sometimes to those about to die."

And the Duke, his vision passed, yet with the air of one who has received the promise of content, turned to the Bishop of Bath and dropping on one knee bared his head and bent it for the extreme absolution. At the end, he took Ratcliffe and De Lacy by the hand.

"You have been friends at a trying time," he said, "and I thank you from the heart." . . . He drew a chain of gold from within his doublet: "Here, Sir Aymer de Lacy, is my George; do you return it to the King--it may suggest to him that you should take my place."

"You are very thoughtful, my lord," De Lacy answered brokenly.

"And I am enjoined by the King," said Ratcliffe, "to assure you that your domains shall not be forfeited or your Line attainted."

The Duke looked at the Master of Horse steadily for a moment.

"Verily, Richard is a mystery," he said. "Is he then greedy of naught save power, that he passes thus my lands and castles?"

"Methinks there are many who misjudge him," Ratcliffe answered.

"Perchance! Yet my judgment is of small import now. Nathless, I thank him for his clemency and consideration toward my wife and son. And touching my body, I trust it may be decently interred."

"It will be laid beside your ancestors; and with every ceremony your family may desire."

"Truly, this death is not so hard," Stafford said, with a bit of a laugh. "You have just robbed it of its only terrors. Farewell, my friends, farewell!"--And again he took their hands.

Turning to the headsman, who had stood motionless the while, he ran his eyes over the stalwart figure.

"Have you been long at the trade, fellow?" he asked.

"These two and twenty years," came from behind the mask, though the man moved not at all.

"Then you should have learned to strike straight."

"Never but once did I miss my aim," was the grim reply.

"Well, make not, I pray you, a second miss with me."

Calmly as though preparing for his couch and a night's repose, he unlaced his doublet and took it off; and laying back his placard, nodded to the executioner.

The sombre figure came suddenly to life, and drawing from his girdle a pair of heavy shears he swiftly cropped the Duke's long hair where it hung below the neck--then stepped back and waited.

"Are you ready?" Buckingham asked.

The man nodded and resumed his axe.

With a smile on his lips and with all the proud dignity of his great House, Stafford walked to the block and laid his head upon it.

"Strike!" he said sharply.

The executioner swung the axe aloft and brought it slowly down, staying it just ere the edge touched the flesh. There, for an instant, he held it, measuring his distance, while the sunlight flashed along its polished face. Suddenly it rose again, and sweeping in a wide circle of shimmering steel fell with the speed of a thunder-bolt.

And at that very instant, from the camp beyond the town, came the music of the trumpets sounding the fanfare of the King.

XXII
THE KNIGHT AND THE ABBOT

When the King returned, Sir John Kendale with Sir Aymer de Lacy hastened to place in his hands the letter containing Buckingham's statement, at the same time detailing the circumstances under which it was made.

Richard read it very carefully, and handed it back to Kendale.

"So!" he said. "Out of the revolt comes the solution of the mystery, even as I thought. Now, De Lacy, you see it was wise not to arrest Darby at Lincoln."

"Aye, Sire, you were right--and I fancy it is no wiser to arrest him now."

"Not unless you would have the Countess hurried to a fresh prison--or perchance put away altogether--ere you could hope to reach her. For be assured, Darby has provided that instant information be forwarded if he be seized."

"Then all I ask is permission to return forthwith to Yorkshire," said De Lacy.

"It is granted," the King replied instantly. "Take with you a few men-at-arms and Raynor Royk; he knows the country as a priest his prayers. As many more as you may need draw from Pontefract or any of our castles--the Ring will be your warrant. Depart quietly and it can be given out that you are on our special service. Meanwhile Darby shall be as much a prisoner as though he were already in the Tower. We march for Exeter to-morrow; and after things grow quiet thereabouts, and a head or two more has fallen, we shall fare back to London. There I trust you will bring, ere long, the Lady of Clare."

An hour later Sir Aymer De Lacy and Giles Dauvrey, with Raynor Royk and four sturdy men-at-arms, rode out of Salisbury and headed Westward. But after a league or so they turned abruptly to the right and circling around gained the main road to the North at a safe distance from the town and bore away toward Yorkshire.

Had De Lacy responded to the eagerness in his heart he would have raced all the way, nor drawn rein save to take refreshment. But no horse nor pair of horses ever foaled could go the length of England at a gallop, and there were none worth the having to be obtained along the way: the army had swept the country clean of them as it marched Southward. And so the pace was grave and easy; and though Aymer fretted and fumed and grew more impatient as the end drew nearer, yet he never thought to hasten their speed; knowing that by going slowly they were, in fact, going fast. But at length, and in due season, the huge towers of Pontefract frowned against the sky line; and presently at the name of De Lacy, the drawbridge fell and they crossed into the courtyard.

In the small room, where first he saw the Duke of Gloucester, De Lacy found Sir John de Bury. The old Knight was slow to rally from his wound; and being scarcely convalescent when Richard drew in his forces, he had been left in command of Pontefract in place of Sir Robert Wallingford, who went with the King. But lately his strength was coming back to him with swift pulsations and he was growing irritably impatient of his forced inactivity and of the obligation of office which held him stagnant while his sovereign rode to the wars. For as yet, no news had reached this distant section of the actual happenings in the South and the bloodless collapse of the rebellion.

"Holy St. Luke! has Richard been defeated!" De Bury exclaimed, springing to his feet.

"Buckingham is dead and Tudor back in Brittany," Aymer answered.

"Parbleu! Stafford dead!"

"Aye--on the block at Salisbury on All-Souls-Day."

"On the block? . . . Poor fool! . . . Poor fool! . . . Come, tell me about it. But first, what brings you hither now?"

"The Countess of Clare."

"Beatrix! You have found her?" De Bury cried.

"No--not her; but her abductor."

"And he is hereabouts?"

De Lacy shook his head. "He is with the army."

"Then in God's Name, why are you at Pontefract?"

"Easy, Sir John, easy," Aymer answered, his hand on the other's shoulder. "Do you think I would be in Yorkshire if Beatrix were not there, also?"--and forthwith he plunged into a narrative of the events from his encounter with Darby at Sheffield to the death of Buckingham.

"A pretty scheme of Darby's, truly," Sir John commented; "and the dog has played it well. He has nerve uncommon so to brave the royal Richard in his very Court. It is well for you there was no battle, or onfall even, else would you have got an arrow or a sword thrust from behind. . . Now as to Beatrix; is she at Roxford?"

"There or at Kirkstall Abbey."

"True enough; and a most likely place to conceal her the instant Darby was suspected."

De Lacy took a quick turn up and down the room. "God in Heaven, Sir John! has Beatrix come through this without injury or insult?"

"What! What! Injury or insult! They would not dare------?" De Bury cried passionately.

"They have dared to seize and hold her prisoner--would they would dare no more."

The old Knight sank back into his chair and covered his face with his hands. . . "The heiress of the Clares--the favorite of the Queen. . . They would not dare.--Yet if they have------"

"Beatrix will be dead," said De Lacy, "and naught left for me but vengeance."

"Aye! she was ever a brave lass and would kill herself without a whit of hesitation. Nathless, the rescue or the vengeance is for me, also--I ride with you tomorrow?"

"But are you strong enough to risk it?"

"By St. Luke! strong enough to ride to Land's End if need be to strike a blow for Beatrix,"--smiting the table with his fist.

"Then together be it, and welcome. Here is to the Countess and her rescue ere the morrow's sun go down!" and he filled two goblets with wine.

"And death and confusion to her captors," Sir John echoed, raising high his glass.

Clad in full mail and followed by threescore men-at-arms and as many archers the two Knights set out from Pontefract the following morning. After due discussion they had determined that the time for cautious indirection was passed and that there would be no quibbling with the Abbot of Kirkstall. He would be called upon to produce the Countess or to disclose where she was hidden, as well as to confess all that he knew concerning the abduction. They were not in a mood to argue or to be trifled with; and ill would it be for Aldam if he tried evasion or grew stubborn.

And that they came in spirit scarce pacific was declared by their first act when the Abbey was reached. With the haft of his battle-axe De Lacy struck the outer gate a resounding blow; and getting no prompt response, followed it with a second that rang among the buildings and corridors within. Straightway there came the shuffle of sandaled feet and a fumbling at the wicket, which opening slowly, disclosed the rotund face and heavy, sleepy eyes of Father Ambrose.

"Well! what means this unseemly bluster?" he began. . . . "Your lordships' pardon--I will open instantly," and hurried to remove the bars.

"We seek speech with the Lord Abbot," said De Lacy, halting beside the lodge, while the soldiers filed into the courtyard and drew into line at the farther side.

The monk watched this proceeding with blank surprise.

"Hear you not?" Aymer demanded sharply, letting his mailed hand fall heavily on the other's shoulder. "We seek the Abbot."

Father Ambrose shrank back in amaze at the tones and action.

"His reverence is engaged at present in a session of the Chapter," he faltered.

"Good--we will interrogate him there," Aymer answered; and Sir John and he galloped across to the church and dismounted.

In the Chapter-house, the brothers, both ecclesiastical and lay, were assembled in convocation. On the dais, in the recess at one side of the hall, sat the Abbot in his great carved chair of state. He was leaning slightly forward, chin on hand, regarding with calm and critical scrutiny the faces of the white-robed throng below him. And the monks, crowded on their narrow oaken benches, felt the stern eyes upon them and grew restless; for none knew how soon he might be called forward for rebuke before them all. And Aldam did not spare words when he administered his corrections; and not one of the Cistercians but would have chosen the heaviest task of the fields for four and twenty hours in preference to a single minute's lashing by his biting tongue.

On the Abbot's right was Father James, the Prior, whose jolly face and ample girth were equalled only by the Sub-prior, Father Albert, the favorite of all the Abbey, who permitted the monks to do their own sweet wills so long as it did not interfere with the necessary labors of the farms and religious ceremonies.

"Let the names of the candidates for admission to full brotherhood in our holy Order be read," the Abbot ordered.

The Chancellor stepped forward and with much rattle of parchment opened the roll and cleared his throat preparatory to intoning. But he got no further. The religious calm was rudely broken by the clash of steel on the bare pavement of the ante-chamber, and as Aldam raised his head in angry surprise the door was flung back and the two Knights, visors up, strode down the aisle.

Instantly there was confusion; the monks, like timid children, drew far away from these impious invaders of their peacefulness; some made as though to flee; and all broke out into cries of alarm and terror.

The Abbot sprang to his feet, his eyes flashing, his face pale with suppressed ire.

"Silence!" he thundered. "Return this instant to your seats, you fearful ones!"

The brothers huddled back into their places, trembling. There was for them small choice between the anger of their ruler and the armed men in their midst.

"Truly this is strange conduct for Sir John de Bury and Sir Aymer de Lacy," the Abbot exclaimed as they halted before the dais. "Since when, pray, has it been deemed knightly to offer such affront to Holy Church?"

"Since a mitred Abbot of Holy Church has shamed his sacred office," De Lacy answered curtly.

"What, sirs!" Aldam cried. "Do you dare insult the Abbot of Kirkstall, here in his very chapter, and hope to go unpunished either in this world or the next?"

Aymer folded his arms over the shaft of his battle axe and laughed grimly.

"In this world methinks small need have we to fear your reverence; and as for the next world we will chance it. But be advised: tax us not with threats; our patience is likely to be short."

"And ours is gone entirely--do you, Sir John de Bury, approve this rash youth's sacrilege?"

"Aye, that I do," De Bury answered, his face set as stone.

"Are you both mad?" the Abbot exclaimed.

"Yea, that we are," replied De Lacy. "Mad with anger and resentment. Can you guess why?"

The monk made no answer save a sneer.

"Listen, and you and your underlings shall hear: One evening a month or so aback--your memory, good father, will serve you whether it was one, or two, or three--a certain demoiselle styled Countess of Clare, Maid to Her Majesty, the Queen of England, while near the Hermit's Cell in the escort of Sir John de Bury, her uncle and guardian, was waylaid and by force and violence seized upon and carried off. And though there was hue and cry and searchings without rest, yet it was unavailing."

"Certes, we know all these matters," Aldam broke in angrily.

"Yes, you know them--and much more."

The Cistercian's face changed its expression not a whit.

"Are you aware, my lord Abbot, that the Duke of Buckingham has died upon the block?" De Lacy questioned.

Aldam shrugged his shoulders. "It was scarce Stafford's death that brought you to Kirkstall," he scoffed.

Aymer laughed derisively. "Think you so? Then are you mistaken woefully. But for it I would be at Salisbury and your foul crime still unsuspected."

"Now has patience run its limit!" the Abbot exclaimed. "Brothers of Benedict! throw me these two godless ones without the gates." And seizing the huge chair beside him, with strength astonishing in one so slender, he whirled it high and brought it down at De Lacy's head.

But the Knight sprang lightly aside, and the heavy missile, tearing itself by sheer weight from the priest's fingers, crashed upon the pavement and broke asunder.

If there had been any possibility of help from his frightened flock it was ended by this ill-timed blow. The Prior and his fellows on the dais made not a single motion; and save for an excited swaying and whispering, the monks sat stolid on their benches, either too frightened to flee or too indifferent to the Abbot's safety to care to aid him. For once had the habit of trembling obedience, yoked upon them by years of stern domination, been loosed by the spirit of fear or the hope of release.

And with a sneer of disgust on his face he surveyed them; and the scorn in his voice must have shamed them to the floor had they been of the blood of such as feel disgrace.

"You cowardly curs!" he exclaimed; "have you no spark of manhood left among you?"

"Perchance they, in their turn, can dub you cur," said De Lacy tersely, springing on the dais and taking hold upon the Abbot's arm; "for here, on the dying word of the Duke of Buckingham, do I accuse you of complicity in the abduction of the Countess of Clare."

Aldam shook off the mailed fingers.

"What! What!" he cried. "Would you lay hands in violence upon one of God's anointed? . . . Stand back, Sir Aymer de Lacy . . . and you, too, Sir John de Bury, lest I smite you both with the Church's anathema."

A gasp of horror came from the monks, and even the two Priors were appalled at the threat--dire enough, indeed, to most men in that age, but little short of Hell itself to such as were cloister-bred.

De Lacy folded his arms again over his battle-axe.

"It was no purpose nor intent of mine," he said, "to offer you violence------"

"Nathless, it was done," the Abbot broke in arrogantly, "and naught but sharp penance can atone for it and for your deeds here this day."

De Lacy smiled contemptuously. "Methinks, lord Abbot, you are strangely dull of brain to fancy you can fright us so. Believe me, we care as little for your curse as for your broken chair. Nor did I speak in apology for my action. I meant no violence then; yet if we do not get true answer to our questions, be assured there shall be violence both meant and done."

The monks groaned aloud; but the Abbot only shrugged his shoulders.

"You have heard," De Lacy went on with steady menace; "and do not think it is an idle boast. Answer! have you the Countess of Clare within the bounds of Kirkstall Abbey?"

Aldam raised his hand in seeming horror. "Think you that the monks of Benedict------?" he began.

"Answer!" cried Aymer, striking the arm of the Prior's chair with his mailed fist so fiercely that its stout occupant, in sudden terror, fled to the rear of the dais.

Instantly the Abbot seated himself in the vacant place.

"I frighten not so easily as the timid Brother James," he said. "But as the lady is not with us, you are welcome to that knowledge."

"Where is she, then?"

The Cistercian leaned back and stared De Lacy in the face. "If I knew I would not tell you."

"You do know--and either you tell or you hang from your own gate beam."

Aldam half arose from his chair; then dropped back and laughed.

"You would not dare," he said; "and were I the abductor himself."

De Lacy faced toward the door.

"What ho! Without!" he called.

A score of men-at-arms burst into the room with drawn swords. The monks set up a fresh cry of terror and fell to chanting prayers, and Father Alfred and the Chancellor sought refuge in the shadow with the Prior. But the Abbot never stirred in his seat, save to shift his gaze to the fresh disturbers of his authority.

At a sign from De Lacy, the soldiers sheathed their weapons and fell into double rank near the door, while Raynor Royk advanced to the dais and saluted. Then the Knight turned again to the Abbot.

"We shall search this Abbey from loft to cellar,'" he said. "If the Countess be not here and you still remain obdurate, then shall you stretch halter, an you were the Pope of Rome himself. . . Raynor, we commit these good fathers to your custody. Let none quit the room--if need be, cut down any who attempt it."

All this time Sir John de Bury was leaning on his long sword, his cold grey eyes fixed on the Abbot. Now he faced about and, silent still, tramped out of the Chapter-house beside De Lacy. And with them went half of the men-at-arms.

XXIII
THREE CHEVRONS GULES

When the Knights had gone Raynor Royk, having posted guards at the three doors, turned the broken chair over with his foot and sitting down on one of the fragments so that he could observe the entire room, fell to polishing his dagger.

The Abbot watched him furtively for a space, then arose.

"Are you of De Lacy's or De Bury's household?" he asked with condescending friendliness.

No answer.

"You hear? I asked if De Bury or De Lacy were your master."

No answer; and the polishing went vigorously on.

"Are you deaf?" the monk exclaimed angrily, and prod the old retainer with his foot.

The next moment the air was full of flying arms and legs and sandals and fluttering robes; and when it cleared Aldam was lying in a heap on the floor--and Raynor Royk was working on his dagger, as placidly as though it were a common enough act with him to seize the foot of a mitred Abbot and whirl him backward to the earth.

And the look of mingled fury and pain on the monk's face when, shaking off the assisting hands of the Prior and the Chancellor, he struggled to his feet, would have made a less hardened soldier feel a bit uneasy as to the fate of his soul. But without so much as a glance at the furious churchman, Raynor returned the dagger to its sheath and went to work on his sword blade.

Never in all the years of his life had the stern Aldam been so crossed and flouted as within this last hour. Speechless with rage, with clenched hands and heaving breast, he paced the dais. And the monks in fresh terror huddled closer together, and told their beads anew and muttered prayer on prayer. Verily, was it a gloomy day for the Cistercians of Kirkstall Abbey; and one sadly unpropitious to those lay brothers whose initiatory rites had been so rudely interrupted.

Presently the Abbot's face grew calmer and he began to prolong gradually his steps toward the rear of the platform, where the wall stones were very large and stood out rough and bare. There he would pause and lean against them as though for rest, his head bent slightly forward, his eyes closed--a figure of dejection deep and heavy. Yet it might have been noticed that he always rested at the same place, and could eyes have pierced his white robe, they would have seen his slender fingers playing with careful pressure over the wall beside him.

At length it happened--when the soldiers had grown accustomed to his pacings and had ceased to watch him, and while Raynor Royk was busy with his sword work, his head bent low--that Aldam halted at the wall and leaned against it in his usual way; and as he did so the huge stone he touched swung back noiselessly, he glided swiftly through the opening and the stone closed back into its place.

An excited exclamation by the Prior caused Raynor Royk to look up. Instantly he missed the Abbot. With a shout he sprang over and seized the Chancellor, who happened to be nearest.

"The Abbot? The Abbot?" he demanded fiercely.

"I know not," the monk stammered, staring about. "I saw him last by yonder wall."

The old soldier loosed him straightway and turned upon the Prior.

"Speak," he thundered, "where is the Abbot?"

Father James stepped forward. "He went through the wall," he said.

"What! thou shaveling! Do you take me for a superstitious fool? Through yonder stones! Think you I believe such nonsense?"

"That you believe or disbelieve concerns me not at all," the Prior answered. "Nathless, through that wall he went, for with my own eyes I saw a part of it roll back and him pass in."

Raynor crossed to the spot in a single bound and fell to pounding with his sword hilt. But only a monotonously dull sound answered to the blows.

"Do you know this hidden door, or whither it leads?"

"Methinks I can answer for myself and all my brothers," said the Prior. "There are certain secret passages in the Abbey which none but our ruler ever knows. Doubtless this is one of them."

"Beware, Sir Monk!" Raynor exclaimed, striding over and glaring down upon him. "If you lie to aid your Abbot you shall hang instead of him."

The Prior crossed himself devoutly. "Holy St. Benedict, be my witness, I speak truth. Nor do we love the Abbot Aldam well enough to shield him at danger to ourselves."

The veteran regarded him keenly for a moment. "I am prone to believe you," he said; "for I myself know something of this Aldam. Yet here is one who will need the convincing," as Sir Aymer de Lacy entered suddenly. And behind him came an archer with a coil of rope.

"Seize the Abbot!" the Knight commanded as he crossed the threshold. . . "Ho, Raynor! Since when are you afraid to touch a Priest? Seize him, I say."

The old soldier advanced and saluted.

"The Abbot has escaped," he said.

"What!--Escaped!--Hell and Furies!" De Lacy cried, and sprang at him with arm raised to strike. But instantly the anger passed; and instead of a blow, his hand fell kindly upon Royk's shoulder. "How did it happen?" he asked. "It was through some trick, I warrant, and by no fault of yours."

"I thank your lordship," Raynor answered, with another salute. "The Abbot escaped by a secret passage in yonder wall when my eyes were not upon him. This monk saw the stone open and close," and he pointed to the Prior.

De Lacy eyed Father James sharply, then nodded for him to speak.

At the end, he sent Royk to make another search of the entire Abbey, and himself turned his attention to the wall. But though he tried pressure both light and heavy and in all possible positions and combinations the stone stood firm.

"Is this the first time you have seen this passage opened?" he asked.

"It is, my lord; this or any other of its kind. It is a violation of the Abbot's vows to use the secret ways in presence of another."

"Do you think he never violated them before?"

The monk shook his head. "Save possibly for certain damsels, I think not; he never before had such occasion. Yet I will inquire. . . Brothers!" he cried, "if there be any among you who knows the trick of this hidden door or whither it leads, I enjoin him, in the name of the blessed Benedict and as the ranking officer in this Chapter, that has not yet been dissolved, to reveal the same."

The monks whispered among themselves. Then one stood forth.

"There is none among us who knows the secret, most reverend Prior," he answered.

"You hear, sir?" said Father James.

De Lacy nodded. "Yet I must trouble you to answer me a little further. Do you know this glove and kerchief? I found them in the room next to the Abbot's."

The Prior took them and after a glance held them inquiringly toward the Chancellor and Father Albert; but each disclaimed all knowledge.

"I fear me, sir, we cannot help you. . . Women are not unknown in the Abbot's quarters; yet none of us has ever seen them close enough to know them. It is thought he uses for them one of the secret passages which opens somewhere beyond the Abbey walls. Leastwise, you may be assured no one has ever ventured to refer thereto in the holy Aldam's hearing. So, my lord, these articles might belong to any of a dozen demoiselles--with religious inclinations," and he chuckled. . . "Yet--here is a cognizance upon the kerchief which may tell much to one acquainted with escutcheons. It is three chevrons gules, I take it."

"They are the arms of Clare, and the Countess is its heiress," said De Lacy.

"Then she you seek has, indeed, been here!"

"And is here still, though I have failed to find her."

"Nay--methinks not. There have been no gentle ones with his reverence these last five days."

"You are sure of that?"

The Prior's broad face expanded in a grin. "Well, sir, you see we have thought it good to keep a religious eye upon our worthy head."

De Lacy drew off his steel gauntlet.

"See you this ring?" he said, holding up the Boar. "In the name of the King I promise you, Sir Prior, the Abbotcy of Kirkstall, and your good fellows each a grade in rank, if you will aid me to capture this Aldam and to recover the Countess of Clare."

Father James's face flushed slightly at the prospect, and the Sub-prior and the Chancellor drew nearer in sudden interest.

"It is a tempting offer," the Prior said; "yet though you promised us all the red hat of a Prince Cardinal, we could give you no more assistance than we have already done. Nathless, fair sir, we shall do whatever lies in our power."

"It is a bargain. When the Abbot is a prisoner or the lady saved, the new dignities are yours . . . Monks of Kirkstall, harken!" he cried to those upon the benches. "For inasmuch as Aldam, Abbot of Kirkstall Abbey, has aided and abetted the enemies of his lawful Sovereign and has furthered and assisted the abductors of the Countess of Clare, Maid-in-waiting to Her Majesty; now, I, Aymer de Lacy, Knight of the Body, under the authority vested in me by this signet and in the name of the King, do hereby publicly degrade and remove the said Aldam from his office and do absolve and release every and all of you from any obligation or duty to him. And further, whosoever shall offer him comfort or sustenance shall be deemed and held traitor and shall suffer death. Heed and obey."

The Prior sprang to the front of the dais.

"Long live the King!" he shouted.

And the monks, wild with joy at release from their hard master, jumped on the benches crying:

"Long live the Royal Richard! Long live the King!"

XXIV
"WHEN YOU HAVE TOPPED THESE STAIRS"

For an hour Raynor Royk and his men searched every nook and corner of the Abbey, sounding walls and floors and making a confusion such as the stately establishment had never known. But they found neither the Countess nor the Abbot. He had either escaped by one of the passages through which he introduced his frail companions, or he was hiding in some secret chamber--whence he would take good care not to issue until the Knights had departed.

And to provide for just such contingency De Lacy, on the morrow when the march was resumed, detailed five of the royal men-at-arms to remain at Kirkstall. The armed retainers of the Abbey, who had been made prisoners the instant De Bury and he entered the place, he now relieved from service there and enrolled them among his own following. They were sturdy soldiers enough, albeit they had little to do but to wax fat and sluggish by inaction and much food and, occasionally, to escort the Abbot when he went abroad. Yet they were glad to be admitted to the service of one who wore the Boar and they donned corselet and casquetel with eagerness and haste--as willing now to fight against the Cistercian as, an hour since, they were ready to defend him.

The Castle of Roxford lay some four leagues northwest of the Abbey. It had been the seat of the Lords of Darby for two centuries and more; and while in no way comparable with the huge Pontefract, in either size or strength, yet it was deemed a formidable fortress and one, when properly garrisoned and defended, well able to withstand attack.

A broad path led from the highway half a league or so through the forest of oaks and beeches to the castle, which stood on a slight eminence in the centre of a wide clearing covered with luxuriant turf, and used for pasturing the domestic animals as well as for the sports of the garrison. But the morning after the events at Kirkstall, when Sir Aymer de Lacy and Sir John de Bury halted near the edge of the timber, this open space was bare of denizen, either brute or human. Nor did the fortress itself show more animation; for though they rode slowly around its entire circle, keeping the while well under cover of the trees, yet not a sign of life did they discover either without or within. Save for the small sable banner with the three golden escallops, which fluttered in gentle waves from the gate-tower, there was no moving thing in all the landscape.

"It is uncommonly queer, this quiet," said De Bury, shading his eyes with his hand to see the better. "It would almost seem they had been warned of our coming."

"Like enough," De Lacy answered. "They would only need to know that I was back in Yorkshire; and that, doubtless, reached them quick enough. There is no hope to catch them with drawbridge down," and they went on to their following.

"You know the castle, Sir John; what is the best point to attack?" Aymer asked.

The old Knight shook his head. "There is no weak spot, so far as I have recollection."

"Where is the postern? I did not note it."

"No postern will you find in yonder walls," De Bury answered. "A secret exit runs beneath the moat known only to the ruling lord himself."

"Another Kirkstall!" commented Aymer.

"Aye--yet as Darby is not within, there will be no escape by it."

With banners to the fore, they marched across the open space to the barbican and the herald blew the parley.

No answer came from the outwork. Riding closer, De Lacy discovered it was without defenders, and passing through he halted on the edge of the causeway.

"Sound again!" he commanded--and this time with quick effect.

A trumpet answered hoarsely from within and a mailed form arose from behind the crenellated parapet near the gate.

"Who summons so peremptorily the Castle of the Lords of Darby?" it asked.

Sir John's herald blew another blast.

"It is a most ignorant warder that does not recognize the arms of Sir John de Bury and Sir Aymer de Lacy," he answered.

"What seek Sir John de Bury and Sir Aymer de Lacy at the Castle of Roxford?" was the demand.

De Lacy waved the herald aside. "We seek the Countess of Clare who, we have reason to believe, is held in durance here. In the name of the King, we require you to surrender her forthwith."

"And if she be not here?"

"Then after due search, we will leave you undisturbed," the Knight replied.

The other laughed tauntingly.

"You must needs have wings, fair sirs, to gain entrance here;" and with a scornful gesture he disappeared below the parapet, and the blast of a trumpet signified that the truce was ended.

De Lacy closed his visor, and for a time surveyed the fortress with careful eye. Before him lay a moat full sixty feet across and two thirds full of water, with no means of passage save the drawbridge, that hung so high on its chains as to seem almost against the outer portcullis. From the farther edge the wall rose solid and grim, and, as he knew from Sir John, with no opening in all its circuit save the gate directly opposite.

"It is evident the garrison is very small," De Bury observed, "else they would not have abandoned the barbican without a blow."

"Undoubtedly; and if we can reach the gate or scale the wall the rest is easy."

"I would we had a bombard or two that are lying idle in the armory at Pontefract."

"They will not be needed," De Lacy answered. "We shall sleep in the castle to-night."

Sir John smiled. "Have you found the wings the warder recommended?"

"We shall not require them; the gate is easier entrance than over the walls--besides being the way naturally intended. This is not the first time I have forced such a castle and won it by sundown. . . Giles, we will try the flagons; let the ropes be made ready, and bid the archers stand to their bows."

Sir John was regarding De Lacy with vexed surprise.

"Flagons!" he broke out. "Do you think to win the castle by pouring wine on the waters of the moat?"

Aymer laughed. "It is a trick I learned among the Italians, though they use hollow iron balls. There were none such at Pontefract, so I substituted flagons; they are filled with powder, the mouth plugged shut save for the fuse, and the whole is wrapped in a bag, also filled with powder."

"How in the name of St. Luke do you expect to use them?"

"Come," said De Lacy, and led the way to the edge of the moat.

The squire was there uncoiling a long, stout rope with a broad iron ball at one end. Fastening the other end to a projection in the barbican, he whirled the weighted one around his head, then suddenly let it fly. Like a bird it soared over the moat, and crossing back of the right lift-chain swung far down near the water. With a wide grappling hook he caught it above the ball, and drawing it in tied the two ends together, forming a great loop around the chain where it was fastened to the bridge.

Hitherto there had been no opposition from the castle; but now there was a change.

As Dauvrey whirled another weighted rope behind the left draw-chain, an arrow whistled from the wall and rapped him hard upon the hauberk near the gorget, piercing the outer mail, but being stayed by the inner shirt of Italian steel. The next instant the shafts came thick and furious, marking De Bury and De Lacy and the squire at every joint and seam of their harness, but without effect.

"By St. Denis, I fancy not those bolts," exclaimed De Lacy, as a quarrel from an arbalest glanced along his helmet near the eye hole. "It came from the left gate tower, methought."

"From the far window," said De Bury.

"Fetch me a bow," De Lacy ordered Royk.

Drawing off his right gauntlet he notched the shaft and waited. Presently a head rose cautiously in the window and the cross-bow was laid upon the ledge. Instantly De Lacy's fingers touched his cheek, the string twanged sweetly, and the arrow flashed across and deep into the brain of the arbalestier.

The cry he gave as death gripped him was answered by the splash of his weapon as it sank into the waters of the moat.

"Bravo! my lord!" Raynor exclaimed. "You are a sight for old eyes."

"It was a lucky shot," the Knight replied, handing back the stave.

Meanwhile Dauvrey, minding the arrows rained upon him no more than so many feathers, had caught the last rope, and so both lift-chains were encircled by a running loop. In a trice a flagon was fastened to a strand of each and drawn quickly over until it rested close against the bridge. All this time the ropes were kept swinging irregularly to prevent them being cut by arrows from the walls; though the defenders had ignored them entirely, thinking, doubtless, they were to be used for crossing and being quite content; for then their assailants' armor must come off and they be easy marks.

But when the bags went over they scented danger, and the darts began to hiss about the ropes. And the gate was flung back and the bridge lowered a trifle, and up it two men worked their way toward the chains. They were protected by the flooring from the fire of those at the barbican, but Dauvrey, foreseeing just such a move, had stationed archers on each side to meet it; and ere the two had reached the middle of the span they were pierced by half a score of arrows and rolled back into the gateway.

"Now!" cried De Lacy. "Up with them"--and seizing the rope nearest him he gave it a quick twist that flung the bag upon the bridge and against the chain; and Dauvrey did the same with the other.

At the command two archers had sprung forward with lifted bows and barbs wrapped with burning tow and oil.

"Shoot!" Sir Aymer ordered; and straight into each bag a blazing arrow sped.

Then came a sullen roar--a burst of silvery smoke--a rush of flying bits of iron and splinters; and as those before the barbican leaped back at the Knight's warning cry, the drawbridge crashed down upon the causeway, its lift-chains torn clean away.

Instantly De Lacy dashed forward with waving axe; and beside him went Sir John de Bury, and at his shoulder were Dauvrey and Old Raynor Royk. And they were none too quick; for already those at the entrance were trying to remove the planks that formed the flooring. But with a cry of "Clare! Clare!" Aymer and the others were upon them and they fled within the walls, swinging the gate shut just as the two Knights flung themselves against it.

"Keep an eye upward lest they loose a turret and destroy the bridge," De Lacy shouted, and fell to work on the gate with his heavy axe, while Dauvrey made haste to prevent the dropping of the portcullis by driving a spike into the grooves in which it worked.

But the gate was made of heavy, seasoned oak, studded thick with iron and bound deep around the edges with well-wrought steel. And though De Lacy's blows thundered upon it until it swayed and rattled on its massive hinges, yet it still stood staunch and firm. Presently he paused, and Giles Dauvrey sprang forward to take his place. But he stayed him.

"It is too strong to waste good time and strength upon," he said. "We must use the powder again."

Twice the flagons spoke without material result; but the third tore the gate from its fastenings, and even before the smoke had risen Sir Aymer de Lacy and Sir John de Bury hurled it back upon its hinges and dashed through--to be brought up short by two men in complete armor, who attacked them furiously.

In the narrow passage, with the walls close on either side and the roof low over head, the fighting was hampered and awkward. De Lacy and De Bury were in each other's way and neither could swing a heavy blow; yet they pressed forward, sword and axe drawing fire as they rasped each other or scraped against the rough stones of the arch.

Meanwhile the men-at-arms led by Raynor Royk had poured across the bridge and were crowding close in the rear.

"Bear aside, my lords!" the veteran shouted high above the din of the clashing steel. "We will sweep the way clean by a rush."

But neither Knight gave heed. Gradually De Lacy was driving his foe before him. Step by step he forced him back, until presently they were free of the wall and into the outer bailey. Then he first noticed that, though his opponent bore no device upon shield or hauberk nor crest upon helm, his armor was scarcely of the sort wont to be worn by retainers or simple men-at-arms; it was far too handsome in its lines and fashion and much too beautifully forged. And as he parried the sword strokes, waiting for an opening when he could end the conflict by a crashing blow, he tried to distinguish the face behind the bars of the visor. At first he had thought it was some retainer masquerading in one of Lord Darby's suits of mail, but the sword play was manifestly that of no common soldier; it was too graceful and too skillful to have been learned amid the turmoil of the camp and battle. And suddenly the great hope came that it was Darby himself--who had eluded the King and, following after, had passed him at Pontefract. Instantly the cool method of his fighting vanished; his fingers took a fresh and tighter grip; his battle-cry "Clare! Clare!" rang out vengefully; and with all the fury of his wrongs and pent-up hate he sprang in close. And as he swept his axe aloft its heavy head caught the other's sword and tore it clean away, sending it far across the bailey where it fell with a clang.

To many, here would have been the conflict's end; yet even as the hilt quit his fingers, the unknown plucked forth his heavy dagger and sprang straight at De Lacy.

Aymer met the attack by facing on his right heel swiftly to the left, and as the other, unable to recover himself, struck wildly at the air, the axe caught him full upon the shoulder, biting through gorget and gambeson and deep into the neck beneath.

Bending over his fallen foe, De Lacy cut the lacings of the helmet and drew it off--then started back in wonder.

Instead of the dark curls and face of Roxford's lord there were disclosed the tonsured head and pale features of the Abbot of Kirkstall.

"Pardieu!" he exclaimed, gazing down into the face already set in death. . . "You were my enemy, yet had I known whom this suit encased, methinks my arm had dealt an easier blow. Nathless, you were a better knight than churchman and, mayhap, it was a proper death for you to die."

Just then, De Bury's antagonist went by, running as easy as though his mail were silk and shouting:

"To the keep! To the keep!" to those upon the walls. And behind him came Sir John, and the squires, and Raynor Royk with all the troop.

Whirling about, De Lacy sprang after. But here had he and all the others met their match; for strain as they might, they gained not an inch; and when the foe reached the steps they were yet fifty feet away.

The door was open for him and rushing in he flung it shut, but with such force that it missed the catch and rebounded--and at that instant, De Lacy thrust in his axe and he and Dauvrey threw themselves against the door and slowly forced it back. Then of a sudden, it yielded and they were near to falling headlong.

Shouting his battle-cry, Aymer strode into the great hall and made for the wide stairway at the opposite end, where the remnants of the garrison were gathered for the final stand. There were but nine and of them only the three in front were garbed in steel; and in the centre was he who had held the gate against Sir John de Bury.

Out-matched and out-armed there could be for them but one end to the melee; for though they held the vantage post yet it counted little against those who were arrayed below them, eager to begin. Nevertheless, they stood calm and ready, leaning on their weapons, and showed no glint of fear. And De Lacy, in admiration and loath to put them to the sword, raised his axe for silence.

"You bear yourselves as men deserving of a better cause," he cried, "and I fain would not have your blood spilled needlessly. Yield yourselves prisoners, and scathless shall you leave this castle within the hour--all save one, if he be among you, the flat-nosed retainer of Lord Darby. Him must I carry to the King."

A gruff laugh came from the figure in the centre and he swung his visor up.

"Aye, sirs, be not surprised. Behold him you have dubbed Flat-Nose--by true name, Simon Gorges--the leader of your assailants, Sir John de Bury, when yon Knight saved you--the abductor of the Countess of Clare--the man who eluded you, Sir Aymer de Lacy, at the house in Sheffield." And he laughed again. "And now do I thank your worship for the proffered clemency to my fellows, and for the honor you have in store for me. Yet am I scarce fit to stand before His Majesty; nor do the followers of the Master of Roxford accept favor or life from the enemy of their lord. Here await we the onslaught, fair sirs, and let it come quickly that it may be quickly done."

"Stay!" cried De Lacy fiercely. "You have many more sins upon your soul, doubtless, than those just vaunted, yet will you not do one redeeming act ere you are sped? For of a verity you shall die ere the shadows yonder lengthen by a span. Where, I ask you, shall I find the Countess of Clare?"

Flat-Nose smiled.

"You will find her when you have topped these stairs," he answered, and snapped his visor shut.

"I claim the villain!" De Bury exclaimed.

"Take him," said De Lacy--and whispered, to Giles Dauvrey: "Keep behind Sir John, and if he weaken take his place until I come."

Then with the old Knight in the middle and Aymer and Raynor Royk on either hand, they advanced to the fight.

But whereas at the gate they were on equal footing, here the assailed had vastly the advantage; for standing on the edge of the landing, where the stairs divided, they were high above their foes. So the conflict began warily; and on the third step below the three halted and made play with the three above, seeking for a chance to rush up and get on even terms. But the others were not to be confused by tricks or taken unaware, and were content to act only on the defensive and wait their opportunity. And so they struggled for a while, with no result on either side save that the strain grew heavy and the breath came harder than at first.

Suddenly, Gorges' heavy blade found an opening, and Sir John de Bury, with a great hole in his helmet, staggered back and sank into the arms of the men behind him. But it brought no respite to the victor, for Giles Dauvrey stepped into the vacant place and his sword and Flat-Nose's rang viciously together.

With a groan De Lacy marked the old Knight's fall; then as for an instant his opponent's eye wandered thither, he sprang up inside his stroke, and gripping him with both hands about the ankles threw him over his head and clean to the pavement below.

At this moment, Raynor Royk cut down his foe and joined his leader on the landing with the men-at-arms at his back. Then, indeed, was the fight quickly ended--save where Simon Gorges still held the squire at bay.

And while they fought a queer thing happened in the hall below, for Sir John de Bury got suddenly upon his feet and came toward the stairs.

"You must strike harder, Flat-Nose, to reach a skull through Spanish bascinet," he said. "Yet of a verity, did you stun me sore and show me stars in millions. Have at him, De Lacy, I resign the rogue to you--my legs are over shaky to stand on yonder stair."

De Lacy motioned all to move back.

"Flat-Nose!" he called. "You shall have one more chance. Will you yield prisoner?"

Instantly Dauvrey stepped down out of reach and grounded blade.

"To dangle in a halter from the gate tower?" scoffed Gorges, facing about. "Not by St. Edward! Cry on your dogs."

"Has life then grown tiresome to you?"

"Marry, no! Yet it is but a change of deaths you offer; and I prefer the one that finds me sword in hand."

"You have said the Countess of Clare is in this castle. Will you accept life from her if she decree it; or in steel harness fight me to the death, if she condemn you?" De Lacy asked.

Flat-Nose flung down his sword and raised his visor.

"I accept the offer, Sir Knight," he said. "I will risk the lady's judgment. Knock upon the door in the farthest corner, and she, herself, will open to you--there is no lock upon it, save that she has inside."

"Will you come with me, Sir John?" De Lacy called, as Dauvrey made haste to unlace his lord's helmet and lift it off.

De Bury shook his head. "Nay, lad, it is your right first. Later will I join you and gladly."

Without further urging Aymer hurried down the corridor and tapped lightly at the door, beyond which, if Flat-Nose spoke truly, he would find his lost betrothed. No answer came, and he rapped again and louder. But within was silence and he waited vainly for response. Then with rising suspicion that he had been tricked by Darby's minion, he struck the panel sharply and with force--and the door swung back until it was open wide.

For a moment he hesitated; but when another knock brought no reply, he ventured across the threshold and into the room a little way. Then as his eyes chanced upon a hat with long plumes, lying on a table, and beside it a veil and a woman's gauntlets, he was seized with sudden fright and turned to flee.

But on the instant, from behind, two arms were flung about his neck and a soft cheek was pressed against his own, and a voice, than which to him the world contained none sweeter, whispered in his ear:

"Aymer, my lord!"

XXV
A PAGE FROM THE PAST

With a cry of deepest gladness he whirled and caught his lost love to him, and kissed her brow and ruddy hair, and his voice broke and his eyes dimmed as he repeated many times:

"Beatrix! . . . Beatrix! . . . Thank God!"

And so for a space they stood. Then of a sudden he held her gently off at arm's length.

"Are you glad to see me, sweetheart?" he asked.

"And need I tell you that, dear?" smiling archly.

"At least you might tell me why my knocks were so ignored," he said, smiling back.

"Perchance, sir, I was curious to know how long you would be content to knock and wait."

"You knew it was I?"

She glanced up with a merry sparkle in her grey eyes.

"Stupid!--do you think the door would have been unbolted to another?". . . Then with a woman's quick mind: "And dear Sir John! It is sweet to see that he has his strength again."

"See? When did you see Sir John?"

She led him to the window and drew aside the curtain.

"I saw everything, my lord!" she cried, with a blithesome laugh. "Everything from when you slew the odious Abbot until the fight ended on the stairs; and you can never know, dear, the joy with which I recognized the Stag upon your jupon."

"Surely you did not see the fight in the hall!" he exclaimed.

"Every stroke. I was leaning on the railing just above you."

"And never spoke to me!"

"Because I feared it might be distracting and do you harm. When all was over I hurried hither . . . to wait . . . though I feared Sir John might come with you," and she blushed bewitchingly.

"His heart is young, if his hair be grey," said De Lacy. "He bade me go alone and he would follow presently. And ere he comes, dear, tell me something of your captivity."

"I will try to sketch it briefly, but if I seem to wander, bear in mind that to me it is years--long years--since that fateful evening by the Hermit's Cell." She paused a bit, and then went on: "The attack upon us was so sharply sudden that Sir John had no chance to defend--the villains seemed to rise from the very turf on every side. Almost instantly he was stricken, and as his horse bolted into the forest, a cloak was flung over my head and wound round about my arms, so that I was helpless. Then at a sharp trot, that grew quickly into a canter, we set out. After a while, how long I had no notion, we halted until the leader--he whom I have come to know as Simon Gorges--had freed me from the cloak, apologizing very humbly for being obliged to use it.

"It would likely have been more maidenly had I been tearful and trembling; but, to my shame then, must I admit that I was neither--only curious to know who had been so desperate as to commit an act that would bring the whole of England down upon him. Had I but guessed the long weeks which were to pass and the sore trials they were to bear, there would have been weeping without stint that night as, indeed, there was later; when it began to seem that you and all else on earth had forsaken me."

"Nay, Beatrix; surely there was never such doubt of me?" De Lacy asked.

"Well; not doubt, exactly--only a growing fear that, having searched for me and vainly, you had given me up for dead."

"Yet all the while, methinks your heart told you that there was one, at least, who sought you still," he said, raising her face so he could look into her eyes.

"I fear me, Aymer, you are still given to occasional conceit. . . No, sir--not another kiss until I have finished--and not then, unless you are good and humble. . . When we arrived before this castle the bridge was down and all things ready for our coming. The place was strange to me, and in the faint glimmer of the torches and the uncertain moonlight I could discern no escutcheon above the gateway and no banner on the tower. Nor did I have much time for observing, for they hurried me out of saddle and through the great hall and up to these rooms. Directly, there came to me an old woman who proffered herself as maid.

"'Maid!' I exclaimed. 'Maid for one with no gown but a riding habit!'

"She opened the closet door and showed me apparel in plenty; and when I said I would wear no other woman's clothes, she told me they were made for me and had been waiting for a week.

"'Does this place then deal in abducted maidens?' I demanded; and got for answer that I was the first woman of quality to cross these halls since the lord's mother was laid in yonder chapel.

"Then suddenly my courage left me, and I grew faint and would have fallen had she not led me to the couch. With the morning came fresh strength; and ignoring the loose chamber robe she laid out and urged upon me, I donned my riding skirt and waited. But that day passed; and the second was in darkness when I heard a trumpet call and then much commotion in the courtyard; and presently there were steps in the corridor, followed by a knock upon the door. When I opened it I gave a cry of glad surprise; instead of the abductor, it was Lord Darby who entered smiling and gay.

"I suppose the sharp shift of feeling was too much for my wrought-up nerves, for I began to cry and laugh by turns; and when I came back to calmness, I found him at my feet and holding my hand, and . . . talking foolishness. But my sole idea was to be gone, and I told him so curtly and started for the door. To my amaze, he stepped in front of me, and as I would have slipped by he caught my arm. I tried to fling him off, but unavailingly. Then he gravely led me to a chair and bowed me into it.

"'Bear with me, Countess, I pray you,' he said, and fell to talking foolishness, again.

"But I told him it was quite useless; that the question had been finally settled between us at Windsor, as he ought to know, and prayed him not to weaken my gratitude for the rescue by pressing the subject further. I did it gently as I could, but I saw his anger rising.

"He had been kneeling; now he arose and stood with folded arms, looking down at me.

"'Tell me, Countess,' he said, 'is this your final answer?'

"'It is, Lord Darby,' I replied, and springing by him I tried to make the door. But he was before me and turned the key.

"It were folly to grow violent in my helplessness, and I swept him a mocking curtsy.

"'Will you tell me if I am captive to Lord Darby or to him who rules this castle?' I asked.

"He bowed back at me until his plume almost touched the floor.

"'To both, fair Countess,' he answered, 'for this is Roxford Castle, and I am its lord and your abductor.'

"'What a despicable scoundrel you are!' I exclaimed, trying to hold my voice steady and keep a brave front--though my heart had suddenly become as lead, and I thanked God for my dagger.

"'It is a pity you should view your future lord with so poor esteem,' he returned. 'For here you stay until the bans are tied as tight as priest can knot them.'

"'The Church mates not the quick with a corpse,' I answered.

"He shrugged his shoulders. 'True, Countess,' he replied. 'But one must risk something; and few women go in search of death. Nathless, it is the only way you can escape me now.'

"'You forget the King,' I retorted.

"He gave his sneering laugh. 'Nay, put no hope in Richard,' he said. 'He soon will have enough of his own troubles, and no time to spare for missing maids. When Buckingham, Stanley, and Darby rise and Richmond lands in England, Richard's rule is ended. Then think you the new King will deny me the Countess of Clare for wife--even though she be a bit unwilling? Meanwhile, it is already ordered that you be treated as the chatelaine of Roxford. When next I come it will be to lead you to the altar, by the kind permission of His Gracious Majesty, King Henry.'

"He went out leaving the key in the lock, and after a while he rode away.

"It would be small profit to detail the weeks that followed. I rarely left this room, though I had the freedom of the castle, and was denied nothing save leave either to pass the gates or to communicate with the outer world.

"Then, one day, I chanced to be at yonder window when Simon Gorges rode from out the gate-arch and across the courtyard; his mount staggering from weariness and both plastered with mud and water.

"That night Gorges carried me to Kirkstall Abbey; some one met him near the gate and I was smuggled, blindfolded, through an underground passage to a small room, furnished in all luxury, and with all the toilet trifles of our sex. There I abode, seeing no one save a shrewish looking woman who paid no heed to my questions and ignored me utterly. And on the third evening Lord Darby entered suddenly, and I cried out in sheer surprise and terror.

"'You are not glad to see me, I fear,' he said, with his short, sneering laugh.

"I made no answer. His return could mean only that Richard was dethroned, Henry Tudor, King, and he come to claim me. My hand sought my hidden dagger; and he must have read my mind, for he laughed again--Merciful Mother, how I hate that laugh!--and bade me be easy.

"'I am here before my time,' he said. 'Richard is yet King, and I stand now with him, and am just come from mustering my following at Roxford. He has promised me your hand when the rebellion is ended. Therefore, I have you sure, whoever conquers; for in the battle I shall so play as to be with him who wins.' . . . He drew back the arras--then paused as though the thought had just come: 'Perchance it will interest you to know that a certain Aymer de Lacy has left England and returned to France.'

"'It is a lie--a lie of your black heart!' I cried.

"But he only smiled maliciously and went out. And thank God, since that evening I have never seen him more.

"And now is my tale most told. For a week longer I dwelt in that room, and saw no person but my dumb attendant. At a strange hour on the night of the seventh day, there came a knock at the door and, without staying for permission, a robed figure entered.

"'Be not alarmed, daughter,' it said, as I sprang up. 'I come to take you hence.'

"It was the Abbot Aldam himself, and my anger arose.

"'Since when, Sir Abbot,' I demanded, 'has the Abbey of Kirkstall become the prison for abducted women?'

"'Since it pleased me to assist a friend in need,' he answered.

"Coming near, he scanned my face and figure; and suddenly he put his arms about me and kissed me on the mouth."

De Lacy struck his gauntlets against his greaves.

"God! I am glad I killed him," he gritted.

"So am I, dear," said the Countess--then went on: "I tried to reach my dagger, but Aldam caught my hands and kissed me twice again.

"'Be not so timid,' he laughed. 'There are many of your sex come to this room, and far different from a simple caress is the toll they pay. But you are Darby's, so must I stop with that . . . yet I would it were otherwise,' and his look was so cruelly devouring I fled to the far side of the room.

"There I waited, ready if he sought again to touch me, to sink my dagger in his breast. But he had bound his passions, seemingly, for he sat down and bade me prepare to leave without delay. And gladly did I comply, caring little where I went, so that I left this vile priest's clutches.

"When I had done, he took my bundle and a candle and led the way through a hidden panel in the corner opposite the door. We passed along a narrow corridor, with the roof almost against our heads, and descended a score of stone stairs into a tunnel, deep and foul. How far we went I cannot even guess, but presently there was another ascent of stairs, and after a bit of fumbling, the heavy door swung back and I felt a rush of night air and saw the moonlight.

"Thrusting the Abbot aside, I sprang through the opening . . . and into the arms of Simon Gorges.

"'Your pardon, my lady,' he said; then freed me, but stood within easy reach. He was alone, and beside his horse was another with a woman's saddle. He saw my eyes upon it.

"'We are for Roxford Castle,' he explained.

"'Listen, Gorges,' I said. 'What will you have to take me back to Pontefract? Name your price, man--I am rich and can pay a royal ransom--and you shall enter the King's own guard.'

"He shook his head. 'I have served the Lords of Darby all my life, and my sire and my grandsire before me. No gold nor rank can buy me from my duty. To me you have been committed, pending my lord's return; and so long as I have power to keep you, I must obey.'

"'It is an ignoble task you are assigned,' I began.

"But he would not hear me. 'You forget, my lady, that I am of those you and your station deem ignoble. Yet, none the less, am I ashamed of this business-- though, since my lord commands, it is not for me to question nor delay. Therefore, I pray you, let us mount and be going?'

"I saw he neither could be bought nor persuaded, so I let him lift me into saddle and we set out for Roxford. On the way, I asked why I was being so moved about, though I had no hope he would tell me; and for a while he made no answer. Then, to my surprise, he said: 'What do you think would be the reason?'

"'Can it be that Lord Darby is suspected of my abduction?' I cried. And the hope that had almost died came back to life with a bound.

"'Will you promise never to betray me to him?'

"'I promise,' I answered, all a tremble.

"So he detailed how, as Flat-Nose, he had been sought over all England; how at Sheffield, you, Aymer, had come upon him and Lord Darby together, and had carried his master to the King at Lincoln; how he, himself, escaping, had galloped back and hurried me to Kirkstall, assuming that Roxford would be visited by Richard's order; how Darby had bested you with the King; and how Buckingham's rebellion had sent you and Darby with the army to the South.

"'For the time Roxford will be in no danger of a searching party, so you are being returned there,' he ended. 'But if I know aught of Sir Aymer de Lacy, my lord has not yet won his bride.'

"'Lord Darby told me that the King had promised him my hand--and that Sir Aymer de Lacy had gone to France.' I said.

"He looked at me with a smile.

"'I never contradict my master,' he replied; but there was vast encouragement for me in his tones.

"And I slept that night as I had not for weeks; nor troubled that I lay once more at Roxford Castle. For after my heavy gloom and dark despair, even the smallest hope was mountain size and promised sure release. And so I waited; confident and strong. Last evening near sundown the Abbot Aldam came; and as I saw him, all bedraggled, cross the courtyard on foot and unattended, I felt that my deliverance was near. No one of his rank and station would travel so, except his life were jeopardized, and I cried out in joy at his undoing. Then I sent for Gorges and learned the Abbot's tale--that he had escaped by the passage used for me, and that you were even then at Kirkstall.

"'To-morrow's sun will see Sir Aymer before the barbican, my lady,' he said. 'And though we shall hold the castle to the final stroke, yet it will be a losing fight;

204 *Beatrix of Clare*

for we are few in number, and when one falls there will not be another to step into his place. And so will it be that you have seen the last of Simon Gorges, whose greatest shame is to have been your jailer.'

"He bowed awkwardly and was going when I stopped him.

"'Your lord and the Abbot of Kirkstall can learn courtesy and chivalry from you,' I said. 'But what profit can your death be to Lord Darby? When I am found here, his end is sure. So when the last hope is gone--the castle lost--promise me that if quarter be offered, you will not let it pass; take your life and you shall have service under me.'

"He was embarrassed by my praise and earnestness. 'Your ladyship is gracious; yet must I think upon the matter,' he stammered; and hurried out as though afraid I might persuade him more.

"Therefore, dear, as on the stairway I heard him accept mercy on my word, you will grant it to him?"

"He is your prisoner, sweetheart, and we will have him here," said Aymer. "You are his judge."

Presently, with helmet in hand and bladeless scabbard by his side, but still in his harness dinted and hacked in the recent fight, Gorges appeared; and halting at the threshold, bowed to the Countess; then saluting the Knight with formal motion, stood at attention.

"Flat-Nose--for by that name I know you best," said De Lacy, "you yielded prisoner to the Countess of Clare. Advance and receive your sentence."

Gorges came forward and knelt at her feet in silence.

"Simon," said Beatrix, "you were kind to me when most I needed kindness; will you now take your life from me in earnest of my gratitude?"

"That will I, my lady, and gladly," Gorges answered frankly and at once.

"And will you wear the badge of Clare and be my chief retainer?"

The soldier hesitated and glanced uncertainly at De Lacy.

"You are bound no longer to Lord Darby's service," Sir Aymer admonished. "He is traitor to the King, and will die on the block within the month."

The Gorges raised the hem of the Countess' gown and kissed it; and taking her hand placed it on his head.

"I am your man," he said. "Henceforth do with me as to you may seem good."

XXVI
THE JUDGMENT OF THE KING

In the Painted Chamber of the Palace of Westminster the Court was gathered. Through the great long room, amid the soft light of scores upon scores of candles, moved the gorgeously attired throng--waiting for the King whose usual hour of entrance was long since past. And curiosity was rife, and uneasiness in the atmosphere.

For the times were sadly unsettled; and among those who had for an instant hesitated between Tudor and Plantagenet--and their number was not small--there was grave anxiety, lest their faint loyalty had come to Richard's ears. And to such it was scarce a comforting reflection that, in Exeter, the headsman had just done his grim work upon St. Leger; albeit he were husband of the King's own sister. If he were condemned for treason, even though it were open and notorious, who that were tainted ever so slightly were likely to be spared?

But all the while, the ladies laughed and chatted gayly, and the knights bowed and smiled and answered back in kind; and the throng as a whole seemed to be without a shred of care.

At one group of young matrons there was much merriment; and as Lord Darby chanced to stroll by, they hailed him banteringly, inviting him to join them. But he declined with sarcastic pleasantry.

"Fie, sir! It was not a gallant speech," cried the Lady Strange, with a toss of her golden locks; "and if your tongue be as acid always, there is small wonder that rumor gave another precedence in the favor of the Countess of Clare."

Darby halted and bowed low and long--very low and very long.

"Your ladyship does me too much honor," he said, with well assumed humility, "in even thinking of the Countess of Clare and my poor self in the same moment."

"Doubtless I do--since your devotion was too feeble even to send you to her rescue."

"And now you do me deep injustice; I sought the Countess from the day following the abduction until all hope was gone. Methinks alas! she has long since been gathered with the Saints."

The Countess of Ware--the Lady Mary Percy that was--laughed with gibing intonation.

"There is one, at least, who has not ceased to hope and to search," she said.

"And has been as successful as myself," he retorted, nor hid the sneer.

"But if he find her?"

Darby shrugged his shoulders. "Think you there is recognition in the spirit world?"

"Then you actually believe the Countess dead?" the Lady Lovel asked.

"Beyond all question, madam. It is near three months since the abduction and a trace of her has yet to be discovered;" and was going on when the Countess of Ware stopped him.

"Can you tell us what detains the King?" she asked.

"I have no notion," he replied. "I saw him an hour or so ago and he was in the best of health and humor."

"Your news is stale," she laughed; "a King's humor an hour old is very ancient."

"True," said Darby, "true indeed, yet here comes one who can doubtless answer fittingly. . . Sir Ralph, what delays His Majesty?"

But De Wilton looked him straight in the face, and with never a word in reply, passed on.

And at that moment the Black Rod entered, and behind him came the King.

Save for the crimson lining of his short gown, he was clad in white from head to foot, an ivory boar with eyes of rubies and tusks of sapphires, pinned the feather in his bonnet, about his neck hung the George, and his only weapon was the diamond hilted dagger at his girdle. With it he toyed, looking neither to the right nor to the left, nor yet to the front; but rather at the mental picture of one engrossed in thought.

Slowly and with the impressive dignity that was the natural heritage of the Plantagenets, he mounted the steps to the Throne and turning faced his Court; and all bowed low, and then in silence waited, while his dark eyes searched them through.

"You may take your places, my Lord Cardinal and Lord Chancellor," he said.

"Her Majesty will not join us until later."

Bowing in response, the Archbishop of Canterbury and the Bishop of Lincoln assumed their stools on the third step of the dais; and the crowd, released from the ceremonial calm, began to buzz softly with conversation, though without taking eye from the King. And they turned quickly dumb again as Richard raised his hand.

"We will have to beg your kind indulgences if, for a while, we delay the games and the dance," he said. "It is a most unhappy chance upon this evening of all others, when we are about to celebrate our safe return from rebellious war, that there has come to us evidences of foulest crime and darkest treason by one high in rank and station, and who is, even now, within sound of my voice."

Over the Court ran a shiver of apprehension; and men eyed one another with misgiving and drew within themselves; while the women, with faces suddenly gone white and lips a tremble, clutched the hands of those most dear, as though to shield them from the doom about to fall. For green in the memory was Hastings, and Rivers, and Buckingham, and St. Leger, and the stern suddenness of their taking off.

"Perchance, it were more suitable," the King went on, "that matters of such import be deferred to the quiet of the council chamber and the Court of the Lord High Steward; and in particular, that there should be none of the gentler sex in presence. Yet for reasons which to me seem adequate and proper, I have determined otherwise. He who is charged with these crimes is now among you; and by you, my lords and my ladies, shall he be adjudged. Stand forth, Henry, Lord Darby of Roxford."

The gasp that soughed through the room as Richard spoke the name was far more of relief than of wonder, and instantly all eyes sought the accused.

And he met them with a shrug of indifference and a smiling face. And down the aisle that opened to him he went--debonair and easy--until he stood before the Throne. There he bent knee for an instant; then, erect and unruffled, he looked the King defiantly in the eye.

"Here stand I to answer," he said. "Let the charges be preferred."

Richard turned to the Black Rod.

"Summon the accusers," he ordered.

As the Usher backed from the room, there arose a hissing of whispers that changed sharply to exclamations of surprise as in formal tones he heralded:

"Sir John de Bury! Sir Aymer de Lacy!"

The elder Knight leaned on the other's arm as they advanced; but dropped it at the Throne and both made deep obeisance. An impatient glance from the King brought instant quiet.

"Sir John de Bury and Sir Aymer de Lacy," he, said, "you have made certain grave accusations touching Henry, Lord Darby of Roxford. He stands here now to answer. Speak, therefore, in turn."

De Bury stepped forward and faced Darby, who met him with folded arms and scornful front.

"I charge Henry, Lord Darby," he said, "with having abducted and held prisoner, in his castle of Roxford and elsewhere, my niece, the Lady Beatrix de Beaumont, Countess of Clare."

A cry of amazement burst from the Court, but Richard silenced it with a gesture.

"You have heard, my lord," he said. "What is your plea?"

"Not guilty, Sire."

At a nod from the King, De Lacy took place beside Sir John.

"I charge Henry, Lord Darby of Roxford," he cried, "with high treason, in that he aided and a betted the Duke of Buckingham in his late rebellion, and stood prepared to betray his Sovereign on the field of battle."

"You hear, my lord," said the King. "What is your plea?"

But Darby did not answer; and for a while Richard watched him curiously, as with half-bared dagger and lips drawn back in rage, he glowered upon De Lacy, forgetful of all things save his hate. And so imminent seemed the danger, that Aymer put hand to his own poniard and fell into the posture to receive attack. And doubtless there, before the Throne itself, would these two men have fought to the death for very lust of the other's blood, had not the clear, stern voice of the King aroused them, like cold water in a sleeping face.

"Do you not hear, Lord Darby? We await your plea!"

"Not guilty," Darby answered in tones husky with rage. "And I demand wager of battle, as against the foul charge of this foreign slanderer and liar."

"I pray you, my Liege, to grant it to the traitor," said De Lacy eagerly.

But Richard waved him back. "The wager is refused. By the evidence shall the judgment be. Proceed, Sir Aymer de Lacy, we will hear you first."

The Knight drew a packet from his doublet.

"I offer herewith," he said, "the dying statement of Henry Stafford, late Duke of Buckingham, touching the part taken in his rebellion by the accused."

"I object to it!" Darby cried.

"For what reason?"

"Because its execution has not been proven; and because, even if genuine, it is incompetent as being by a condemned traitor."

"Let me see the paper," said the King. . . "It is regular, on its face--signed by Stafford under his own seal and attested by Sir Richard Ratcliffe and Sir John Kendale. Do you wish their testimony?"

Lord Darby bowed.

"Sir Richard Ratcliffe and Sir John Kendale," the King said, as they stood forth, "do you each testify on honor that these are your respective signatures, and that you saw Henry Stafford sign and affix his seal hereto?"

"We do, upon our knightly honor," they replied.

"It would appear, Sir John, that the body of this document is in your handwriting."

"It is, Your Majesty. I wrote it at request of Stafford and at his dictation."

"Where?"

"In his room in the Blue Boar Inn in the town of Salisbury."

"When?"

"On the afternoon of the second day of November last. When the Duke had signed it he went direct to execution."

"And this document?" the King questioned.

"Was kept by me until presented to Your Majesty that same evening; and by your direction deposited among your private papers, whence I took it a few minutes since to give to Sir Aymer de Lacy."

Another murmur of astonishment went up from the Court, but died quickly under Richard's glance.

"Methinks, my lord," he said addressing Darby, "the paper has been sufficiently proven and is competent as a dying declaration of a co-conspirator. Therefore, we admit it. . . Read it, my Lord Chancellor."

The Bishop arose and spreading out the parchment began:

"I, Henry Stafford, Duke of Buckingham, being about to suffer on the block (which even now stands ready before my window) do hereby make, publish and declare this as and for my dying declaration; trusting that thereby I may be of service to one who, though my foe in war, has been my friend in peaceful days, and now, as well, when all others have forsaken and betrayed me--and may, at the same time, bring to justice a pair of caitiffs. By these presents, do I denounce and proclaim Henry, Lord Darby, and John Morton, ycleped Bishop of Ely, as perjured and forsworn traitors to Richard, King of England, as well as betrayers of their plighted faith to me. Further, do I hereby admonish Richard Plantagenet that this Darby (whom I have but this hour observed among his forces in this town) and the aforesaid priest, Morton, are the instigators of my rebellion; that these two aided me in all the scheming of the plot; that to Darby was assigned the proclaiming of Henry Tudor in Yorkshire and the North; and that, within one week of the day set for the rising, he was at Brecknock and completed the final details. That he was a double traitor I knew not until I saw him here in the courtyard this day. Also, I denounce----"

"Stay, my Lord Bishop!" the King interjected. "Read no further for the present."

"Since when, I pray, Sire, has it become the law of England to admit only such part of a paper as may suit the prosecution's plan?" Darby cried.

"You wish it read entire?" Richard asked.

"Marry, that I do. Since I am already judged, it can work me no hurt."

Richard looked at him fixedly. "You are overbold, sirrah!"

"Those who speak truth to a King must needs be so," was the curt rejoinder.

"Steady your tongue, Lord Darby," said Richard sternly, "else may the Tower teach you respect for England's King."

"Think you, then, I should find the young Fifth Edward there------alive?" sneered Darby.

For a moment, Richard's eyes flashed like sparks springing from the clashing of two angry swords. Then he smiled; and the smile was more ominous than the sparks.

"Be easy, sir; the remainder of the declaration shall be read in season," he said very quietly. "But first, will you reply now to Stafford's allegation, or shall we proceed with Sir John de Bury's charge?"

If this were all the evidence of treason Darby was in small danger and it behooved him to change his bearing.

"I did Your Majesty grave wrong in presuming you had prejudged me," he said with a frank smile, "for well I know that on such shallow falsehoods no man could ever be condemned. And here do I place my own knightly word against the traitor Buckingham's; and do specifically deny all that has been read by the Lord Chancellor. And further, do I solemnly affirm that neither by voice nor deed have I been recreant to my oath of allegiance, nor false to you. Moreover, Sire, my very action in the rebellion attests my truth: Did I not hasten to join your army with all the force at my disposal? Have I not been ever honest and faithful?"

And with arms folded proudly on his breast, he waited for the acquittance that seemed to be his due.

"As the case stands now, it would be our duty and our pleasure to pronounce you guiltless," Richard replied. "But it so chances that there is still another witness on the charge of treason, whose testimony deals also with the abduction. Wherefore, we shall be obliged to mingle somewhat the two matters and so to withhold our judgment until the trial is ended and all the evidence is in. . . My Lord Chancellor, proceed with the reading."

The Bishop resumed:

"Also, I denounce the said Henry, Lord Darby, as the abductor of the Countess of Clare whom, he told me, he by pre-arrangement with her had seized one night in September and had carried to his castle--she loving him, but being coerced by the King into marrying another. And I, believing him, promised that he should wed her and receive her lands and title when Henry Tudor became King. Only to-day did I learn that he had taken the maid by force, and that his story of her love for him was pure falsehood. And it gratifies me much that, perchance, these words may aid in the lady's rescue and her dastardly abductor's punishment. In testimony to the truth whereof, and in full appreciation of impending death, I hereunto set my hand and affix my seal of the Swan. Given at the Inn of the Blue Boar, in the town of Salisbury, this second day of November, in the year of Grace 1483."

The Chancellor folded the parchment. "I have finished, Sire," he said.

"Now, Lord Darby, you have had your wish and heard the statement full and entire," the King admonished. "If it has not improved your case, the next witness, methinks, is scarce likely to better it."

At a sign, the Black Rod again withdrew, and once more there was profoundest silence; and upon the doorway in the corner all eyes were turned, save those of the accused. He stood stolid and defiant glaring at De Lacy. Then a cry went up, and after it came cheers and loud applause. Nor did Richard offer to rebuke it, but himself leaned forward smiling.

Aroused at this, Lord Darby glanced around--and suddenly his face went pale, and red, and pale again; and he staggered slightly, passing his hand across his forehead in a dazed-like way. For there, advancing toward the Throne, hand in hand with the Queen, was the woman he thought securely hid in far distant Roxford Castle.

Then sharp panic seized him and he turned to flee.

But close behind him was the wall of courtiers, and beyond flashed the halberds of the guard. Straightway, the terror passed, and he was again the cool soldier, contemptuous and indifferent--though he saw full well the case would go against him and that death was drawing near. And so he waited, utterly forgotten for the moment, amid the gladsome welcome for the Countess of Clare, whom all long since had given up for dead.

At the foot of the dais Beatrix stopped, but the Queen would not have it so, and with gentle insistence she drew her up the steps. And Richard met them half way, and with him on one side and the Queen on the other, she stood before the Court.

Then the King raised his hand for silence.

"Behold!" he said, "the lost Lady of Clare!" and kissed her finger tips, while the cheers swelled forth afresh.

She curtsied low in response, and sought to descend to her place. But Richard detained her.

"Fair Countess," he said, "the Lord Darby stands here accused of your abduction, and of complicity in the late rebellion; we have sent for you to testify your knowledge in these matters."

Beatrix's face grew grave, and for a little while she made no answer.

"I implore you, Sire, relieve me from the duty," she said. "Safe now and freed from my captor's power, I want never to look upon him nor to speak his name, being well content to let God in His Providence punish the crime against me."

"Your words are earnest of your gracious heart," said the King. "But for the honor and name of fair England, it may not be settled so. If Lord Darby be guilty, then must he suffer punishment, were it for no other reason than that our laws demand it. If he be innocent, it is his bounden right to receive full acquittance here in the presence of those before whom he has been arraigned. Speak! as your Sovereign I command. Who was your abductor?"

The Countess clasped her hands before her and hesitated. Then for the first time, she let her eyes rest upon Darby; and the sight of him seemed to nerve her; and she raised her arm and pointed at him with accusing finger, while her voice rang out full and strong:

"There he stands--Lord Darby of Roxford! By his orders I was seized and carried to his castle, where he came and sought first to persuade, and then to force me into marriage with him. And when I scorned him, he swore with words insulting he would hold me prisoner until he and Buckingham had made a King of Henry Tudor, when he would wed me whether I wished or no. Later it seems he somewhat changed his plans, and instead of joining openly with Henry he remained with you, Sire; yet with full intention, as he, himself, assured me, to cleave to whatever side was winning in the battle. So was he sure, he said, to be in favor with whomever wore the crown. Of all these crimes and treasons is yonder false lord guilty. And had not Sir John De Bury and Sir Aymer de Lacy carried by storm his Castle of Roxford, I would yet be a prisoner to him."

And the very thought brought quick reaction and her courage ebbed, and turning her back upon the Court, she covered her face with her hands.

Through the swift denunciation Lord Darby had stood with impassive face and eyes that never flinched, looking straight at the Countess; then he shifted his glance to the King. He knew that the words just uttered had confirmed his doom--that in all that throng there was no friend for him, nor even one to do him favor. A score of lies or a flood of denials would be unavailing to win so much as a glance of sympathy. He had essayed a game with Destiny; he had lost and must pay penalty--and he never doubted what that penalty would be with Richard Plantagenet his judge. But at least, he would wring a cry of pain from the heart of his enemy--and he smiled and waited.

Then the King spoke: "We will hear you now, Lord Darby."

"I thank Your Gracious Majesty for the stern impartialness of this trial," he said with biting sarcasm. "It was planned as skillfully as was a certain other in the White Tower, adown the Thames, when Hastings was the victim"--and he gave his sneering laugh; and then repeated it, as he remarked the shudder it brought to the Countess. "Nathless I am not whimpering. I have been rash; and rashness is justified only by success. For I did abduct the Countess of Clare, and have her carried to my Castle of Roxford. So much is truth." Then he faced Sir Aymer de Lacy and went on with a malevolent smile. "But she was not a prisoner there, nor did I take her against her wish. She went by prearrangement, and remained with me of her own free will. I thought she loved me, and believed her protestations of loathing for the upstart De Lacy who, she said, was pursuing her with his suit, And when she begged me to take her with me and risk your Majesty's anger, I yielded; and to the end that we might wed, I did embark, in the plottings of the Duke of Buckingham, upon his engagement, for the Tudor Henry, that our union would be sanctioned. Later, when the lady seemed so happy with me at Roxford, methought the marriage could bide a bit, and so resolved to wait until the battle to choose between Plantagenet and Tudor. Having the girl, I could then get the estates as payment of my service to the victor. But it would seem I risked too much upon the lady's love. For while I was at the wars, either she tired of me and so deserted Roxford, or having been found there by De Bury and the Frenchman, as she says, she deemed it wise to play the innocent and wronged maiden held in durance by her foul abductor. Leastwise, whoso desires her now is welcome to her," and he laughed again.

Then could De Lacy endure it no longer; and casting off De Bury's restraining arm, he flashed forth his dagger and sprang toward Darby. But as he leaped Sir Richard Ratcliffe caught him round the neck and held him for the space that was needful for him to gather back his wits.

"For God's sake, man, be calm!" he said, as he loosed him. "Let Richard deal with him."

And the Countess, as Darby's vile insinuations reached her ears, drew herself up and gently putting aside the Queen, turned and faced him. And her mouth set hard, and her fingers clenched her palms convulsively. So, she heard him to the end, proudly and defiantly; and when he had done, she raised her hand and pointed at him once again.

"Though I am a woman," she exclaimed, "here do I tell you, Lord Darby, you lie in your throat!"

"Aye, my lady! that he does," a strange voice called; and from the doorway strode Simon Gorges, the anger on his ugly face flaming red as the hair above it.

"May I speak, Sire?" he demanded, halting before the Throne and saluting the King in brusque, soldier fashion.

"Say on, my man," said Richard.

"Then hear you all the truth, touching this dirty business," he cried loudly. "I am Flat-Nose. At Lord Darby's order, I waylaid and seized by force the Countess of Clare, and carried her to Roxford Castle. Never for one moment went she of her own accord, and never for one moment stayed she willingly. She was prisoner there; ever watched and guarded, and not allowed outside the walls. In all the weeks she was there Lord Darby saw her only once. And when he spoke to her of love, she scorned and lashed him so with words methought he sure would kill her, for I was just outside the door and heard it all."

"Truly, Sire, you have arranged an entertainment more effective than I had thought even your deep brain could scheme," Darby sneered, as Gorges paused for breath. . . "What was your price, Simon? It should have been a goodly one."

"Measure him not by your standard, my fair lord," said the King. "He held your castle until none but him was left; and even then yielded not to his assailants, but only to the Countess."

"And upon the strict engagement that I should not be made to bear evidence against you," Flat-Nose added. "But even a rough man-at-arms would be thrice shamed to hear a woman so traduced and not speak in her favor. Therefore, my lord, I, too, say you lie."

But Darby only shrugged his shoulders and bowed to the Countess.

"Your ladyship is irresistible," he said, "since you have wiles for both the master and the man."

"Shame! Shame!" exclaimed the grey-haired Norfolk, and the whole throng joined in the cry.

Then forth stepped Sir Aymer de Lacy.

"I pray you, my liege," said he, "grant me leave to avenge upon the body of yonder lord the wrongs the Countess of Clare has suffered."

Beatrix made a sharp gesture of dissent and turned to the King appealingly.

With a smile he reassured her.

"Not so, De Lacy," he said kindly. "We do not risk our faithful subjects in combat with a confessed traitor. There are those appointed who care for such as he. . . Nay, sir, urge me not--it is altogether useless." And he motioned Aymer back to his place.

Then he faced Lord Darby, who met him with a careless smile.

"Out of your own mouth have you condemned yourself," he said. "And there is now no need for verdict by your Peers. It remains but to pass upon you the judgment due your crimes. And first: for your foul wrong to the Countess of Clare and through her, to all womankind, here, in her presence and before all the Court, you shall be degraded."

Darby's face flushed and he took a quick step backward, like one stricken by a sudden blow. But he made no reply, save from his angry eyes.

"What say you, Flat-Nose; will you execute the office?" the King asked.

"And it please you, Sire, I cannot do such shame upon my former master," Gorges answered bluntly.

"It does please me well, sirrah; though truly your face belies your heart. . . What, ho! the guard! . . . Let the under-officer come forward."

In a moment the tall form of Raynor Royk stalked out from the throng, and halting in the open he raised his halberd in salute.

"Hew me off the spurs from yonder fellow," the King ordered, with a move of his hand toward the condemned.

Saluting again, the old soldier strode over and with two sharp blows of his weapon struck the golden insignia of Knighthood from Lord Darby's heels.

Nor did Darby make resistance; but with arms folded on his breast he suffered it to be done, though his bosom heaved in the fierce struggle to be calm, and the flush left his face and it grew gray and drawn, and bitter agony looked out from his eyes. And many turned away their heads. And on the dais the Countess had faced about, and the Queen and she were softly weeping.

Lifting the spurs from the pavement Raynor Royk held them up.

"The order is executed, Sire," he said.

"Fling them into the ditch," the King commanded. "They, too, are stained with dishonor."

Then in tones cold and passionless, and wherein there was no shade of mercy, he went on: "And now, Henry Darby--for Lord and Knight you are no longer--you have suffered penalty for one crime, hear the judgment for the other: As false to your oath of fealty and traitor to your King, the sentence is that you be taken hence to Tyburn and there hanged by the neck until dead--and may the Lord Omnipotent have pity on your soul. Remove him."

"Come," said Raynor Royk, and led him through the crowd, which drew shudderingly aside to give him passage.

And Darby--stunned by the stern justice that had sent him to die a common felon on Tyburn Tree, instead of as a Lord and Peer of England, on the block on Tower Hill--went with dazed brain and silently; and ere his faculties returned, he was among the guards in the rear. Then with a sudden twist he turned about and shouted with all his voice:

"Long live Henry Tudor!"

It was his last defiance. The next instant he was dragged outside and the doors swung shut behind him; while from all the Court went up the answering cry:

"Long live Plantagenet! God save the King!"

And when silence came the Countess and De Lacy were gone.

"So," said Sir Aymer, as Beatrix and he reached the quiet of the Queen's apartments, "your troubles end--the sun shines bright again."

The Countess sank into a chair and drew him on the arm beside her.

"My troubles ended when you crossed the courtyard of Roxford," she replied, taking his hand in both her own, "but yours have not begun."

"Wherefore, sweetheart?" he asked. "I thought mine, too, had ended there."

"No," with a shake of the ruddy head . . . "no. . . Your heaviest troubles are yet to come."

He looked at her doubtfully. . . "And when do they begin?"

She fell to toying with her rings and drawing figures on her gown.

"That is for you to choose," she said, with a side-long glance. . . "Next year, may be, . . . to-morrow, if you wish."

"You mean------?" he cried.

She sprang away with a merry laugh--then came slowly back to him.

"I mean, my lord, they will begin . . . when you are Earl of Clare."

THE END

The Codes Of Hammurabi And Moses
W. W. Davies

The discovery of the Hammurabi Code is one of the greatest achievements of archaeology, and is of paramount interest, not only to the student of the Bible, but also to all those interested in ancient history...

Religion   **ISBN:** *1-59462-338-4*

QTY

Pages:132
MSRP $12.95

The Theory of Moral Sentiments
Adam Smith

This work from 1749. contains original theories of conscience amd moral judgment and it is the foundation for systemof morals.

Philosophy   ISBN: *1-59462-777-0*

QTY

Pages:536
MSRP $19.95

Jessica's First Prayer
Hesba Stretton

In a screened and secluded corner of one of the many railway-bridges which span the streets of London there could be seen a few years ago, from five o'clock every morning until half past eight, a tidily set-out coffee-stall, consisting of a trestle and board, upon which stood two large tin cans, with a small fire of charcoal burning under each so as to keep the coffee boiling during the early hours of the morning when the work-people were thronging into the city on their way to their daily toil...

Childrens   ISBN: *1-59462-373-2*

QTY

Pages:84
MSRP $9.95

My Life and Work
Henry Ford

Henry Ford revolutionized the world with his implementation of mass production for the Model T automobile. Gain valuable business insight into his life and work with his own auto-biography... "We have only started on our development of our country we have not as yet, with all our talk of wonderful progress, done more than scratch the surface. The progress has been wonderful enough but..."

Biographies/   ISBN: *1-59462-198-5*

QTY

Pages:300
MSRP $21.95

The Art of Cross-Examination
Francis Wellman

QTY

I presume it is the experience of every author, after his first book is published upon an important subject, to be almost overwhelmed with a wealth of ideas and illustrations which could readily have been included in his book, and which to his own mind, at least, seem to make a second edition inevitable. Such certainly was the case with me; and when the first edition had reached its sixth impression in five months, I rejoiced to learn that it seemed to my publishers that the book had met with a sufficiently favorable reception to justify a second and considerably enlarged edition. ...

Pages:412

Reference **ISBN:** *1-59462-647-2* *MSRP $19.95*

On the Duty of Civil Disobedience
Henry David Thoreau

QTY

Thoreau wrote his famous essay, On the Duty of Civil Disobedience, as a protest against an unjust but popular war and the immoral but popular institution of slave-owning. He did more than write—he declined to pay his taxes, and was hauled off to gaol in consequence. Who can say how much this refusal of his hastened the end of the war and of slavery ?

Law **ISBN:** *1-59462-747-9* **Pages:48**

MSRP $7.45

Dream Psychology Psychoanalysis for Beginners
Sigmund Freud

QTY

Sigmund Freud, born Sigismund Schlomo Freud (May 6, 1856 - September 23, 1939), was a Jewish-Austrian neurologist and psychiatrist who co-founded the psychoanalytic school of psychology. Freud is best known for his theories of the unconscious mind, especially involving the mechanism of repression; his redefinition of sexual desire as mobile and directed towards a wide variety of objects; and his therapeutic techniques, especially his understanding of transference in the therapeutic relationship and the presumed value of dreams as sources of insight into unconscious desires.

Pages:196

Psychology **ISBN:** *1-59462-905-6* *MSRP $15.45*

The Miracle of Right Thought
Orison Swett Marden

QTY

Believe with all of your heart that you will do what you were made to do. When the mind has once formed the habit of holding cheerful, happy, prosperous pictures, it will not be easy to form the opposite habit. It does not matter how improbable or how far away this realization may see, or how dark the prospects may be, if we visualize them as best we can, as vividly as possible, hold tenaciously to them and vigorously struggle to attain them, they will gradually become actualized, realized in the life. But a desire, a longing without endeavor, a yearning abandoned or held indifferently will vanish without realization.

Pages:360

Self Help **ISBN:** *1-59462-644-8* *MSRP $25.45*

QTY

☐ **The Rosicrucian Cosmo-Conception Mystic Christianity** *by Max Heindel*   ISBN: *1-59462-188-8*   **$38.95**
The Rosicrucian Cosmo-conception is not dogmatic, neither does it appeal to any other authority than the reason of the student. It is: not controversial, but is: sent forth in the, hope that it may help to clear...   New Age/Religion Pages 646

☐ **Abandonment To Divine Providence** *by Jean-Pierre de Caussade*   ISBN: *1-59462-228-0*   **$25.95**
"The Rev. Jean Pierre de Caussade was one of the most remarkable spiritual writers of the Society of Jesus in France in the 18th Century. His death took place at Toulouse in 1751. His works have gone through many editions and have been republished...   Inspirational/Religion Pages 400

☐ **Mental Chemistry** *by Charles Haanel*   ISBN: *1-59462-192-6*   **$23.95**
Mental Chemistry allows the change of material conditions by combining and appropriately utilizing the power of the mind. Much like applied chemistry creates something new and unique out of careful combinations of chemicals the mastery of mental chemistry...   New Age Pages 354

☐ **The Letters of Robert Browning and Elizabeth Barret Barrett 1845-1846 vol II**   ISBN: *1-59462-193-4*   **$35.95**
by Robert Browning and Elizabeth Barrett   Biographies Pages 596

☐ **Gleanings In Genesis (volume I)** *by Arthur W. Pink*   ISBN: *1-59462-130-6*   **$27.45**
Appropriately has Genesis been termed "the seed plot of the Bible" for in it we have, in germ form, almost all of the great doctrines which are afterwards fully developed in the books of Scripture which follow...   Religion/Inspirational Pages 420

☐ **The Master Key** *by L. W. de Laurence*   ISBN: *1-59462-001-6*   **$30.95**
In no branch of human knowledge has there been a more lively increase of the spirit of research during the past few years than in the study of Psychology, Concentration and Mental Discipline. The requests for authentic lessons in Thought Control, Mental Discipline and...   New Age/Business Pages 422

☐ **The Lesser Key Of Solomon Goetia** *by L. W. de Laurence*   ISBN: *1-59462-092-X*   **$9.95**
This translation of the first book of the "Lemegton" which is now for the first time made accessible to students of Talismanic Magic was done, after careful collation and edition, from numerous Ancient Manuscripts in Hebrew, Latin, and French...   New Age/Occult Pages 92

☐ **Rubaiyat Of Omar Khayyam** *by Edward Fitzgerald*   ISBN:*1-59462-332-5*   **$13.95**
Edward Fitzgerald, whom the world has already learned, in spite of his own efforts to remain within the shadow of anonymity, to look upon as one of the rarest poets of the century, was born at Bredfield, in Suffolk, on the 31st of March, 1809. He was the third son of John Purcell...   Music Pages 172

☐ **Ancient Law** *by Henry Maine*   ISBN: *1-59462-128-4*   **$29.95**
The chief object of the following pages is to indicate some of the earliest ideas of mankind, as they are reflected in Ancient Law, and to point out the relation of those ideas to modern thought.   Religiom/History Pages 452

☐ **Far-Away Stories** *by William J. Locke*   ISBN: *1-59462-129-2*   **$19.45**
"Good wine needs no bush, but a collection of mixed vintages does. And this book is just such a collection. Some of the stories I do not want to remain buried for ever in the museum files of dead magazine-numbers an author's not unpardonable vanity..."   Fiction Pages 272

☐ **Life of David Crockett** *by David Crockett*   ISBN: *1-59462-250-7*   **$27.45**
"Colonel David Crockett was one of the most remarkable men of the times in which he lived. Born in humble life, but gifted with a strong will, an indomitable courage, and unremitting perseverance...   Biographies/New Age Pages 424

☐ **Lip-Reading** *by Edward Nitchie*   ISBN: *1-59462-206-X*   **$25.95**
Edward B. Nitchie, founder of the New York School for the Hard of Hearing, now the Nitchie School of Lip-Reading, Inc, wrote "LIP-READING Principles and Practice". The development and perfecting of this meritorious work on lip-reading was an undertaking...   How-to Pages 400

☐ **A Handbook of Suggestive Therapeutics, Applied Hypnotism, Psychic Science**   ISBN: *1-59462-214-0*   **$24.95**
by Henry Munro   Health/New Age/Health/Self-help Pages 376

☐ **A Doll's House: and Two Other Plays** *by Henrik Ibsen*   ISBN: *1-59462-112-8*   **$19.95**
Henrik Ibsen created this classic when in revolutionary 1848 Rome. Introducing some striking concepts in playwriting for the realist genre, this play has been studied the world over.   Fiction/Classics/Plays 308

☐ **The Light of Asia** *by sir Edwin Arnold*   ISBN: *1-59462-204-3*   **$13.95**
In this poetic masterpiece, Edwin Arnold describes the life and teachings of Buddha. The man who was to become known as Buddha to the world was born as Prince Gautama of India but he rejected the worldly riches and abandoned the reigns of power when...   Religion/History/Biographies Pages 170

☐ **The Complete Works of Guy de Maupassant** *by Guy de Maupassant*   ISBN: *1-59462-157-8*   **$16.95**
"For days and days, nights and nights, I had dreamed of that first kiss which was to consecrate our engagement, and I knew not on what spot I should put my lips..."   Fiction/Classics Pages 240

☐ **The Art of Cross-Examination** *by Francis L. Wellman*   ISBN: *1-59462-309-0*   **$26.95**
Written by a renowned trial lawyer, Wellman imparts his experience and uses case studies to explain how to use psychology to extract desired information through questioning.   How-to/Science/Reference Pages 408

☐ **Answered or Unanswered?** *by Louisa Vaughan*   ISBN: *1-59462-248-5*   **$10.95**
Miracles of Faith in China   Religion Pages 112

☐ **The Edinburgh Lectures on Mental Science (1909)** *by Thomas*   ISBN: *1-59462-008-3*   **$11.95**
This book contains the substance of a course of lectures recently given by the writer in the Queen Street Hall, Edinburgh. Its purpose is to indicate the Natural Principles governing the relation between Mental Action and Material Conditions...   New Age/Psychology Pages 148

☐ **Ayesha** *by H. Rider Haggard*   ISBN: *1-59462-301-5*   **$24.95**
Verily and indeed it is the unexpected that happens! Probably if there was one person upon the earth from whom the Editor of this, and of a certain previous history, did not expect to hear again...   Classics Pages 380

☐ **Ayala's Angel** *by Anthony Trollope*   ISBN: *1-59462-352-X*   **$29.95**
The two girls were both pretty, but Lucy who was twenty-one who supposed to be simple and comparatively unattractive, whereas Ayala was credited, as her Bombwhat romantic name might show, with poetic charm and a taste for romance. Ayala when her father died was nineteen...   Fiction Pages 484

☐ **The American Commonwealth** *by James Bryce*   ISBN: *1-59462-286-8*   **$34.45**
An interpretation of American democratic political theory. It examines political mechanics and society from the perspective of Scotsman James Bryce   Politics Pages 572

☐ **Stories of the Pilgrims** *by Margaret P. Pumphrey*   ISBN: *1-59462-116-0*   **$17.95**
This book explores pilgrims religious oppression in England as well as their escape to Holland and eventual crossing to America on the Mayflower, and their early days in New England...   History Pages 268

www.bookjungle.com *email: sales@bookjungle.com fax: 630-214-0564 mail: Book Jungle PO Box 2226 Champaign, IL 61825*

QTY

The Fasting Cure *by Sinclair Upton*   ISBN: *1-59462-222-1*   **$13.95**
In the Cosmopolitan Magazine for May, 1910, and in the Contemporary Review (London) for April, 1910, I published an article dealing with my experiences in fasting. I have written a great many magazine articles, but never one which attracted so much attention... New Age/Self Help/Health Pages 164

☐

Hebrew Astrology *by Sepharial*   ISBN: *1-59462-308-2*   **$13.45**
In these days of advanced thinking it is a matter of common observation that we have left many of the old landmarks behind and that we are now pressing forward to greater heights and to a wider horizon than that which represented the mind-content of our progenitors... Astrology Pages 144

☐

Thought Vibration or The Law of Attraction in the Thought World   ISBN: *1-59462-127-6*   **$12.95**
by William Walker Atkinson   Psychology/Religion Pages 144

☐

Optimism *by Helen Keller*   ISBN: *1-59462-108-X*   **$15.95**
Helen Keller was blind, deaf, and mute since 19 months old, yet famously learned how to overcome these handicaps, communicate with the world, and spread her lectures promoting optimism. An inspiring read for everyone... Biographies/Inspirational Pages 84

☐

Sara Crewe *by Frances Burnett*   ISBN: *1-59462-360-0*   **$9.45**
In the first place, Miss Minchin lived in London. Her home was a large, dull, tall one, in a large, dull square, where all the houses were alike, and all the sparrows were alike, and where all the door-knockers made the same heavy sound... Childrens/Classic Pages 88

☐

The Autobiography of Benjamin Franklin *by Benjamin Franklin*   ISBN: *1-59462-135-7*   **$24.95**
The Autobiography of Benjamin Franklin has probably been more extensively read than any other American historical work, and no other book of its kind has had such ups and downs of fortune. Franklin lived for many years in England, where he was agent... Biographies/History Pages 332

☐

Name	
Email	
Telephone	
Address	
City, State ZIP	

☐ **Credit Card**   ☐ **Check / Money Order**

Credit Card Number	
Expiration Date	
Signature	

Please Mail to: *Book Jungle*
PO Box 2226
Champaign, IL 61825
or Fax to: *630-214-0564*

ORDERING INFORMATION

web: *www.bookjungle.com*
email: *sales@bookjungle.com*
fax: *630-214-0564*
mail: *Book Jungle PO Box 2226 Champaign, IL 61825*
or PayPal *to sales@bookjungle.com*

Please contact us for bulk discounts

DIRECT-ORDER TERMS

**20% Discount if You Order
Two or More Books**
Free Domestic Shipping!
Accepted: Master Card, Visa,
Discover, American Express